"SPOCK, DO YOU SEE THAT KLINGON STANDING NEAR THE SIDE DOOR?"

He indicated the officer he had seen earlier. "Does he look familiar to you?"

Spock took a moment to study the Klingon, after which his right eyebrow rose in the manner Kirk knew meant his friend was intrigued.

"He is wearing the uniform insignia of a ship captain," Spock noted. "Therefore it is reasonable to presume that he commands one of the two escort vessels used to bring the Klingon delegation to the conference. According to the intelligence reports made available to us while en route, he is either Captain K'tran or Captain Koloth."

Koloth?

STAR TREK®

IN THE NAME OF HONOR

Dayton Ward

Based upon STAR TREK®
created by Gene Roddenberry

POCKET BOOKS
New York   London   Toronto   Sydney   Singapore

This book is a work of fiction. Names, characters, places and incidents are products of the author's imagination or are used fictitiously. Any resemblance to actual events or locales or persons, living or dead, is entirely coincidental.

An *Original* Publication of POCKET BOOKS

POCKET BOOKS, a division of Simon & Schuster, Inc.
1230 Avenue of the Americas, New York, NY 10020

STAR TREK is a Registered Trademark of Paramount Pictures.

This book is published by Pocket Books, a division of Simon & Schuster, Inc., under exclusive license from Paramount Pictures.

ISBN: 0-7434-1225-7

First Pocket Books printing January 2002

10 9 8 7 6 5 4 3 2 1

POCKET and colophon are registered trademarks of Simon & Schuster, Inc.

For information regarding special discounts for bulk purchases, please contact Simon & Schuster Special Sales at 1-800-456-6798 or business@simonandschuster.com

Printed in the U.S.A.

For Mom and Dad,

who taught me that nothing
in life worth having is
easy to obtain, but
that the rewards of
perseverance are
unparalleled.

And for my wife, Michi,

who makes life itself an
unparalleled reward.

Acknowledgments

Let's get something straight here: I am not much more than a lifelong fan of *Star Trek* riding a wave of incredible good fortune. Without the contributions, assistance, and support of the following people, you would not be reading this book today:

John Ordover and Carol Greenburg at Pocket Books: For providing the opportunity of this fan's lifetime, and for shepherding this rookie through his first novel with an enthusiasm that provided me an enjoyable and invaluable learning experience. Everyone should have a boss who can make work this much fun.

Dean Wesley Smith and Paula M. Block: Along with John, for blazing a new trail with the *Strange New Worlds* writing contest in 1997. If I'd known how fun the journey could be, I'd have started out sooner.

Kevin Dilmore: It started as one *Star Trek* geek interviewing another, and it's evolved into a great friendship and one heck of a writing partnership. Thanks for everything, bro, and I promise I'll return that DVD you loaned me one day.

Deb Simpson: Who convinced me to enter the first *Strange New Worlds* contest. See what you started?

The many friends I've made along the way: Be they "real world" or "online," there are too many of you to mention here. You know who you are, but a special "Howdy!" goes out to the volunteers of the *Star Trek* Club on America Online. And how can I forget the "USS *Fortyish*" gang? Geezer Trekkers Rule!

**Stardate 7952.4, Earth Year 2279
Near the Federation-Klingon Border . . .**

Chapter One

EVEN AS THE ORDER to raise shields left her mouth, Captain Gralev knew she'd given it too late. On the main bridge viewscreen of the *USS Gagarin*, the Klingon K'tinga-class battle cruiser had barely finished emerging from under cloak as her first pair of torpedoes spat forth.

The ship shuddered as the torpedoes tore into the *Gagarin*'s hull. Gralev gripped the arms of her command chair as the bulkheads and floor plates protested the attack and artificial gravity wobbled momentarily.

"Break orbit, evasive starboard. Where are my shields?"

Commander Stephen Garrovick, the ship's first officer, said from behind her, "One torpedo impacted on the secondary hull. Engineering reports heavy damage to the shield generators and life-support. The second torpedo damaged the port nacelle." His eyes locked with hers. "Captain, we can't go to warp."

Gralev could see the Klingon ship veering away on the

bridge's main viewscreen, a sliver of gleaming metal contrasting against the dark curtain of space. She knew only seconds remained until their attackers would be in position to launch another strike. With warp drive unavailable to them, her options were dwindling rapidly.

"Stand by weapons," she called out. "I want to smack him across the mouth this time." She glanced over her shoulder to the communications station. "Transmit a general distress call. We don't have a big enough stick to go up against them alone."

As her crew worked around her, Gralev ignored the alarm signals coming from nearly every station on the bridge. Her people knew their jobs, but it was up to her to provide the calm and control they would draw from to guide them through the next few minutes. Despite her anger at having been ambushed for reasons unknown, a display of her legendary Andorian ire wouldn't serve her crew too well just now.

At the forward tactical station, located just to the left of the main viewscreen, Lieutenant Commander Dorthan nodded in her direction. The Bolian, one of the first to graduate from the Academy, was also a proven tactical officer. He'd served previously on the *Bozeman,* his assignment there having ended only weeks before that vessel's mysterious disappearance near the Typhon Expanse the previous year. As a border patrol ship, the *Bozeman* had seen its fair share of scrapes, giving Dorthan plenty of opportunity to sharpen his skills. Gralev for one was grateful for his presence.

"And you told me survey duty was boring." His attempt at humor fell flat. "Where the hell did they come from?" It was a question Gralev was pondering herself.

One moment, the *Gagarin* had been orbiting Nuvidula IV, a barren and unexplored planet situated a mere three-hour cruise at warp two from the Klingon Neutral Zone. The region was only sporadically patrolled, but unmanned sensor probes of Nuvidula had detected trace amounts of dilithium near the planet's surface. It was the *Gagarin*'s job to determine whether or not greater quantities of the valuable mineral were indigenous to the planet's makeup, thereby justifying the establishment of a mining operation as well as greater security. After all, one couldn't be too careful this close to Klingon space.

But the enemy cruiser's torpedoes had decimated the *Gagarin*'s quiet, uneventful survey mission, and if Captain Gralev didn't take action her ship would soon suffer a similar fate.

The Klingons had been uncharacteristically quiet of late, without so much as hostile words exchanged over subspace. Monitoring stations along the Neutral Zone had reported only sporadic ship movement on the Klingon side of the border for months. Rumors had run rampant, theorizing everything from a virulent plague ravaging the Empire to an unknown alien race attacking them from the other side of Klingon space. Gralev, like many seasoned veterans, believed it to be something simpler. In all likelihood, the Klingons merely hadn't had a reason to be bothered with the Federation.

Until now.

Dilithium was just as valuable to the Klingons as it was to the Federation. Unfortunately for the Empire, there were fewer planets rich in the ore within its borders than there were in the Federation. Inevitably the Klingons would have to branch out beyond their territory in search of additional resources. It made sense for them to target remote planets on the fringes of neighboring regions of space.

"They're coming around again," said Lieutenant Linda Parker from the helm, indicating the main viewer. She checked her small tactical display to confirm the Klingon ship's position relative to the *Gagarin*. "Port side forward."

Gralev studied the viewscreen where the Klingon ship had arced around in its flight path and was maneuvering for another pass. The viewer relayed every detail of the enemy ship's hull as it approached. Light glowed from various portholes, and Gralev briefly imagined she saw Klingons in some of those portals, all waiting in anticipation for the opportunity to storm aboard a Federation starship, lay waste to its crew, and plunder its contents.

For an odd instant, she wished that the sensor imaging systems weren't quite so refined.

At the communications console, Lieutenant Sinak turned in his seat. "Captain, we have received a response to our distress call. The *Protector* is the only vessel in any position to render assistance, but they are three hours away at maximum warp," the Vulcan said, maintaining his typical stoic expression.

Gralev grimaced at the news. She knew that her Oberth-class science vessel on its own stood no chance against the Klingons. In fact, Gralev had to wonder why they were still here as the enemy ship was capable of destroying them in a single attack run. Without warp drive, the *Gagarin* had no hope of outrunning their attacker, either.

Maybe she couldn't run, but she could still get her licks in before they took away her ability to fight back.

"Torpedoes locked," Dorthan called out from tactical.

"Fire!" Beneath her feet, Gralev felt the nearly imperceptible vibration in the deck plating as the torpedoes where fired.

Twin hellstorms of orange energy erupted from the *Gagarin*'s forward torpedo launchers, followed almost immediately by a second pair. Everyone on the bridge watched as the first two torpedoes slammed into the Klingon cruiser's forward shields, energy clashing as irresistible force met immovable object.

As the third torpedo impacted, Gralev watched the defensive screens flicker, blinking while the *Gagarin*'s fourth strike passed through the barrier and continued on until it found the cold metal of the cruiser's hull.

The rest of the bridge crew cheered when they saw the result of Dorthan's strike, though the Bolian himself didn't pause to admire his handiwork. His fingers were moving across his tactical console, already firing the ship's phasers and ordering up another spread of torpedoes.

"We're too close. Get me some room, Parker," Gralev ordered. On the screen, the Klingon ship was coming about, already recovering from whatever slight damage Dorthan's attack might have done. Then the stars shifted violently as the *Gagarin* clawed for maneuvering room, her hull plates groaning in objection to the abuse. The vessel simply wasn't constructed for combat. Compared to a battle cruiser, her vessel was a lethargic slug even when functioning at full efficiency.

Gralev saw the cruiser's forward torpedo launcher already glowing red as it prepared to fire in retaliation. Her eyes darted to the tactical status display on the helm console, realizing with horror that the upper section of the *Gagarin*'s primary hull was facing the enemy. At this distance, the Klingons' next strike would be devastating.

"Stand by for impact!" Once again, Gralev knew it was too little too late.

Without shields to protect it, the *Gagarin* was vulnerable as another torpedo slammed into the saucer section. On the bridge, anyone without a secure handhold went flailing as the ship rocked under the assault. The overhead lighting flickered, monitor screens across the bridge blinked, alarms wailed; the noise on the compact bridge was deafening. The acrid smell of smoke assailed the captain's nostrils, followed almost as quickly by the odor of fire-suppressant chemicals as they were automatically discharged to fight console fires.

Sparks and shrapnel erupted from the helm console as it exploded. Gralev twisted her chair around and threw her arms up to protect her head, gritting her teeth at the sudden, intense pain of hot metal tearing through the material of her uniform and into her skin. She could hear other impacts across the side of her chair and even the bulkhead at the back of the bridge as debris from the explosion searched for unwitting targets.

Good God. Parker . . .

Ignoring her own wounds, Gralev vaulted from her chair to kneel over the form of the fallen helm officer, who had been thrown savagely to the deck by the explosion. Her fingers moved to find a pulse but she stopped them as she looked into Parker's open, unseeing eyes.

The captain felt her face flush with rage. Hadn't she been talking to Parker not fifteen minutes ago, discussing the lieutenant's upcoming wedding? The helm officer had been planning to take leave in the coming weeks in order to return to Earth for her marriage ceremony.

Gralev angrily forced the thoughts away. There wasn't time for this.

Garrovick had already jumped down into the command area and had taken over the helm, trying to coax cooperation out of the damaged console.

"I'm rerouting systems, but she's sluggish, Captain."

Gralev didn't have to hear his unspoken addition. They weren't going to be able to maneuver to defend themselves against the next attack. When the Klingons swung around again, the *Gagarin* would be dead in the water.

"Here they come!" Dorthan shouted over the wailing of the alarms. He jabbed the firing controls as the enemy ship grew larger on the main viewer yet again.

Another pair of torpedoes hurtled away from the *Gagarin,* impacting on the Klingon cruiser's shields as the enemy vessel fired. Gralev held on to her chair as her ship was pummeled once more.

"Warning," the ship's computer reported with its emotionless female voice. "Outer hull breach, deck seven, section eighteen."

Gralev pulled herself into her chair. "Have we hurt them at all?"

Dorthan shook his head in disgust. "Not enough." Suddenly he pounded his console with his fists. "Weapons control is offline!"

That's it, then.

Without weapons, without shields, without the ability to maneuver, the *Gagarin* had run out of time. The next attack from the Klingons would likely be the last.

"Captain," Sinak said from communications, "I am receiving an incoming hail from the Klingon ship. They are ordering us to surrender and prepare for boarding."

All eyes on the bridge turned to Gralev. She studied the haunted faces of her crew and wanted to say something, anything to comfort them. She wanted to reassure them that they would get out of this, that they would get home. But she knew it was a lie. So did they.

"They're after something." Only with effort was she able to keep her voice steady. "If they'd wanted us dead, we'd be vaporized by now." She considered the possibility that the Klingon ship commander was simply calling to gloat before he delivered the final killing blow.

"On screen."

The image of a Klingon officer replaced that of the enemy ship. Obviously the captain of the vessel, the Klingon was a large male, with dark skin and narrow eyes that Gralev immediately found menacing.

It took her a moment to realize that this was a variety of Klingon that she hadn't seen in quite some time. He, along with other Klingons she could make out on their bridge, didn't possess the high cranial ridges she'd seen with increasing frequency during the past several years. Instead of the long flowing hair and full beard she'd come to associate with Klingons, this captain kept his hair cut fairly short. A thin goatee and a long, drooping mustache surrounded a wicked smile, full of teeth reflecting the dim illumination offered by the ship's bridge lighting. It was the expression of one who knew he had his prey cornered, and Gralev wanted to plant the heel of her boot squarely in the middle of it.

"Federation ship, I am K'lavut, commanding the Imperial cruiser Vo'taq. *Our scanners show that you are crippled. However, I must commend you on withstanding my attack better than I anticipated."*

Gralev rose from her chair, glaring at the image of the Klingon commander. "This is Captain Gralev of the *Starship Gagarin.* Why have you attacked us in Federation space without provocation?"

The smile disappeared from the Klingon's face. *"By the right granted to those with the power to conquer the weak, Andorian. You would be wise to hold your tongue and restrict your responses to simple acknowledgment of my orders. Stand down what remains of your pathetic defenses and prepare to receive my crew. If you do not comply, I will destroy you."*

Chapter Two

GRALEV COULD BARELY keep her anger in check as she watched K'lavut casually stroll about the upper level of the *Gagarin*'s bridge. He walked slowly, his hands clasped behind his back, as if he had all the time in the world. Light from the overhead illumination reflected off the gold sash draped over the Klingon's shoulder as well as the knife attached to his belt. Gralev's eyes followed the weapon while her mind gave her suggestions on what she might do with it.

Other Klingons guarded the remainder of the bridge personnel, and Gralev knew that all over the ship the rest of the crew was being similarly rounded up. How many of them had been injured or killed during the initial attack? If what she'd heard about Klingon treatment of prisoners was true, she suspected those members of her crew who were already dead might end up being the lucky ones.

K'lavut was moving counterclockwise around the

bridge, his eyes taking in the vast array of polished consoles, padded chairs, even the soft, unobtrusive lighting that illuminated the various bridge stations. Gralev watched him shake his head in apparent disgust.

"It is no wonder your vessels are crewed by weaklings," he said. "You rely too much on technology to fight your battles for you. That is why you will ultimately fall before the Klingon Empire."

"I imagine you'd get more than a bit of debate on that subject," Gralev countered. She knew the risk she was taking on, goading the K'lavut like that. There were few races that the Klingons did not detest, and the Andorians were most definitely not in that select group.

K'lavut laughed softly. "If the decision were mine, this ship and your crew would already be destroyed. I have no use for prisoners, but my superiors are concerned that the Federation might be making a push into this region of space. If that ball of dirt you were studying is any indication, there are rich resources to be exploited in this area. The Federation cannot be allowed to hoard them for themselves."

"I don't know what you're talking about," Gralev said. It was a lie, of course. Federation survey teams had come to the same conclusion about this sector that the Empire obviously had.

K'lavut gave no indication that he believed Gralev, didn't believe her, or cared either way. He continued his inspection of the bridge, passing the main viewer and coming to a stop at the tactical station where Dorthan stood under guard. He appraised the Bolian as if measuring the worth of a possession and deciding whether to keep or discard it.

"You are the tactical officer," he said.

Dorthan nodded. "That's right."

"You are the one who fired the torpedoes so expertly at my ship. Quite an impressive display for someone relegated to a science vessel." The Klingon's face broke into a wide smile. "You have obviously seen combat before. Tell me."

The Bolian cast a quick glance in Gralev's direction, who nodded for him to continue. "I served on a border patrol ship before being assigned here. We had a few run-ins with Klingons and pirates from time to time."

"Ah, yes," K'lavut said. "Border ships. I've heard about such skirmishes. Well fought, for the most part. The fact that you stand here today is a testament to your abilities."

The Klingon's hand was a blur as it curled into a fist and shot forward, striking Dorthan across the jaw. The attack was so powerful that the weapons officer was slammed into an unyielding wall panel. He fell to one knee before he caught himself, one hand reaching up to wipe blood from the corner of his mouth.

"You pathetic worm," K'lavut hissed. "Giving up a position on a ship of battle for this." He waved his hand to indicate the bridge. "Was your stomach too weak for the challenge? Was it necessary to seek shelter from the hard realities of war?"

Gralev, ignoring a Klingon guard and the disruptor he was pointing at her, stepped forward. "That's enough."

K'lavut turned to face the *Gagarin*'s captain, still smiling. "And now the woman comes to the rescue." He threw another look at Dorthan. "Tell me, Bolian. Do you enjoy taking orders from an Andorian, and a female one at that? There are Klingons who would rather choose *Hegh'bat* rather than a life of such loathsome servitude. Then again, making such a choice would require courage, something you obviously do not possess."

"I said that's enough," Gralev repeated, a hard edge to her voice now. "I've surrendered to you out of regard for the safety of my crew. What more do you want?"

K'lavut stepped down into the command area, walking with the confidence of one who knows he's in control of the situation until he was less than a pace from Gralev. He leaned closer still, so close that Gralev could smell the pungent odor of his breath, mute testimony to the vile meal he had recently consumed.

"You will transfer command of this ship to me, Andorian, so that I may present it to the Empire as a trophy. If you refuse, I will present them your head instead, as well as the heads of every member of your crew."

"And if I comply?" she asked. "What about my people?"

K'lavut shrugged. "They will not be harmed."

Gralev knew better than to look for any hint of a bluff in the Klingon's eyes. She held no illusions that anything other than a slow, painful death awaited her. Klingons loathed Andorians even more than they hated most of the species that composed the Federation.

Satisfied with that knowledge, all she had to worry about now was looking out for her crew.

Exhaling in defeat, Gralev nodded. Turning back to her command chair she indicated the control pad set into the chair's arm.

"What are you doing?" K'lavut asked, a hint of warning in his voice.

"Accessing the ship's computer," Gralev replied. "My chair provides a direct link for the captain and the first officer."

K'lavut nodded in approval. "Excellent. I trust the procedure to revoke your codes is a simple one?"

Nodding, Gralev pointed to the control keypad on the

chair's right arm. "Once I give the order to the computer, it will prompt me for a command sequence that I enter here."

Suspicion clouded the Klingon's expression. As much as he hated Andorians, he knew they never willingly ended a fight while there was still a chance that they could either win or at least deliver a last-ditch sneak attack. "You would surrender so easily?"

"We're talking about my crew, K'lavut," she countered. "I don't take chances when it comes to them."

The Klingon seemed to accept that. "Very well, Andorian. You have purchased their lives, at least for the time being. However, they will pay dearly for your actions if you attempt to deceive me." He indicated the chair with a nod of his head. "Enter the code."

Drawing a calming breath, Gralev tapped a control on the chair arm. "Computer, this is Captain Gralev requesting security access. Enable command protocol Alpha Omega Three Nine Five Five."

Dutifully, the computer responded. *"Request acknowledged. Self-destruct sequence has been activated. Detonation in sixty seconds."*

"Oh," Gralev offered casually as K'lavut's expression turned to one of shock, "the computer is also programmed to destroy the ship to keep it from falling into enemy hands. I seem to have given it that code by mistake."

She smiled in satisfaction. Commander Garrovick had at first been hesitant to her idea of scuttling the ship, but understood her reasoning and supported her as he always had. The plan, hastily put into action in the minutes before the Klingons had boarded, would save the *Gagarin* crew from years of torture and abuse at the hands of their enemy.

As she listened to the computer counting down the seconds until detonation while ignoring K'lavut and the scrambling Klingons around her, her thoughts turned to her mates. Would they ever learn the truth about what happened here? Probably not, she realized, just as the families of her crew would in all likelihood never know how bravely their loved ones had performed today. Though she'd never get the chance to tell her own clan, she knew that the sacrifice she and her crew were about to make was worth the larger cause that they served. She had only to see the dismayed expression on K'lavut's face to know that. If she could take that to her grave, she could indeed die happy.

Stardate 8461.7, Earth Year 2287

Chapter Three

ONLY THE FADING strength in the tips of his fingers separated James Kirk from a nasty fall. Thankfully, he'd found purchase with his feet and was able to take some of the strain from his protesting arms and shoulders. Sweat stung his eyes, but his tenuous position didn't afford him the luxury of wiping the perspiration from his face.

Looking up, he spied his next handhold, just above and to the right of his head, and another just above that. To reach the closer of the two he would have to stretch his arm almost to the limit, with the movement leaving him momentarily off balance. Kirk looked to his right side and saw another promising perch for his foot. If he was careful, the combined actions of reaching for the first opening, moving his leg over, and then climbing to the second crevice would pull him almost a meter closer to his goal. He might just make it.

He removed his right hand from the small crevice he'd been gripping and slid it up the side of the wall, searching for the new handhold he'd spotted. As he moved, his left arm protested the extra exertion demanded of it to support the remainder of his weight. He felt his left shoulder starting to tremble, a clear sign of muscle fatigue.

His right hand found the tiny opening and he pressed his fingers into it, securing his hold long enough to push his right foot over to the next crevice and pull his body up those precious centimeters. His left foot hung free and his left hand pressed into the face of the wall, his balance now truly unstable. Kirk looked for the second handhold, just above his right hand.

Time was running out. He couldn't afford niceties. With the muscles of his right arm screaming for relief, Kirk lunged upward, pushing his left hand along the wall until his fingers felt the opening. He grabbed the handhold and with his body secured, at least temporarily, allowed himself a sigh of relief.

"Exercise complete," the feminine voice of the *Enterprise*'s computer said. "Time remaining: 4.07 seconds. Congratulations on a successful ascent. For your next exercise, you may wish to attempt a higher difficulty level."

"Fat chance," Kirk breathed.

Below and behind him, he heard applause. Cautiously he turned his body in order to look in the direction of his heretofore-unknown audience and saw the lanky frame of the ship's chief medical officer, Leonard McCoy, clapping his hands appreciatively. Looking down on his friend from three stories above the *Enterprise* gymnasium's main floor made Kirk realize that to truly complete the exercise with a passing grade, he would of course have to climb back down the wall.

As he began his descent, Kirk called out toward McCoy, "Don't you have anything better to do?"

Strolling toward the wall, the doctor replied, "The fitness of the ship's commanding officer is always a high priority with me, Captain sir. I'm glad to see you finally taking my advice, and I've asked Uhura to enter this momentous occasion in the ship's log. However, your choice of exercise leaves a lot to be desired."

"How so?" Kirk asked, now almost halfway down the wall and continuing to descend.

"Climbing the walls of the ship is normally something I'd relate to a mental disorder. Although after El Capitan, I suppose I should be thankful." McCoy made a show of looking about the room before adding, "Don't lose your grip, Captain. I don't see any flying Vulcans around here to save you this time."

Kirk sighed in resignation, knowing full well it would be a long time indeed before McCoy let him forget the nearly fatal incident at Yosemite National Park during their shore leave the previous month. While attempting to free-climb El Capitan, Kirk had slipped and fallen from the face of the mighty granite mountain. Had it not been for the fortunate presence of Spock and the pair of antigravity boots he'd been wearing, Kirk would have died that day. McCoy had chewed him out over the mishap that night over dinner, and had found every opportunity to remind Kirk of the foolhardiness of his actions since then.

Kirk's left foot touched the mat and he stepped away from the wall to a new round of applause from McCoy, which he ignored as he reached for a towel. Aside from the aches in his muscles that he knew would assert themselves with greater authority in the morning, he felt the sense of elation he always experienced at a task successfully completed. Maybe he wasn't in his thirties any longer, but he was still in decent physical condition for a man . . .

. . . *older than thirty.*

"So what really brings you down here, Doctor?" Kirk asked as he wiped his face. "Coming to see how the captain is fairing with a shipload of politicians? Worried that I might be thinking of throwing one or two of them out an airlock?"

McCoy shrugged. "It wouldn't be the first time you'd considered it."

The captain grinned in agreement. He'd lost count of the times he'd been tasked to ferry an ambassador or some other such Federation representative during his career, just as he'd forgotten how many of those same passengers had caused him some form of headache or misery along the way. Truth be told, however, Kirk considered the *Enterprise*'s current mission to transport a Federation diplomatic team to Starbase 49 as one of the more quiet and uneventful assignments he'd undertaken.

With the doctor at his side, Kirk began a leisurely stroll across the gymnasium floor, occasionally speaking to a member of the crew as he passed them or acknowledging an offered greeting.

"I don't think this round of peace talks is going to be like others we've had in the past, Bones," Kirk said as they walked. "For one thing, this was the Klingons' idea, not ours."

"Got to hand it to that General Korrd," McCoy replied. "Even though he's not exactly high on the Klingons' list of favorites, he still managed to convince their High Council that new peace talks were in order."

Kirk nodded. General Korrd had been the Klingon diplomatic representative to Nimbus III, the site of the *Enterprise*'s most recently completed mission. The planet, a failed experiment in diplomacy sponsored by the Federation, the Klingons, and the Romulan Empire, had been dubiously labeled "the Planet of Galactic Peace."

The name had proven to be a misnomer within a few short years after the founding of the planet's shared colony. Each of the three governments eventually withdrew their support of the project once it became clear that achieving peace would be more difficult than simply having colonists share the meager resources Nimbus III provided. Representatives of each government remained and made several feeble attempts to keep order, but these individuals, more often than not, were usually politicians who had lost some measure of favor with their respective governments. An assignment as diplomatic attaché to Nimbus III was almost always a sign that one's political career was over.

Nearly two decades after the colony's inception, a fanatical Vulcan, Sybok, seized the colony's main settlement, Paradise City, taking Korrd and the other governmental representatives hostage. Demands were made for their safe release, and Starfleet sent the *Enterprise* to investigate and attempt a rescue operation. Once there, it became apparent that the hostage situation was a ruse initiated by Sybok so that he could hijack a starship to take him to Sha Ka Ree, a planet located at the center of the Milky Way galaxy and believed by many to be a myth.

And if things were not complicated enough, Sybok had turned out to be Spock's half brother.

Additionally, Kirk had also been forced to deal with a rogue Klingon bird-of-prey, whose young and eager commander, Klaa, had seen an opportunity to gain glory from a battle against the *Enterprise* and Kirk himself. The intervention of General Korrd had prevented Kirk's death at the hands of Klaa.

"Hopefully Korrd has gained back some favor with the Council after all of this," Kirk said. "He's right when he says our two governments need to sit down and talk.

There are a lot more young excitable ship commanders out there, on both sides. Sooner or later, there'll be another incident and it might not end as peacefully as ours did."

McCoy replied, "Do you really think that one day, all this aggression with the Klingons might be behind us?"

Kirk shrugged. "It's a strange galaxy out there, Bones. I suppose anything's possible, even peace with the Klingons." He doubted the words as soon as they were spoken, and could tell by the look on McCoy's face that the doctor wasn't convinced, either.

The men slowed as they reached the entrance to the locker room. McCoy asked, "So, now that you're finished with your impression of a Degebian mountain goat in heat, what say we rustle up some supper? I think I may still have some of that secret ingredient for my famous beans lying around somewhere."

Wiping his face with the towel once more, Kirk shook his head. "I promised Spock a game of chess tonight. I think he's spent the last couple of weeks developing a defense to the moves I pulled on him last time."

Their conversation was interrupted by the *Enterprise*'s intraship communications system blaring to life. The familiar whistle was followed by the voice of Commander Uhura, who Kirk knew was still on bridge duty for the next hour or so.

"Bridge to Captain Kirk."

Kirk strolled over to a nearby comm panel set into the wall near the entrance to the locker room and opened the channel with his thumb. "Kirk here. What is it, Uhura?"

The tiny display next to the comm panel activated, displaying an image of Uhura sitting at her bridge station.

"Sir, we're receiving a high-priority subspace commu-

niqué from Admiral Bennett on Earth. He wishes to speak with you immediately."

Frowning, Kirk exchanged looks with McCoy. Robert Bennett, Chief of Staff at Starfleet Command, rarely contacted ship commanders himself, choosing instead to leave such tasks to his small army of assistants. The fact that this was the second time he had done so with Kirk was not lost on the captain, the first such contact having happened during the Nimbus III incident. Kirk believed that whatever the reason for this latest communiqué, it must be equally serious.

"I'll take it down here, Commander," he said.

The image on the screen shifted to that of Robert Bennett. The admiral was a severe-looking man with dark, narrow eyes that peered out from beneath a heavy brow made more prominent by his receding line of thin brown hair. A mischievous smile almost always seemed to be lurking just beneath the surface of the stony expression that dominated his features.

Upon seeing Kirk dressed in his sweat-soaked workout attire, Bennett's brow furrowed even more and the smile began to play at the corners of his mouth.

"Captain Kirk," he said, *"I seem to have this habit of catching you in various states of casual relaxation. Do you even own a Starfleet uniform?"*

Kirk laughed, remembering his last communication with Bennett just after returning to the *Enterprise* from his camping trip with Spock and McCoy at Yosemite. He had been filthy and badly in need of a shower and a change of clothes, not exactly the professional appearance one might want to project to a Starfleet Chief of Staff.

"Just a little workout to ease the tension, Bob," Kirk replied. "A shipload of diplomats gets your shoulders in a knot. You remember how it is."

Bennett nodded. *"I do, which is why I let myself get promoted. Maybe you'll get smart and change your mind one day."*

"Over my dead body," McCoy said, just loud enough for the comm's speaker to transmit. Kirk looked sideways at his friend, though he'd long since given up being surprised by anything McCoy might say in a given situation. The doctor had never been one for Starfleet protocol, after all.

Bennett said, *"Jim, I don't think I have to tell you how important the Federation Council views this meeting with the Klingons. We have a chance to bury some hatchets, maybe even once and for all."*

"I'd be lying if I didn't say I'm more than a little skeptical about the whole thing."

"For what it's worth, you're not alone in your feelings, and it's not just grumbling amongst us old-timers minding the store back home. We've got reason to believe this isn't a popular idea with a lot of people."

"Now why do I think he's about to tell us this might not turn out to be just another quiet assignment?" McCoy asked. He had crossed his arms and his face was set in that expression Kirk knew his friend adopted when he was listening to something he didn't want to hear in the first place.

"Your doctor's right," Bennett said. *"We've gotten intelligence reports that suggest someone may try to sabotage the conference."*

"Klingons?"

"Possibly, though I wouldn't rule out people from our side, either. Subspace has been jammed with people speaking out against any sort of treaty with the Empire. You may have your work cut out for you this time, Jim, so watch your aft shields on this one. My people will stay on

top of this and pass on any information we can get our hands on, but I'm counting on you to keep things under control. Good luck. Bennett out."

As the screen went dark, McCoy sighed. "Well, just another boring day, eh, Jim?"

Kirk didn't answer. Instead, his thoughts were racing ahead to the conference, so peaceful and noble in intent, and the consequences of any incident that might harm the proceedings there or, more important, anyone involved. He knew that with the heightened tensions between the Federation and the Empire in recent years, some of which he had contributed to, it wouldn't take much to set off conflict between the two powers.

He recalled the party they had thrown aboard the *Enterprise* following the incident with Klaa and his ship near Sha Ka Ree. With the misunderstanding ironed out to the satisfaction of both sides, the crews had intermingled that evening and Kirk had idly wondered if there was indeed a possibility of a lasting peace between the Federation and the Klingon Empire.

His gut, however, told him such a lasting peace would be a longer time in coming.

Peace talks had not prevented him from being forced to stand helpless aboard the bridge of his crippled ship while David Marcus, his only son, had died at the hands of a Klingon. Though time had eased the agony of that horrible day, the pain remained, suppressed as it was so that only his closest friends could sense anything other than the persona of the proud, confident starship commander that he normally projected.

Still, from time to time he could sense it, lingering deep within him, jading his soul and clouding his hopes for peace with his enemies, perhaps forever. It was only with supreme force of will that he kept the feelings buried and his focus on his command, not allowing his personal distrust of Klingons to intrude on his sworn duty to uphold the principles of Starfleet and the Federation.

Feeling the doctor's eyes on him, Kirk looked up and smiled. "Well, that's why we have a shipload of diplomats. It's up to them to make this all work out."

McCoy snorted. "I think I trust the Klingons more than I do the diplomats. At least with a Klingon you know where you stand most of the time."

Chapter Four

TENTATIVELY AT FIRST, but with unrelenting perseverance, the first rays of sunlight pierced the thick, humid jungle and chased the darkness away. The melodic chorus provided by countless insects diminished with the approaching dawn as nocturnal predators sought shelter until nightfall returned. Water dripped liberally on the lush undergrowth from the towering canopy of trees above.

Rising from the jungle floor was a modest-sized mountain. Formed from granite out of the belly of the planet, its peak was shrouded by a thick layer of clouds. No one had ever bothered to venture to the top of the mountain, the simple reason being an overwhelming lack of interest to see what might await an intrepid explorer there. The mountain did not even have a name. It was, like the rest of the planet from which it had sprung, unremarkable in the eyes of those who called this world home.

At the base of the mountain was a mammoth stone wall, fifteen meters tall and forming a U-shape that used the sheer face of the mountain itself to create an enclosed compound half a kilometer in diameter. The wall's straight lines and smooth finish stood in stark contrast to its surroundings, its artificiality made evident by the tell-tale hum of the powerful energy shield encompassing the compound. Generated by a series of large metallic columns rising out of the ground outside the wall at regular intervals, the shield was all but impenetrable to weapons, sensor scans, and transporter beams.

The wall itself had but a single entrance that was blocked by a pair of massive metal doors, their polished finish long ago dulled and inundated with rust by the jungle's ever-present moisture. Inside the wall, a massive opening formed an entrance into the mountain. The resulting tunnel was lit by rows of dim, yellow-tinged light fixtures hanging from wire attached to the sides of the subterranean passage. To either side of the entrance, twenty-five two-story structures made of equal parts stone and metal composites lined the massive wall's interior perimeter. A single building was different in construction from the others, this one a freestanding structure that housed a lone short-range transport craft. There was room for more than one, but given the circumstances, one was all that was needed. Despite the compound's large population, the only way the majority of the inhabitants would travel aboard the ship would be as cargo, not passengers.

Decades old, the prison had been refurbished several times over the years in response to the long-term deteriorating effects of jungle moisture and harsh weather. Prior to the hot season and its oppressive heat, violent storms would ravage the region for months. The heavy monsoon season had ended and temperatures were already on the rise. In a few weeks, the heat would become potentially deadly to all but the hardiest of life-forms. Given such conditions as well as the fact nothing even remotely resembling civilization could be found anywhere in this hemisphere, the area made an ideal location for a prison.

With the exception of five buildings that housed the prison's control center, armory, and billeting for the staff, the rest of the structures were used to quarter prisoners. Each of the barracks buildings were comprised of forty cells, each of those secured by a door constructed from heavy tritanium. The gray, unpolished doors were identical, one meter wide, two meters tall, and half a meter thick. A single narrow slot, perhaps two centimeters high and fifteen centimeters long, broke the surface of each door half a meter from the top.

Inside one of the cells forming the structure known to the prisoners as Barracks 6, Stephen Garrovick lay awake in the upper bunk of a two-tier bed. More like a hammock than an actual bed, the rough-woven material that formed his mattress sagged beneath the weight of his body. It was comfortable enough though, and better than other places he had slept in during his captivity.

Sunlight filtering through the door slot had washed across his face and awakened him minutes earlier, just as it did nearly every morning. It was a rare occurrence for Garrovick to sleep until the guards sounded the three shrill horn blasts signaling the start of each new day.

Lying in the near-darkness he listened, trying to determine whether or not his cellmate, Sydney Elliot, was still sleeping in the lower bunk. Her breathing pattern indicated that she wasn't, but he didn't say anything. It was their longtime unspoken agreement that neither would speak until the horn sounded, on the off chance that either one of them was still sleeping. A few hours of uninterrupted slumber was something to treasure in places as devoid of peace as the various hellholes they had called home during the past several years.

Eight years.

Out of necessity, Garrovick had long ago given up any sense of incredulity that came with realizing how long he had been in captivity. The duration of his confinement was a simple fact now, best accepted at face value and nothing more. After the first three years had passed, he had surrendered any hope of ever returning home or of seeing his family again. To dwell on the feelings of despair that almost always accompanied such dreams was hazardous in an environment such as this, where the guards and even fellow prisoners would be watching for any sign of weakness to exploit. Better to just accept the reality of the situation and cope with it.

His thoughts were interrupted by the sound of the horn located in the prison courtyard. Three blasts echoed through the damp morning air, resounding off the interior of the cell.

"Rise and shine," he said as he sat up, his right hand reflexively moving to rub the smooth top of his head. In an attempt to keep various species of mites and fleas from overwhelming the prison population, every prisoner was depilated of all body hair at least once every two weeks, more often when the weather grew warmer as it was beginning to do.

"Yeah, yeah," Sydney Elliot replied, her voice not dulled by sleep and confirming for Garrovick that she had indeed been awake. "Another glorious day in Shangri-la."

Garrovick smiled at the dry humor as Elliot rose from the lower bunk, taking a moment to stretch the kinks out of tired muscles. He couldn't help but notice her shrunken form in the paltry light provided by the slot in their door, as well as the circles under her eyes that contrasted even against her ebony skin. He guessed that she'd suffered another bout of insomnia, the third time in the past five days. The attacks had come more often in the last year or so, but Elliot never complained about it. Garrovick had asked her about it when he'd first begun noticing her condition, but she dismissed the inquiries. "I like to stay up late reading a good book," she had quipped on one occasion.

A native of the harsh environment found on Mars and a security officer on the *Gagarin,* Elliot had once been the epitome of prime physical conditioning. Aboard ship she had been a fierce athlete, making a reputation for herself in many good-natured sporting competitions. Her prowess in unarmed combat had given her a reputation of another kind, the type that crewmates bestowed on someone they knew could be counted on in a sticky situation. Be it suspicious locals on a first-contact mission or a bar brawl on Argelius, the *Gagarin* personnel had always considered it a tactical advantage to have Sydney Elliot watching their backs.

However, just like Garrovick and the other captives here, Elliot's body had long ago succumbed to the ravages brought on by years of abuse and improper diet. While the last few years had seen a marked improvement in their treatment, they were still fed only enough to survive and remain sufficiently healthy to work and to fend off various diseases.

The sound of the door lock disengaging caught Garrovick's attention just as the door swung open, flooding the tiny cell with morning sunshine.

"Chow time," Elliot said, clapping her hands to emphasize the point as the pair made their way from the cell. "I guess it's too much to hope for an omelet made from Ktarian eggs and a nice tall glass of orange juice."

Garrovick snorted as they stepped out onto the catwalk running the length of their cell block level. "Keep dreaming, Syd."

A former security officer himself, Garrovick had liked the younger officer from the moment she had joined the *Gagarin*'s crew. Fresh from the Academy and Starfleet Security School, Elliot had displayed more brashness and confidence than he had during his first assignment aboard the *Enterprise*. While he had been forced to find his sense of self-assurance during his initial tour, Elliot simply oozed it. It wasn't arrogance or cockiness, but the cool demeanor displayed by someone confident in her own abilities.

Along with a thousand or so other prisoners, they waited for the morning routine to begin. Every day, they would line up and the prison's central computer would verify that everyone was accounted for. This was done by means of a metallic band worn by each prisoner. On humanoids, the device was worn around the right ankle. Embedded in each band was a tiny transceiver monitored by the computer.

It was an effective means of observation given the fact that on any one day, the prison population could be spread out over several kilometers, both above and below the surface of the planet. No means of removing the bands had ever been discovered, short of severing the limb it was attached to. This rendered most thoughts of escape moot. Even if an escapee somehow got away from the guards, through the prison's lone entrance or over the wall and through the forcefield surrounding it, the computer was capable of tracking that person anywhere on the planet.

"jaH!"

The single barked command, the order for the prisoners to begin moving down from the catwalks and into the line from which they would receive their morning meal, came from one of the Klingon guards in the small courtyard below them. No matter where the prisoners went, be it the mess hall or the mines or to the bathing area, they always did so in line. Except when working in the mines or on some other detail, prisoners were not allowed to move about independently unless given permission to do so. Violating this most basic rule invited harsh retaliation by the guards.

As he shuffled along behind a Rigelian prisoner, Garrovick looked across the courtyard to the building opposite his. There he could make out the forms of Robert Kawaguchi and Sinak, two more *Gagarin* crewmen. They were also looking his way and the three men greeted one another with subtle nods.

Lived to see another day.

He knew he wouldn't see the other two survivors of the *Gagarin* until they made it to the mess hall, where they would gather at a single table and take comfort in each other's company. While he had no evidence to support his theory, it was Garrovick's belief that the six of them were all that remained of the *Gagarin's* fifty-person complement.

Despite Captain Gralev's having set the ship's self-destruct sequence into motion, the Klingon commander had managed to thwart that daring plan. With members of his own crew having taken over most of the *Gagarin's* vital areas, Captain K'lavut had used his ship's massive cargo transporters to move the surviving crew to his own vessel before the *Gagarin's* warp core exploded. When Garrovick had been able to get a headcount, he found that twenty-eight of the crew had been beamed out. As he had feared eight years ago, he considered the twenty-two left behind to be the fortunate ones.

After their capture, the surviving crew members had been segregated into small groups. Except for those in his own group, Garrovick had never seen anyone else from the *Gagarin* since that day. Of the seven people that had been brought to this prison with him, one had died from disease and the other from extreme physical torture. Garrovick's dreams were still haunted by the gruesome death that had befallen Captain Gralev soon after their arrival here.

Gralev had been a target for extreme prejudice simply for being an Andorian, but her fate had been sealed when she had outwitted K'lavut, albeit temporarily, in front of his subordinates on the *Gagarin*'s bridge. She had been tortured and finally killed at the hand of the prison commander as the rest of her crew had watched helplessly, a horrifying demonstration of the penalty for disrespectful behavior.

The prisoners continued to march, moving out into the courtyard to form a series of columns, one for each cell block. Klingons strolled about the groups of prisoners, their sharp haircuts, trimmed beards, and shiny uniforms contrasting against the prisoners' shaved heads and drab gray coveralls. While none of the guards were armed with disruptor pistols or even bladed weapons, each guard carried a stun baton in hand. It wasn't a weapon that conveyed any overt threat, but Garrovick knew from experience that the baton could deliver electrical shocks of varying intensity capable of incapacitating or even killing its victim.

Garrovick caught sight of one Klingon in particular, Khulr. The leader of the guards, Khulr was known among the prisoners for his exceptional cruelty. In spite of the camp's policies on treatment of prisoners which had been enacted a few years previously, Khulr still took great pleasure in administering beatings and other harassment, most of which appeared to go unnoticed by the prison's commander. He had been reprimanded for exceeding his authority on occasion, but never severely.

The reason for that was simple. Despite his harsh behavior toward the prisoners, Khulr was quite effective at keeping them productive, insuring that the regular quota for mined dilithium was continually met. His hatred of humans was all-encompassing, and his favorite targets for abuse were the *Gagarin* survivors, Elliot in particular.

Stealing a glance over his shoulder at Elliot, Garrovick whispered, "Syd. Khulr's coming. Behave yourself."

Elliot noticed the approaching guard as well, and Garrovick saw the slight tightening along her jawline. He knew that subtle display of emotion was the only sign of fear she would show to any of the Klingons. Despite years of imprisonment, Elliot had refused to allow her captors the satisfaction of seeing her give in to the situation. Though Garrovick and her other shipmates had helped to protect her from the worst of prison realities over the years, they had failed to convince her that adopting a less provocative nature would benefit her in the long run. Instead, Elliot had maintained an unrelenting air of irreverence, showing no fear toward the guards regardless of the consequences. Garrovick suspected that the former security officer had simply accepted the grim reality of her existence here, deciding that she alone would dictate her future. If she died here, then it would be on her terms, not a Klingon's.

Garrovick watched as Khulr turned away from them, his attention drawn by something the *Gagarin* first officer couldn't see. He exhaled audibly, relief evident in the look he shared with Elliot.

"Looks like he's found somebody else's morning to brighten," she said. "Lucky me." It had been nearly a week since her last run-in with Khulr, and she knew it was only a matter of time before the head guard found some excuse, real or imagined, to harass her.

A sharp cry of pain from behind them caused Garrovick's head to snap around in time to see a female Bolian prisoner slump to the ground in a disjointed heap while clutching at her midsection. A Klingon stood over the fallen prisoner, stun baton in hand. Garrovick recognized him as one of the newer guards, probably fresh out of whatever school prison guards went to before taking their first assignment and not yet acclimated to the camp's routine. Garrovick figured he was out to impress Khulr and the camp commander with his enthusiasm and ability to control helpless, unarmed prisoners.

"Move when you're told, *petaQ!*" The guard's foot lashed out, striking the hapless Bolian in the chest. More kicks followed and the prisoner tried to fend off the attack, howling in pain as she failed. Around them, other prisoners cowered in fear from the raving guard as his brutal assault intensified.

If his attention had not been so drawn by the altercation, Garrovick would have realized what was coming next. By the time he realized what was happening, Elliot had exploded from her place in line and was rushing toward the fallen Bolian and her tormentor.

"Syd!" Garrovick yelled even as he moved to follow.

Chapter Five

THE KLINGON'S FOOT was drawn back to deliver yet another vicious kick to the defenseless prisoner just as Elliot crashed into him.

Though the massive Klingon outweighed her, she slammed into him with enough force to drive them both to the ground. As the guard fell, the stun baton dropped from his hand. Around them, other prisoners scattered away from the impromptu melee, a few of them pulling the fallen Bolian away from the scuffle as Elliot regained her feet.

"How's it feel, Klingon?" she yelled as she struck a furious kick to the still-downed guard's face. She was readying another attack when Garrovick caught up to her from behind, grabbing her by the arms and pulling her away from the guard.

"What the hell are you doing?" he screamed at her, turning her around to face him. From farther down the line of prisoners, he saw other guards closing on them.

Elliot ripped one arm from his grasp. "He would have killed her, Stephen!"

Garrovick's next words were lost to an agonizing jolt from behind, every nerve ending in the small of his back exploding as his legs went numb. It was all he could do to throw his arms out as he tumbled forward to the ground. No sooner had he hit the dried dirt surface of the prison courtyard than he saw Elliot fall in a similar fashion, her face screwed up in agony.

Gritting his teeth against the pain, Garrovick turned onto his side in time to see a gleaming pair of polished black boots step in front of him.

"Commander Garrovick," Khulr said as he drew circles in the air before the prisoner's face with the end of his baton, "have you forgotten the rules about prisoners staying in line?" The Klingon's voice was calm, with no trace of anger or menace. He was a master at keeping his composure and bearing, and that was what made him so dangerous. One never knew when he might lash out in a violent fury.

Khulr turned to face Elliot, still lying prone in the dirt, though her eyes burned with hatred as she turned her head to look up at the Klingon. "And Ensign Elliot, I haven't had the opportunity to chat with you for quite a while. Thank you for giving me reason to correct that oversight."

"STOP!"

The voice from above them halted everyone in their tracks. Garrovick turned his head to search for the source of the voice, and found it on the second-floor balcony of the prison's command center. Standing there in full military regalia was the camp commander. The morning sunlight glinted off the heavy gold sash he wore over his stark black uniform, the gray in his hair and beard giving him a more regal appearance than a prison commandant had any right to have.

"Bring them to me," the commander said before turning sharply on his heel and retreating through the doorway into his office.

Garrovick didn't let the sigh of relief escape too audibly as he was hauled from the ground by two of the guards. No sooner had he regained his feet than the dark, menacing face of Khulr filled his vision.

"We will finish this conversation later, human." Garrovick knew there was no mistaking the Klingon's tone. He was none too happy about having his plans derailed by the prison commander, and he would find some means of restitution, most likely before the day was out.

As he returned to the relative comfort of his small yet functional office, Korax shook his head in disgust and a vile oath slipped from his lips. While he craved any opportunity to disrupt the mundane daily routine that so characterized the operation of this prison, dealing with a handful of disruptive prisoners wasn't what he had in mind.

How long had it been since the last time a prisoner had caused a disturbance? A week? Two? He supposed he should be thankful for the diversion. Any break from the unending stream of mind-numbing tasks he was used to overseeing would normally be welcome. He took in his surroundings, not for the first time cursing the cruel fate bestowed upon him.

Korax was certain that not all of the Klingon gods had been slain by noble warriors all those centuries ago, but that one had survived and was now taking out a millennium's worth of divine anger by sentencing him to this life of mediocrity and humiliation.

And to make it worse, it had to be the Earthers.

He hated humans and always had. Despite his many meetings with them, however, the memory of one particular encounter never failed to generate a bitter taste in his mouth.

Stardate 4524.2, Earth Year 2268

Even with his hands covering his ears, Korax could still *hear* them. The shrieks were deafening, penetrating the meager protection his hands provided and driving straight through into his skull.

Tribbles.

Beyond the doors leading to the engineering section of the IKS *Gr'oth*, Korax could see almost nothing but an ocean of the cursed furry animals. White ones, brown ones, tan ones, they had overtaken the enormous compartment. He also saw three engineers trying to wade through the screaming, shivering mass of hair. Near the door, dozens of the tribbles were falling into the corridor, where they immediately sensed the Klingons' presence and began squealing and scurrying in every direction.

Kicking out at one tribble that dared to venture too close, Korax yelled at a junior officer near the door. "Seal the room! Don't let any more of those cursed vermin escape!" The subordinate moved to comply and in a moment only the shrieks of the few dozen tribbles that had made it to the corridor could be heard.

"Korax!"

The booming voice echoed in the passageway behind him, and Korax turned to see Captain Koloth stalking toward him. He had seen his captain angry enough times in the past to know that this was a level of fury that was rarely displayed.

"What in the name of Kahless is this?" he asked, seeing the tribbles fleeing away at his approach. "How did these things get aboard my ship?"

"Our sensor logs show that the *Enterprise* activated her transporter just before we engaged our warp engines," Korax replied.

As Koloth cursed at the report, Korax glanced about the corridor. Tribbles were scattered across the floor, attached to the walls, and a few had even managed to work themselves into the overhead support beams. How fast did the damnable things move?

"It isn't enough that I've failed in my mission to sabotage the Federation's plans for developing Sherman's Planet," Koloth roared, waving at the tiny, writhing masses of purring fur littering the corridor. "Nor is it sufficient that these disgusting things had anything to do with my failure. Now you're telling me that I am the victim of a petty deceit no more refined than one executed by a child?"

"It had to have been that Earther, Kirk," Korax said. He had heard of the human captain's penchant for unorthodox tactics.

Koloth shook his head. "No. With no battle being fought, I doubt that Kirk would take such underhanded action when there was nothing to gain from it."

But someone else certainly had, Korax knew. Even as the *Gr'oth* accelerated away from Federation Deep Space Station K-7 toward Klingon space, someone aboard the *Enterprise* had foisted these evil cretins upon them. If the reports on the tribbles' reproductive capabilities were accurate, the ship would soon be overflowing with the damned things.

Koloth slammed his fist into a nearby wall communications panel, an action which sent the closest tribbles scurrying and squealing away in apparent terror. The Klingon captain scowled, but otherwise ignored the creatures.

"Bridge, order the transporter operators to their stations. I want these godless creatures off my ship. Beam them into space."

"It was the engineer," Korax said suddenly.

Looking to his first officer, Koloth replied, "What?"

Korax nodded now, not looking at his captain as he pieced the puzzle together. "That wretched Earther. This is his revenge for losing our fight in the station bar."

"From the report I received," Koloth said, "it was the Earther who was victorious. He succeeded in attacking first, did he not?"

His face burning with anger and embarrassment, Korax nodded. "His attack was cowardly, striking out when my attention was elsewhere."

"You mean while you were drunk and unaware of your surroundings," Koloth corrected. "Because of your idiocy, my ship is being overrun by these filthy maggots." He indicated the tribbles scattered across the deck of the corridor with the wave of his hand. Korax frowned as he took in the scene once more. Was it his imagination, or were there more of them than there had been just a few moments ago?

The purrs and squeaks of the tribbles almost drowned out the sound of a beep from the ship's intercom system, followed by a filtered voice. *"Captain Koloth, this is the bridge. I have a report from the transporter officer."*

Crossing the corridor to the communications panel set into the far wall, Koloth thumbed the switch to open the connection. "What is it?"

"We are able to lock on to the tribbles occupying the engineering section. However, others have moved into the

ventilation systems. Many of these pass through shielded areas of the ship, preventing a transporter lock."

Koloth glared at Korax as he spoke into the comm panel. "Are you saying that we can't get rid of them all?"

"That is correct, Captain."

Without bothering to end the conversation, Koloth severed the connection and turned on Korax. Waving his arms to indicate the tribbles, he said, "These *Ha'DIbaH* will continue to breed until they replace the very air. By the time we reach our nearest base, they will be the only thing left manning this ship!"

Korax stared at the floor and the tribbles covering it, some of which would resume their hateful squealing whenever one of the other officers came too close to them. He shook his head in disbelief. It seemed ridiculous that such a pathetic-looking animal as a tribble could pose so great a threat. Of course, it wasn't the single tribble that gave cause for concern.

Rather, it was the hundreds of thousands of siblings it brought along for company.

He had no doubt that their superiors would be less than pleased when the *Gr'oth* returned to base. Korax wouldn't be surprised if Koloth simply didn't have the ship destroyed, tribbles and all.

Chapter Six

IN THE AFTERMATH of the embarrassing incident over Sherman's Planet, Koloth was able to regain favor with the High Council, due in no small part to his having many loyal supporters in the Klingon government. Korax, however, possessed no such luxury. With no one willing to speak on his behalf, not even Koloth, he knew that his chances for redemption were small and that they dwindled with each passing year. As Koloth continued to advance through the ranks and was given more responsibility, Korax soon found himself shuttling from one mediocre assignment to another. Though he served faithfully, ever the loyal soldier, he remained unnoticed or worse yet, ignored by those in power.

All because of humans, and the cursed tribbles.

Since that incident, Korax's encounters with humans had been rare and fleeting. Even here, very few Earthers had been brought to him. Humans or members of other Federation races were taken prisoner only rarely, as the engagements between Starfleet and Klingon ships either yielded minor damage to the involved vessels or else resulted in complete destruction of one of the combatants.

Korax looked on as order was reestablished in the courtyard below. He could hear guards directing the prisoners back into line, loud commands carrying over the collected murmuring of inmates still trying to determine what had caused the disruption in their morning routine. Within moments their attentions would be focused on the workday ahead, leaving him to deal with the two humans currently being escorted to his office.

Ordinarily, he would relish the opportunity to deal with a human prisoner, but as soon as he had seen which inmates were involved, he knew that resolving the situation would be anything but simple. It had been that way since he had arrived at the prison and been briefed about the *Gagarin* survivors and the circumstances surrounding their captivity. Once more he cursed the politicians who, from their lofty perch hundreds of light-years away on the homeworld, dared to interfere with how he ran his prison.

The door chime sounded, rousing Korax from his reverie.

"Enter." The office door opened to admit the two prisoners, Garrovick and Elliot, escorted by Khulr and another guard, Moqlah.

Korax studied the two humans in silence for several seconds. Substandard nutrition and occasional bouts with disease had aided in the deterioration of their bodies that was the normal result of years spent in conditions such as they had endured. Still, the camp commander detected a residual fire in the eyes of the humans standing before him that had refused to be quelled by their long captivity.

"So," he said almost casually, "what is the problem here?"

Indicating Elliot with the tip of his unpowered baton, Khulr said, "This one attacked a guard who was administering punishment to another prisoner." Korax knew that Khulr despised the humans, with a special emphasis on Elliot.

Khulr brought with him his own unique set of concerns, though. The senior guard had made well known his dissatisfaction with many of Korax's policies since the camp commander's arrival. Korax had disciplined him for disobedience in the past, and if he hadn't been so effective at keeping the prisoners in line, Korax would have already killed him. However, with manpower concerns the way they were, executing Khulr or even transferring him from the prison wasn't a viable option.

Moving around the corner of his desk, Korax eyed Elliot thoughtfully. In response, the prisoner glared back at him, defiance gleaming in her eyes.

"Interfering with a guard in the performance of his duty is a serious offense," he said. "Attacking a guard is grounds for execution."

"Duty?" Elliot spat the word. "He was beating on that woman."

"She did not move quickly enough when ordered by the guard," Khulr offered.

"How fast was she going to move after you finished beating her?" Garrovick snapped. Turning his attention back to Korax, he added, "He damned near killed her. She couldn't defend herself from the attack, and this thug was enjoying the whole thing. You could see the smile on his face."

Korax nodded, not saying anything. The human's story was accurate, at least as far as he was concerned. After all, he had observed the entire incident from the balcony outside his office. He turned his attention to Khulr.

"Why did this happen?"

"The guard is new, Commander," Khulr replied. "Replacement officers are almost always too enthusiastic. I will correct his behavior."

"Are you saying he was improperly trained upon his arrival here?" Korax asked, knowing full well the response the question would generate. Khulr himself was in charge of training new arrivals to the guard detachment.

"No," the head guard said, and Korax heard the anger enveloping the single word. Khulr was bristling at the direct challenge of his ability to indoctrinate the men in his charge.

"He was briefed on prison policies?" Korax pressed. "Specifically, my orders regarding the treatment of prisoners?"

Nodding, Khulr's eyes flared in growing anger. "Yes, Commander."

"Then obviously," Korax replied, "this soldier willfully disobeyed your orders and mine. See to it that he is executed immediately."

He saw the effect his blunt command had on Garrovick and Elliot, and smiled inwardly. He watched as the humans exchanged looks, each reading the question in the other's eyes: How little were their own lives worth if he could so easily order the execution of one of his own guards?

Equally surprised by the order, Khulr's slow-burning anger evaporated, replaced by astonishment as he blinked several times before a single word tumbled from his own lips.

"Commander?"

Knowing that the guard would resent being ignored in such a fashion, Korax didn't respond immediately. Instead he began to pace the width of his office, his hands clasped easily behind his back. Stopping before his desk, he reached out and casually ran one finger along its worn wooden surface, noting the trail created in the light film of dust. His personal servant apparently needed to be reminded about attention to detail when cleaning his office.

Finally, after a few more moments studying his desk and the trappings of his position scattered atop it, he turned to face Khulr once again.

"The prisoners cannot possibly be productive in the mines if they are beaten to near death over minor incidents. That is the reason for my orders regarding their treatment, and I will not tolerate disobedience. You will gather your men, Khulr, and execute the disloyal guard as an example to them. The same fate awaits anyone who chooses to defy me as he did. Further, the next time I must make an example of someone, it is I who will execute you. Now, get out."

He watched Khulr's eyes smolder as he listened to his commander's tirade. Korax knew that being forced to endure such a dressing-down in the presence of prisoners, Earthers no less, would make the guard even angrier than he already was. Khulr stood that way for several more seconds before directing a look of pure hatred at Garrovick and Elliot. Then he turned on his heel and left the office without another word.

Not even bothering to watch him leave, Korax instead returned his attention to Elliot. "There is still the matter of your having attacked the guard."

Garrovick stepped forward, making the remaining guard, Moqlah, reach for his baton, but the human kept his arms at his sides and made no further moves.

"Commander, I am responsible for the actions of my people. If anyone should be punished, it's me."

"Stephen," Elliot began.

"As you were, Ensign," he snapped, cutting her off. "I'm still your superior officer."

Korax watched the brief exchange, noting the added layer of emotion beneath the short, terse words spoken aloud. As Elliot clamped her mouth shut he saw her eyes flare in anger, her volatile nature threatening to spill forth yet again. He knew that Garrovick was the highest-ranking of the remaining Starfleet prisoners, and as such had taken the responsibility for the actions of his crewmates on many occasions. Korax respected the fact that the human had not relinquished his duty even in the face of the adversity he endured here.

"I alone decide who is responsible," he said finally. "And I alone decide who is to be punished."

What was he to do here? He couldn't just overlook the incident. Unfortunately, the usual penalty for attacking a guard, death, wasn't available to him. The Chancellor of the High Council himself had made that quite clear to Korax when he had first taken charge of the prison and custody of the *Gagarin* prisoners. Korax had therefore been forced to modify camp policies so that all of the prisoners were treated the same way. Instead of the brutal existence that normally characterized life in a Klingon gulag, inmates here were spared unnecessarily harsh treatment. Only in the most extreme of circumstances was a prisoner tortured or killed. He'd been forced to train his guards to display total authority and control while at the same time refraining from acting in accordance with their past experience and training.

Still, this incident demanded special attention. Korax couldn't simply ignore standing policies on the penalty for assaulting a guard just to protect the six Starfleet officers. It would arouse suspicion among the other inmates almost immediately. One could never discount the intelligence, ingenuity, or determination of anyone held against their will. Other prisoners would soon deduce that the Earthers held some value that they themselves did not, and might even take steps to utilize the information for their own gain. Korax couldn't risk any harm coming to the *Gagarin* survivors, either from his own guards or other inmates.

"Commander, if I may," said Moqlah, who had been standing silently from the time he had first entered the office.

Korax looked to his subordinate, slight surprise registering on his face. "Yes? What is it?"

"Sir, these two have been trained to operate our larger mining machinery. There are only a handful of prisoners who can perform such tasks. If they are killed, our quota could be affected."

Yes!

Korax managed to keep the relief from his face. Moqlah had unknowingly provided a solution to his dilemma, but it wasn't enough to justify not retaliating for Elliot's actions.

"Very well," he said, schooling his features so as to appear the annoyed prison commander. "Put them in isolation, three days."

The isolation cells were in no way a pleasant experience. When a prisoner was placed inside one of the small, coffin-like booths, the contraption succeeded in cutting off all outside stimuli. The occupant could see nothing, could hear nothing save the sound of his own breathing. After prolonged periods, the booths were quite capable of destroying a prisoner's mental health. Korax knew that Elliot had experienced the isolation firsthand and knew its effects and potential as well as any other prisoner. She'd endured punitive isolation for a lot longer than three days, so Korax was certain she could handle the punishment he had handed to her and Garrovick. His suspicions were confirmed when he saw the momentary relief flash in her eyes. That had to be dealt with quickly if the illusion he was working to create was to be maintained. Stepping toward her, he glowered as he leaned in close.

"But remember this, Earther," he said in a low voice filled with a menace that he hoped was convincing. "The next time, there might not be an alert, sympathetic guard watching out for you. Take care that you do not disrupt my prison again."

The route to the isolation cells appeared to have been deliberately constructed so as to add to the total effect of this particular punishment. Moisture clung to walls crudely cut from the bedrock just beneath the surface of the prison compound, chilling the air of the underground passage. Small lamps hung intermittently along the corridor provided dim illumination. Though Garrovick had traversed this path once before, the sense of foreboding was just as intense as it had been that first time.

"Thank you," Garrovick said to Moqlah as the Klingon escorted he and Elliot to the isolation booths. "You could have easily let Korax execute us."

"No, I could not," Moqlah answered simply.

The blunt reply stopped Elliot in her tracks. She pivoted to face the guard. "What is that supposed to mean? Surely two lowly prison workers can be replaced easily."

"Syd," Garrovick hissed in warning.

"You are not the same as the others incarcerated here," Moqlah said. "You are prisoners of war, taken during battle. To execute you would be dishonorable and disobedient to the teachings of Kahless."

"Kahless?" Garrovick frowned at the name, one he had not heard since his history classes at the Academy. He recalled that Kahless was supposed to have been a mythical figure of major importance in Klingon culture.

Moqlah nodded. "Kahless, the creator of the Klingon Empire." His expression turned somber as he added, "You were denied the right to die in battle. Kahless would not approve of executing warriors like criminals, and it is he who will decide whether you are to join him in *Sto-Vo-Kor* or be banished to the depths of *Gre'thor* with the other *petaQ* who possess no honor."

Moqlah's words chilled Garrovick almost as much as the damp, cool air surrounding them. He had never seen Klingons display such rich devotion to something other than the heat of battle. It provided a different facet of their culture, one he had never expected to encounter.

"I don't think Khulr feels the same way that you do," Elliot said.

"There are those in the Empire who reject beliefs such as those held by Khulr. We are growing in number, and our message is sweeping across the Empire. Khulr is a dog, and when he dies he will spend eternity with those who share his dishonor."

Elliot nodded in satisfaction. "Now you're talking. If *Gre'thor* is anything like Hell, then it's still too good for him."

As they moved further along the clammy, dark corridor, Garrovick pondered what Moqlah had told them. If other Klingons felt the same way as the guard did, then how far did it go? He wondered if an entire race of beings could change their culture at such a fundamental level. Notions of honor and valor hadn't been hallmarks of Klingon behavior in Garrovick's experience.

If change was indeed on the horizon, his only hope was that he might live long enough to see it.

Chapter Seven

NORMALLY CONSERVATIVE and austere in both form and function, the VIP lounge on Starbase 49 had undergone a remarkable transformation. Gone were the Starfleet-regulation sofas, chairs, tables, and other standard furnishings, all replaced with lavish banquet facilities. Buffet tables lay overstuffed with foods representing dozens of Federation worlds as well as many Klingon delicacies.

At the entrance to the lounge, Kirk took in the scene with the air of a gladiator about to do battle before the frenzied masses. The room bustled with activity as Starfleet officers and Federation diplomats along with Klingon military officers and governmental representatives moved about the room. Though the atmosphere seemed congenial on the surface, one had only to look closer to see a discernible segregation taking place. While politicians from either side were making efforts to mingle and converse, those in uniform were conspicuously separated into small camps, each eyeing the other with varying degrees of suspicion and distrust.

"Lord how I hate these state dinners," McCoy said in a low voice as he stood beside his friend.

"What are you complaining about?" Kirk asked. "You're not the one the Klingon ambassador is going to single out before we eat." He had never been comfortable with being publicly honored or praised, content instead with knowing that he performed his duties to the best of his ability.

"Well, I know just the cure for that," McCoy replied. "The bar looks to be well stocked, Captain sir. Might I suggest a Saurian brandy to take the edge off? We can celebrate your making it through the entire week without jettisoning a single Federation diplomatic blowhard into space."

True enough, the journey to Starbase 49 had been free of incident, one of the rare times during his career that Kirk could remember such an anomalous event occurring. None of the dignitaries traveling aboard the *Enterprise* had been the least bit of trouble. On the contrary, Kirk had even struck up a friendship with one diplomatic aide, himself a retired Starfleet captain with a penchant for racquetball. The muscles in Kirk's arms and legs reminded him of how intense the friendly game between the two men had quickly become.

Noticing the bustle of activity as people began to move to their tables, Kirk said, "Looks like our celebration will have to wait, Bones. The party's about to start." He led the way to their table, situated near the raised dais at the front of the room.

As he moved through the gathering of people, Kirk noticed one Klingon in particular. Tall even for a Klingon, the officer had long dark hair streaked with gray, which flowed about his broad shoulders and highlighted the high brow ridges on his head. The leather of his immaculate uniform gleamed in the reflected overhead lighting, as did the heavy sash he wore draped over his right shoulder.

Kirk realized the Klingon was looking at him. Their eyes locked, and the *Enterprise* captain was teased with the notion that he'd met this impressive warrior somewhere before.

"Something the matter, Jim?" McCoy asked quietly. It wasn't until the doctor had spoken that Kirk realized he had stopped moving. The words startled him into continuing his path toward their table.

"It's nothing, Bones," he replied. "Just thought I recognized someone, that's all." He cast a final look toward the Klingon, who bowed his head formally in Kirk's direction. A small smile played across the warrior's lips.

Kirk shrugged off the moment as he and McCoy arrived at their table to find Captains Spock and Scott, along with Commanders Uhura, Chekov, and Sulu already there. The officers began to rise at their captain's approach but he smiled and indicated for his comrades to remain seated.

"Good evening, Captain, Doctor," Spock offered, a sentiment repeated by the others at the table.

Kirk took the seat next to his first officer and leaned in closer to the Vulcan. "Spock, do you see that Klingon standing near the side door?" He indicated the officer he had seen earlier. "Does he look familiar to you?"

Spock took a moment to study the Klingon, after which his right eyebrow rose in the manner Kirk knew meant his friend was intrigued.

"He is wearing the uniform insignia of a ship captain," Spock noted. "Therefore it is reasonable to presume that he commands one of the two escort vessels used to bring the Klingon delegation to the conference. According to the intelligence reports made available to us while en route, he is either Captain K'tran or Captain Koloth."

Koloth?

"Captain," the Vulcan said, "we met another Klingon named Koloth, nearly twenty years ago on Deep Space Station K-7. At the time, he was commanding a border patrol ship, the IKS *Gr'oth.*"

"Tribbles," Scotty said, having overheard the captain and Spock's comments.

Spock nodded. "That is correct, Mr. Scott. As I recall, the incident ended with you falling somewhat out of favor with the crew of the *Gr'oth.*"

"That's putting it lightly," Uhura added, a smile brightening her face as she saluted the *Enterprise* engineer with her raised glass.

"You don't think he might still be holding a grudge?" Sulu wondered, the end of his sentence dissolving into a chuckle.

McCoy turned back in his seat to face his companions. "Somebody correct me if I'm wrong, but I don't remember Koloth looking anything like that the last time we saw him."

Not saying anything, Kirk was nevertheless sharing the doctor's confusion. During his career in Starfleet, he had encountered two distinctly different types of Klingons. As the years passed, he had assumed, as he figured most people might, that the Klingon Empire was made up of several different species, just as the Federation was composed of hundreds of races occupying an even larger number of worlds.

But what about Koloth?

Looking past the delegates and other people milling about the room, Kirk returned the Klingon's scrutinizing gaze. Though their paths had crossed occasionally since the incident at K-7, it had been several years since he had last seen Koloth. Still, as he studied this Klingon warrior, looking past the longer hair, fuller beard, and yes, even the pronounced forehead ridges, the piercing eyes that Kirk remembered as one of Koloth's more defining characteristics were decidedly familiar.

"As crazy as this sounds," Kirk said after a moment, "I think that's the same Koloth."

The thought was interrupted as he noticed a distinct diminishing of the various background conversations and other activity taking place around him. A hush gradually fell over the conference hall and his attention was drawn to movement on the dais holding the head banquet table. In addition to the Federation and Klingon ambassadors, the table also held a handful of high-ranking Starfleet personnel. As the audience waited, Ambassador Catherine Joquel, the Federation envoy to the current peace proceedings, made her way to the podium positioned at the front of the dais.

"May I have your attention, please," Joquel said once she had reached the podium, her voice amplified by the lounge's audio system. After giving the audience a few moments to take their seats and direct their attention toward the front of the room, she continued.

"For many years, you and those who came before you, whether you be officers of Starfleet or the Klingon Empire, have sworn oaths to serve your people in defense of their enemies. Unfortunately, for that same number of years, your enemies have been each other. However, after decades of distrust, hostility, and conflict, we have arrived at a crossroads. The leaders who guide you, those you have sworn allegiance to, have decided that it is finally time for change. They have arrived at the conclusion that we are stronger if we join together than if we continue to hold each other at arm's length as enemies."

She indicated the Klingon ambassador, seated to her left at the head table. "Along with Ambassador Kaljagh and our respective teams, we have traveled here today to begin that process. Hopefully, our efforts will place us all on the path to that day when we will no longer refer to each other as enemy, but as friend."

Kirk noted the murmurs of approval that filtered through the room, barely audible but there nonetheless. One thing was certain: Catherine Joquel knew how to work a room.

"And now," she continued, "it is my great honor to introduce the Klingon special envoy to the Federation and one of the architects of the effort which brings us here today, Ambassador Kaljagh."

Applause erupted as the mighty Klingon ambassador rose from his chair and made his way to the podium. He nodded respectfully to Joquel as he moved beside her, though his face was that of the typical, hardened Klingon warrior.

"He looks like he could fight us all single-handedly," Chekov muttered in Sulu's direction.

The helmsman nodded in agreement. "Well, you're the chief of security. It's your job to handle him. I can't risk damaging my hands, you know."

At the podium, Kaljagh stood absolutely still, staring out into the audience and waiting for the applause to die down. When he spoke, it was with a deep, resonating voice that was used to being heard.

"Greetings, Federation officials, Starfleet officers, and warriors of the Empire. It is with a profound sense of honor that I address you this evening. I have been charged by the High Council to represent our people at these historic proceedings, during which we will forge the beginnings of a bond with our former enemies. There are many who believe such a union is long overdue, but there are also those who believe we are somehow undermining those things which made our Empire what it is. I stand before you today as an emissary of the former viewpoint. It is time to cast aside our distrust, our anger, our fear, and embrace one another as brothers. May the negotiations we pursue here lead to that momentous event."

There were more applause, though Kirk couldn't help noticing that there was decidedly less enthusiasm shown by the Klingon attendees than by those wearing Starfleet uniforms. In addition, many of the more senior Starfleet officers, captains, and admirals sprinkled among the audience were more reserved in their appreciation than their more junior counterparts. As with Kirk himself, experience had jaded the perspective with which the more veteran officers were viewing the current proceedings.

"Before we go any further," Kaljagh continued, "I must perform one important duty. Our coming here today, as many of you know, was prompted by an unfortunate course of action undertaken by a spirited yet inexperienced Klingon officer. Were it not for the prudent actions of a tested Starfleet captain and his crew, we would possibly be at war today, rather than discussing peace."

The ambassador looked up at Kirk as he spoke, and the *Enterprise* captain felt eyes on him as audience members turned in their seats to face his table. Though the life he'd chosen had long ago accustomed him to being an object of scrutiny, he found himself growing uncomfortable with the sudden heightened attention Kaljagh had foisted upon him.

"There is a man among us who is regarded by many as a prime enemy of the Empire. He is a man whose death would bring celebration in our capital cities. It is the height of irony that he is also the one most responsible for seeing to it that the rash actions of an ambitious youth did not cascade into disaster for us all. The High Council extends its most sincere apologies and gratitude to Captain James Kirk and the crew of the *USS Enterprise*."

Applause engulfed the room once more as, following Kirk's lead, the command staff and those officers from the *Enterprise* who were in attendance stood. Kirk took in the mixed reactions of those around him, most especially the Klingons. While some clapped heartily, many others were more subdued. Peace, trust, and harmony might be the goals of the conference, but none of those qualities were in abundance at the moment.

McCoy leaned closer. "Ready for that drink yet?"

Chapter Eight

FOLLOWING THE OPENING SPEECHES, the dinner had officially been declared under way. Admiral LeGere, the commander of Starbase 49, and his staff had created a buffet menu featuring selections from across the Federation as well as the Klingon Empire. At first LeGere had been worried about the informal setting, but the Klingon ambassador had quickly put him at ease, in his own way of course.

"The weak will starve," Kaljagh had said, allowing the remark to hang over the admiral's head for several seconds before a tremendous wolfish grin enveloped his face.

The lines moved slowly, and Spock had elected to wait before eating. He was moving about the outskirts of the room, studying the paintings and other artwork adorning the walls, when a voice called out from behind him.

"Captain Spock?"

He turned to see a Klingon, dressed not in the uniform

of a soldier but rather the flowing robes of a delegate. They were not as rich or colorful as those worn by the Klingon ambassador and the other dignitaries in his party.

"Yes?" the Vulcan replied.

A smile broke out on the Klingon's face. "Excellent. I am Toladal, aide to Ambassador Kaljagh. It is an honor to meet you, Captain. Your reputation is well known within the Empire."

Spock's eyebrow rose at that. "Indeed?" In actuality, he was quite aware that he was a target of scrutiny, given the *Enterprise*'s numerous encounters with Klingons over the years.

Toladal nodded. "We have followed the careers of several Starfleet officers for many years, and you are among that select group. Your interactions with members of the Empire have always been forthright and honorable, even during battle."

"Klingons appear to value such traits, particularly in battle," Spock replied.

"That may not have always appeared so, Captain, but rest assured that the Empire has grown beyond the warlike band of savages that the Federation first encountered many years ago. We too have evolved as a species. While there is still much work to be done, many of us believe we have progressed far enough to make this effort at negotiation worthwhile."

Spock absorbed Toladal's words, noting how strange such sentiments sounded coming from a Klingon. He knew that McCoy would relish the thought of his having allowed, even fleetingly, a notion of suspicion as he listened to the aide.

He scolded himself for his moment of doubt. Toladal's words, odd as they may have sounded coming from the mouth of a Klingon, could not be discounted. If one did not listen to the words, then one could not understand the ideas behind them.

Spock formed his own response with practiced care, effortlessly conforming to the diplomatic atmosphere permeating the conference hall around him. "It cannot be forgotten that the Klingons are a proud people, with a rich history of tradition and military successes. In our haste to put aside our differences, the Federation must also be conscious of the Klingon culture and take steps to see that it does not fall victim to dishonor or disrespect. The peace process must be beneficial and agreeable to all concerned, or we are doomed to failure before we even begin."

Toladal smiled in unabashed appreciation. "You give voice to thoughts shared by an increasing number of my people, Captain, including some members of the High Council." The aide paused momentarily, and Spock watched his body language shift noticeably as the Klingon insured that no one might be overhearing their conversation. When he resumed speaking, it was in a much softer voice.

"One of our more recently elected members, Gorkon, frequently speaks of the need for peace and cooperation between our peoples. While some of his ideas bring resistance, others have been rapidly gaining support. In fact, it was Gorkon who led the initiative to bring about this conference."

"Fascinating," Spock said. "This Gorkon sounds like an individual I would very much like to meet one day, circumstances permitting."

"Perhaps if you were to enter the political arena, Captain," Toladal replied, indicating the conference hall and its abundance of diplomats with a wave of his massive arms. "It is common knowledge that your father is a formidable and well-respected ambassador in his own right. You would do well to consider following the path he has traveled when your career in Starfleet is finished."

Not for the first time, Spock was intrigued by the idea of diplomacy as a second career after Starfleet.

"There are always possibilities."

"I don't see the famous McCoy beans anywhere, Bones."

McCoy cast a disparaging look at Kirk as they moved through the serving line. "It's not my fault the cooks on this starbase have no idea what constitutes good Southern cooking." He indicated one dish with a wave of his fork. "Now, will somebody tell me what that's supposed to be?"

Behind him, Uhura eyed the platter. "Whatever it is, it's moving."

"It is *gagh*," a voice said from behind them. "And it is always served best when still alive."

Though the voice sounded confident, almost arrogant, there was a certain lyrical quality that Kirk immediately recognized. Turning around, he found himself staring into the dark, calculating eyes of Captain Koloth.

A huge Klingon smile, replete with jagged teeth, greeted him. "My dear Captain Kirk, it has been entirely too long. It is my good fortune that our paths should cross again on such a glorious occasion." The mighty warrior was carrying a plate of food, including a generous helping of . . . whatever it was he had called it.

"The pleasure is mine, Captain," Kirk replied. For a brief moment, he didn't comprehend that he was staring at the Klingon. Though his appearance had indeed changed drastically since their first encounter twenty years ago, it was still undeniably Koloth.

Kirk indicated his companions with a sweeping gesture

of his arm, introducing Uhura, Scott, Sulu, and Chekov. "And I believe you may remember Dr. McCoy."

Koloth greeted each of the *Enterprise* command staff as pleasantly as he had Kirk. "Yes, the good doctor. As I recall, it was you who played a rather instrumental part in that little encounter of ours on your space station. I never did get to congratulate you on your powers of deductive reasoning."

"Just my lucky day, I guess," McCoy replied.

The Klingon laughed. Casting a quick glance over his shoulder, he returned his attention to Kirk. "I must be getting back to my men, Captain, but we will regale one another with tales of our glorious battles before our duties take us from this place." He indicated the banquet table with a nod of his head. "Be sure to sample some of the Klingon cuisine. It is food fit for a warrior."

The writhing substance on the Klingon's plate beckoned to Kirk. Koloth saw the expression on the *Enterprise* captain's face and laughed again. Taking a fork, he speared a small helping of the food, and Kirk imagined he could hear the squirming mass scream in agony.

"Come now, Captain. Surely the battle-tested commander of a Federation starship can handle a little *gagh*, no?"

The *gagh* was still wriggling on the end of the fork, and Kirk swallowed the nervous lump that had formed in his throat.

"You know," McCoy said, "the last time I ate something that was still alive, I was eleven and it was a double dog dare. I lost that bet, by the way."

Ignoring the comment, Kirk shrugged. "What the hell," he said as he took the fork from Koloth. Giving the wormlike food a last look, he closed his eyes and put the fork into his mouth.

It was still wiggling as Kirk swallowed. He felt it hit his stomach, where it continued to move somewhat for a few more seconds before the acids in his stomach prevailed. The flavor was one he couldn't identify, though it wasn't unpleasant.

"Actually," he said after a few more seconds, "it doesn't taste that bad."

"I'll take your word for it," Scotty said, watching the proceedings with a mixture of disgust and awe.

Kirk smiled at Koloth, intending to thank the Klingon for introducing him to the delicacy, when a sudden feeling of weakness rushed over his body. He felt sweat break out across his forehead, chest, and back. The color washed from his vision and he reached out for the banquet table to steady himself.

"Jim?" he heard McCoy say, the concern evident in his voice. "Are you all right?" A chorus of similar entreaties followed from Uhura and the others.

"Queasy," was all Kirk could stammer before the universe spun away from him and he fell like a rag doll to the floor.

The transporter beam faded around the kneeling form of McCoy, who held the head and shoulders of an unconscious Kirk in his arms. The technician manning the transporter console rushed from behind the protective shield to offer assistance.

"Where the hell's that damned stretcher?" McCoy snapped. His fingers moved to check Kirk's pulse and confirmed again that it was rapid, the captain's heart beating much too fast.

"Medics are on their way right now, Doctor," the technician replied. He exhaled in relief when the doors to the transporter room opened and a pair of medical assistants charged in, each carrying one end of an emergency anti-gravity stretcher.

As the medics loaded the captain onto the stretcher, McCoy grabbed for the medical kit they'd brought and retrieved a portable scanner. In seconds he had activated the unit and was running it over Kirk's chest and abdomen.

"Acute allergic reaction," he noted from the scanner's readings. He reached into the kit again and extracted a hypospray. Setting the injector to deliver a general sedative, McCoy jammed the hypospray into Kirk's arm and injected the drug.

"That'll get his heart rate down," he said. "Get him to sickbay on the double. I'm going to want to treat him for food poisoning, along with the reaction he's having to that Klingon slop he ate."

The ship's intercom system flared to life. *"Spock to Dr. McCoy. What is the captain's condition?"*

As the medics moved Kirk into the passageway on the anti-grav stretcher, McCoy smacked a wall intercom unit with the heel of his hand. "Jim's had a reaction to Klingon food, Spock. I'm on my way to sickbay with him now. I'll let you know when I find out something."

McCoy didn't even bother to close the connection, stalking out of the transporter room and leaving the technician to deactivate the intercom. As he made his way to the nearest turbolift, he cursed Koloth, *gagh,* and Jim Kirk, though not necessarily in that order.

Kirk was already up on a diagnostic table when McCoy entered sickbay. Nurse Laria, a Deltan, looked up at the doctor's approach.

"His body temperature is up two degrees just since he was brought aboard, Doctor. Pulse is thready."

With growing puzzlement, McCoy studied the readings displaying the captain's vital signs. Kirk had never shown such a violent allergic reaction to anything, including Retinax 5, the drug that treated eyesight problems due to advancing age and which Kirk was particularly sensitive to.

McCoy's gut told him that something else was at work here.

"We'll start by treating him for food poisoning," he told his staff. "Prepare twenty cc's of . . ."

The rest of his order was cut off as the doors leading to the corridor outside sickbay opened to admit Spock and Koloth. Laria saw the Klingon first, her eyes widening in disbelief.

"Doctor" was all she could get out before her voice failed her, so she simply pointed.

Eyeing the new arrivals only briefly, McCoy returned his attention to Kirk. "I don't have time to conduct a tour," he snapped.

Koloth stepped forward until he stood beside the doctor. He held up his hand, which contained a small vial of dark red liquid.

"Give this to Kirk," he said.

"What the hell is that supposed to be?"

The Klingon looked almost pleased with himself. "Antidote to the poison I gave him."

"Doctor, it is quite all right," Spock said. "Captain Koloth has explained the situation to me."

"Well, before I pump him full of some blasted Klingon witch's brew," McCoy barked, "somebody had better explain it to me."

Koloth growled in anger. "There is no time to discuss this now. Administer the drug or Kirk will die."

McCoy looked to Spock, who merely nodded. This

was *insane!* Koloth poisoning Kirk, only to stand here, now, arguing over a treatment to save his life?

"I see the question in your eyes, Doctor," Koloth said. "Rest assured that if I wanted to kill Kirk, I would not have done so using such cowardly means. A true warrior kills his enemies face-to-face. Honor demands no less. Now, give him the antidote."

McCoy considered the words, then finally shook his head in disgust. "Give me that," he said, snatching the vial from the Klingon's mammoth hand. Loading a hypospray with the drug, he pressed it to Kirk's neck.

The effect of the drug was startling. Almost immediately McCoy noticed a reduction in the captain's heart rate as well as his temperature.

"What the hell's in that stuff?" the doctor asked even as he reached for another hypospray, this one containing a general vitamin compound to compensate for the fluid loss Kirk had suffered when his temperature had elevated so rapidly.

Koloth didn't answer, his attention drawn to Kirk's eyes as they fluttered open. The captain abruptly rolled onto his side and began coughing.

"Take it easy, Jim," McCoy cautioned. "You gave us a nasty scare there. How do you feel?"

Running a hand across his face, Kirk managed to croak out an answer. "Throat's dry, and my head feels like someone set off a photon grenade inside my skull."

McCoy indicated for Laria to administer treatment for the headache and to fetch some water. Turning back to the diagnostic table, he directed a scathing glance at Koloth. "You have your friend here to thank for that."

Seeing the look of confusion in Kirk's eyes, Koloth said, "Forgive me for my abrupt methods, Captain, but it was necessary. I had to find a way to meet with you and this was one of the few options open to me that might avoid suspicion."

"You could have scheduled an appointment with his yeoman," McCoy offered sarcastically.

Ignoring the doctor's comments, Koloth began to pace the room. "Given the delicate nature of the peace conference, I am sure that I am under surveillance. Meeting with Kirk under anything resembling normal circumstances might attract attention we cannot afford to have." Reaching into his belt, Koloth produced what looked to be a data cartridge.

"What is that?" he asked.

Koloth held the cartridge out to Spock, who reached out and took it, his eyebrow raised.

"This cartridge is a type that hasn't been widely used in Starfleet for several years, Captain," the Vulcan said. "Specifically, it is of a type used in ship's disaster recorders." Directing his gaze to Koloth, he said, "Might I ask where you obtained it?"

"Access the data stored on the cartridge, Mr. Spock," Koloth said. "I think you will find it to be self-explanatory."

Looking to Kirk, who nodded ascent, Spock turned on his heel and moved to a worktable and its computer access terminal. Kirk was already rising to a sitting position in an effort to get off the diagnostic table when McCoy reached out to block him.

"Where do you think you're going?"

"I want to see what this is about." McCoy started to protest but saw the look in Kirk's eyes that he knew too well. Sighing in resignation, the doctor withdrew his arm.

"If you collapse and die," he said, "don't complain to me."

As they moved to join Koloth and Spock, the terminal's display screen flared to life and the men gathered around the table saw a barely legible scroll of computer text.

"Spock? What have we got?"

"It is an extract from the captain's log of a Federation starship," Spock said. Tapping a series of commands into the small console, he added, "According to the registry imprint, it is the log of the *USS Gagarin*."

Chapter Nine

"THE *GAGARIN* WAS AMBUSHED by Klingons in Federation space eight years ago," Kirk said. "She was destroyed, all hands lost." Looking down at Spock, he asked, "Can you verify the cartridge's authenticity?"

"I have already done so, Captain. I have run a check against our own data banks and retrieved the data-encryption algorithm used by the *Gagarin* to encode her disaster recorder. It is a match. Our computer has verified that there is little chance this could be a fabrication."

Kirk remembered the report he had read about the *Gagarin,* pieced together from fragmentary distress calls received by other ships.

A fleeting moment of dizziness washed over him, and he involuntarily reached out for the back of Spock's chair to steady himself. As he wiped his face with his free hand, he noted McCoy's concerned expression.

"I'm fine, Bones," he said, smiling slightly. "Just a little aftershock, I think."

McCoy glanced at Koloth, irritation evident on his face. "Once we're done here, I'll check you over one more time, just to make sure that Klingon swill is completely out of your system." Koloth did not acknowledge the barb and neither did Kirk, instead returning his attention to the matter at hand.

"Even though we know from her distress call that she was attacked by Klingons, the Empire never acknowledged the attack. They claimed it was the work of renegades, operating without government sanction." The venom in Kirk's voice increased with each word, and the discomfort he had been experiencing to this point was almost forgotten as new feelings came to the forefront.

Koloth nodded at Kirk's recitation of the events. "Correct. The High Council as an entity never authorized any attack on a Federation ship. However, that did not preclude a few ambitious Council members from taking matters into their own hands for their own personal gain." He indicated the data cartridge with a wave of his hand. "That was part of the disaster recorder retrieved by the ship which attacked the *Gagarin*."

"Which explains why the ship's buoy was never recovered from the debris later found by other vessels sent to investigate," Spock said.

"With no proof," Koloth replied, "the Empire could state that it had no knowledge of the incident, just as they would deny any of what happened afterward."

Leaning forward, McCoy asked, "And what exactly did happen afterward?"

Koloth hesitated, as if contemplating the ramifications of what he might say next before nodding to no one in particular, appearing to come to an agreement with himself.

"There were survivors of the attack, and they were taken into custody."

The statement, simple and straightforward, crashed into Kirk with the force of a physical blow. "Survivors? After all this time? How? How many? What proof do you have?"

By way of reply, Koloth produced another data cartridge from his belt, though this one was not Starfleet in origin. "Captain Spock, I believe you will be able to access this. I've had it translated into a standard format used throughout the Federation."

Spock inserted the cartridge into the reader. As the terminal's viewscreen shifted images, the group of officers weren't treated to text pages this time. Instead, it was a visual recording.

"This image was obtained from a Klingon prison facility eight years ago," Koloth said. "It's a planetoid located near the border on our side of the Neutral Zone, a staging area for prisoners before they are sent to more permanent facilities. Ordinarily you would never find a human there, or any other individual belonging to a race that would easily be identified as being part of the Federation. But watch closely."

The screen depicted a prison work detail laboring to clear a trail of brush and undergrowth in what looked to be a forest or jungle. Kirk recognized the heavy tools as similar to those he'd used as a boy on his parents' farm. The prisoners on the detail represented dozens of species, some of which Kirk couldn't identify.

Then one prisoner walked into the image and Kirk recognized him as a Vulcan male. He appeared younger than Spock, and it was obvious that he had not been treated well after his capture. He was haggard, slumped in posture, and limping noticeably. His left arm was bandaged and suspended in a crude sling, with dark green blood covering much of the Vulcan's injured arm and left side.

"Oh my god," McCoy breathed.

Kirk stood up to face Koloth. "Are any of them still alive? Where are they?"

Koloth shook his head. "They would have been moved within days of arriving at that facility, Captain. But I do know that there were many who survived the attack on the *Gagarin,* though most of them are almost certainly dead by now."

"Dead?" McCoy said. "What happened to them?"

"I would imagine their fate to be similar to many prisoners of the Empire, Doctor," Spock said. "The ship's surviving command crew were probably interrogated for any useful knowledge they might possess, while the rest were in all likelihood interred in one or more Klingon gulags. As such facilities are known throughout the quadrant for the harsh, cruel conditions under which they operate, it is logical to assume that many of the *Gagarin* crew succumbed in one way or another to that unfortunate existence."

Kirk could tell from the doctor's body language and the expression on his face that McCoy's ire was beginning to rise. "Spock, we're talking about men and women who were captured and killed hundreds of light-years from their homes, and whose families never learned the truth about what happened to them. Can't you be the least bit sympathetic to that?"

Turning away from the table and the discussion that was escalating into an argument between his two friends, Kirk began to slowly pace the length of sickbay, digesting the information he'd just been given. The idea that such an unkind fate had been visited on anyone, particularly fellow Starfleet personnel, grated on him.

When the *Gagarin* had been reported lost, he had traveled to Earth in order to visit the mother of Stephen Garrovick, the *Gagarin*'s first officer and a former member of the *Enterprise* crew. He remembered the devastation that had overcome Anne when she learned that her son had been killed in service to Starfleet just as her husband had several years previously.

Kirk understood the pain. As he walked past the suite of patient beds, all thankfully unoccupied at the moment, his mind dredged up the memory of another sickbay that decades ago had been littered with the bodies of the injured and the dead.

It had been aboard the *USS Farragut,* during his first deep-space assignment, and Anne Garrovick's husband had been Kirk's commanding officer. An encounter with a gaseous entity near a remote planet called Tycho IV resulted in massive damage to the ship and the deaths of almost half the crew, including Captain Garrovick. Kirk had nearly been overwhelmed with grief over his captain's death, blaming himself for not being able to stop the creature's attack when he'd had the chance.

He carried that guilt for many years, until a chance second encounter with the creature gave him the chance at redemption. Had it been fate or mere coincidence that Garrovick's son, Stephen, had been aboard the *Enterprise* at that time? The younger Garrovick helped Kirk defeat the creature, demonstrating the same character traits that Kirk had admired in the man's father. Kirk ended up taking young Garrovick under his wing, their bond becoming almost that of father and son and continuing even after Garrovick's career path took him away from the *Enterprise* and on to other assignments.

As he walked past the sickbay beds, Kirk wondered how many casualties the *Gagarin* had suffered on the day of its destruction. Had Garrovick died, or was he one of the survivors, rotting away somewhere in a Klingon prison? The very thought angered Kirk. Turning on Koloth, he made no attempt to hide the disdain in his voice.

"Assuming that recording is also authentic, I thought Klingons didn't take prisoners during battle," he challenged.

Stepping away from the workstation, Koloth nodded. "In battle, that is correct. However, some Klingons have been known to take prisoners if it served their needs." His eyes narrowed as he added. "I am not one of those people. As for the recording, I'm sure Captain Spock can confirm its validity."

"So why the *Gagarin?*" Kirk asked.

"There are those on the Council who believe war with the Federation is inevitable and that some leverage may be necessary. Only a few of the Council members even know about the *Gagarin* incident and that there are survivors. These are the same Klingons who held Council seats when the original attack took place. All of the newer members except for one are oblivious."

"Secrets among members of the High Council?" McCoy asked. "What's to gain by that?"

Koloth ignored the question. "Those who keep the secret feel that with the new round of talks, it might be better to simply dispose of the survivors and go on pretending they never existed." The Klingon's upper lip curled in disgust. "It was disgraceful enough to attack the *Gagarin* for no reason, but the crew should at least have been permitted to die in battle as warriors. Instead, they were kept as bargaining chips by a handful of loathsome glob flies who dare to call themselves Klingon."

Rising from his seat at the computer terminal, Spock

clasped his hands behind his back. "Apparently there are those who don't share your views, Captain."

"But I am by no means alone," Koloth countered, pointing to the workstation. "That data cartridge was discovered by Gorkon, a recently elected member to the High Council. He found it by accident while performing some other research. The entire matter disgusts him as it would any true Klingon, and he wants it resolved. However, he is afraid that if he attempts to bring it to the attention of the rest of the Council, those who are responsible for this travesty of honor will see to it that the survivors are killed."

"So he wants you to get them out," Kirk said, piecing the puzzle together even as Koloth had spoken. "He wants you to stage a covert operation to retrieve the prisoners, and then what?"

"Not exactly," Koloth replied. "He instructed me to give this information to a Starfleet officer whom I believed could be trusted to handle the matter with the delicacy it requires. I believe that officer is you, Kirk."

The sheer audacity of the statement almost made Kirk laugh. "I'm supposed to waltz into Klingon space, stage an assault on a Klingon prison that I don't even know the location of, snatch however many survivors there might be, and then what?" He shook his head in disbelief.

"Return them to the Federation," Koloth said simply. "The official story will be that they were discovered on a remote planetoid in Klingon space, having managed to land there in escape pods from their ship. It is the only way to get them home without sending the High Council into a panic or jeopardizing the current round of negotiations between our governments, Captain."

Kirk looked to Spock, who nodded. "There is logic to what he suggests, Captain. If what he says is true and if the peace talks currently under way are successful, those members of the High Council who have the most to fear from the situation would undoubtedly kill the prisoners to preserve their position."

McCoy stepped forward at that. "Then we can't take this to the Federation Council either, Jim. That would endanger the prisoners, too."

Kirk knew his friends were right, of course, proving again why he trusted their counsel so readily and so often. The only option that didn't immediately endanger the prisoners, if they were still alive, appeared to be a covert action. But he couldn't just take the *Enterprise* into Klingon space, nor could he use one of the ship's shuttlecraft. Even if he could get authorization to use a small, long-range vessel from Starfleet, there weren't any nearby.

Turning away from the others, he was once again greeted by the cold, sterile environs of sickbay. Glancing about, he reminded himself how much he hated this part of his ship. Despite the undeniable talents of his friend Leonard McCoy, who had saved more lives in rooms like this one than he could easily remember, sickbay to Kirk represented nothing more than suffering and death. It meant failure, something he personally despised and fought against with every fiber of his being.

Failure. Odds were that it awaited him should he decide to undertake this mission. He already knew, however, that it would not be enough to keep him from trying.

"If we're going to do this," he said, "then we'll have to move quickly. If what you say is true, Koloth, then the only way this can work in a short time is if we go in undercover. I need access to a Klingon vessel."

Koloth smiled wickedly. "I thought you might, Kirk," he replied. "My ship stands ready to assist you. Of course, if you're discovered aboard a Klingon vessel in our space, we will all be executed as spies."

Kirk nodded, but execution for spying was the least of his concerns. The potential consequences to the peace process currently under way, as well as the future stability of this entire quadrant of the galaxy, could well be resting on his shoulders.

Not just my shoulders, he reminded himself, thinking of the poor souls who had been made pawns in the grand game being played between two interstellar superpowers. What if there were any *Gagarin* survivors? Kirk was certain there were those individuals, on both sides, who would view the sacrifice of a few forgotten prisoners on some backwater planet to be a worthwhile investment if it kept things stable between the Federation and the Empire.

But for Kirk, that price was simply too high.

Chapter Ten

"WELL, I HAVE TO tell ya, laddie, the admiral in charge of this starbase is a man after my own heart. Only someone of refined taste could see fit to make sure his bar is stocked with scotch as smooth as this."

Montgomery Scott held up the glass in his hand, appraising its contents. With a satisfied smile on his face, the engineer brought the glass to his lips and drank deeply.

Standing next to him at the bar, Pavel Chekov shook his head and smiled. After all, he'd long since become familiar with Scotty's penchant for judging the quality of drinking establishments across the quadrant by the scotch they served. He was right much more often than not, which was why Chekov stuck with him when they visited a new bar, pub, or tavern.

The dinner had progressed without incident, and the *Enterprise* officers now found themselves amid a mingling throng of Federation and Klingon delegates,

Starfleet personnel and Klingon military officers. The meal seemed to have had a relaxing effect on the group, as Chekov now noticed more interaction between the two parties than before.

Scotty saw the distant look on his friend's face. "What's the matter?"

The security chief shook his head. "I was just thinking how nice it would be if this was a normal gathering and not a special event. Us, friends with the Klingons. Do you suppose it's really possible?"

"Aye lad, anything's possible," Scotty replied. "Peace with the Klingons wouldn't be the strangest thing we've run into now, would it? I'd have thought you'd know that by now. Have ye not been payin' attention all these years?"

Chekov couldn't suppress another grin as the engineer turned back to the bar for a refill. Behind him, the Russian could hear an animated voice talking.

"I hear the mighty Captain Kirk lost a fierce battle with a plate of *gagh*. Such a great warrior bested by so pitiful an enemy. No wonder the humans want peace. They know they have no chance against a real adversary!"

Chekov turned toward the source of the voice and discovered that it was not he who was being spoken to. Instead, he saw a group of four Klingons, all wearing the heavy leather uniforms of soldiers, standing in a circle. The comments made by one of them, Chekov wasn't sure which one, were rewarded by hearty laughter from the entire group.

"I wonder how strong his stomach would be with my boot in it," he said softly, though Scotty overheard it.

"Ah, that's just the drinks talkin'," Scotty said. His brow furrowed as he added, "Ye wouldn't be thinkin' of introducin' yourself now, would ya? I seem to recall another occasion where you didn't like what some Klingon had to say about the captain in a bar."

Remembering the bar brawl that had erupted all those years ago on space station K-7 between members of the *Enterprise* crew and that of a visiting Klingon ship, Chekov laughed out loud at Scotty's comment. "You didn't want to fight then, either, at least not until they started insulting the *Enterprise.*"

" 'Twas the principle of the thing, laddie," the engineer replied. "It's no different than a mother lookin' after her children. Anyway, if it's all the same to ya, I'd appreciate it if you'd keep it civil. My days of bar brawlin' are a wee bit behind me."

Chekov nodded. He wasn't exactly the excitable young ensign of twenty years ago, either. Besides, he didn't want to find out what Captain Kirk might say about two of his command staff being hauled away by Starbase Security for starting a fight at an important state dinner.

Especially if we didn't win, Chekov reminded himself.

"What are you drinking there, human?"

Scotty and Chekov turned at the new voice and found themselves staring up, way up, into the face of a Klingon officer. A large tankard filled his enormous, leather-gloved hand. The Klingon's eyes appeared to be more than a little glazed over, a sure sign that he had been enjoying the plentiful refreshments.

The *Enterprise* engineer held up his glass proudly. "This is scotch. You'd appreciate it, you know. It's a drink fit for a warrior."

"Oh please," Chekov said just loud enough for Scotty to hear. "Don't get me started."

The Klingon reached forward and took the glass from Scotty's hand, brought it to his lips, and downed its contents in a single swallow. Pursing his lips momentarily, the Klingon then nodded and smiled appreciatively.

"Not at all unpleasant," he said. Then he held up his own tankard to the engineer.

"What is it?" Scotty asked warily.

"Bloodwine," the Klingon answered. "A true drink for warriors."

Sensing a bond forming, Scotty reached out to take the tankard from the Klingon. It was heavier than it looked and the Scotsman almost had to use his other hand to support it. Gaining control of the oversized drinking vessel, Scotty brought it to his face and sniffed the dark red liquid it held. Finally, he took a drink.

And promptly coughed once, twice, three times. His face turned red as he sucked air in an effort to regain some self-control.

Chekov leaned in closer. "Scotty, are you all right?"

"Bloody hell," the engineer wheezed between labored breaths. "That's got quite a kick." He then regarded the tankard for a moment, shrugged, and took another drink. This time the heavy liquid went down without incident and Scotty raised the tankard to the Klingon, smiling.

Laughing, the Klingon clapped Scotty on the shoulder, nearly dislocating it from its socket. "Bartender," he said toward the service attendant behind the bar, "more bloodwine for my friend and I."

Scotty cast a worried look at Chekov, and the *Enterprise* security chief gave silent thanks that he wouldn't have his friend's skull in the morning.

In another area of the room, Uhura and Sulu were having a different encounter with Klingons.

"I understand you are a communications specialist," a large Klingon said to Uhura in a voice she could barely hear over the room's background noise. The soft-spoken delivery seemed decidedly out of character for the burly, thick-muscled soldier. Of course, the Klingon himself appeared decidedly out of place amid the throng of diplomats and other civilians milling about the conference hall.

Clearing her throat, Uhura nodded nervously before replying. "Yes, that's right. I'm Commander Uhura, the chief communications officer of the *Enterprise.*"

Teeth seemed to erupt all over the Klingon's face as a wide smile appeared. "Excellent!" He stuck out a massive hand in a gesture of greeting. "I am Murgh, communications officer of the Imperial Klingon Cruiser *Terthos*. It is an honor to meet you." Uhura's hand disappeared into the Klingon's as they shook, and she braced herself for the bones in her hand to be crushed in the warrior's powerful grip. It never came, and she realized her expression must have conveyed her concern when a hearty laugh erupted from Murgh's lips.

"I have learned that humans shake hands in this manner when they are first introduced," he said. "It seems a foolhardy thing to do, leaving oneself open to attack."

Sulu stepped forward at that. "Actually, the handshake does have its origins in battle. On Earth many centuries ago, when two strangers would encounter one another, they would offer their empty hands to show they were unarmed. It was a greeting designed to invoke trust."

Releasing Uhura's hand, Murgh's eyes narrowed and his smile thinned into a sinister sneer as he said, "Ah, but suppose one of them has a weapon in the other hand?"

The expressions on the faces of Uhura and Sulu had begun to change to that of slight concern before the Klingon's wide grin returned and he let loose another howl of laughter.

"Fear not, new friends, I am unarmed this day." With that, Murgh stuck his hand out to Sulu, who shook it while trying not to look too relieved.

As he released the Klingon's hand, Sulu felt a tap on his shoulder. He turned to see an *Enterprise* security officer with a harried expression on his young face. The helmsman sympathized with the man, who was only one of many such personnel tasked with insuring the safety of the delegations. Sulu briefly imagined the headaches his friend Pavel Chekov would be enduring over the next several days, certain that the *Enterprise* security chief would look far worse than this poor ensign by the time the conference was over.

"Yes," Sulu prompted the other man. "What is it?"

The ensign looked nervously over Sulu's shoulder at Murgh as he replied. "Sorry to disturb you, Commander, but Captain Spock just called from the ship. He is requesting that you report back to him at once."

"Did he say why?" Sulu asked, a frown creasing the lines around his mouth. "Does this have anything to do with Captain Kirk?"

Shaking his head, the ensign replied, "Sorry, sir. I wasn't given any specifics. Only that you were to report back on the double."

Sulu finally shrugged and placed his wineglass on a nearby table. "Duty calls, I'm afraid," he said to Uhura. Casting a quick glance toward Murgh, he asked, "You'll be all right?"

Uhura waved him off. "I'll be fine. I've got my new friend here to keep me company." The mammoth Klingon smiled proudly at the pronouncement.

"Great," Sulu said. "See you later, then." With that, he turned and followed the ensign out of the room.

As the helmsman quickly vanished into the throng of

dignitaries and military personnel crowding the conference hall, Murgh returned his attention to Uhura. "Commander, I am in need of some assistance. Our communications array is malfunctioning, and I am unable to determine the cause. I have already spoken to the communications officer of the *Gal'tagh,* but like me, she is new to her posting. I thought that perhaps a new perspective might be helpful."

Uhura couldn't help her surprised expression. "You want my help in fixing a Klingon communications system?" She knew the request wasn't all that unreasonable in reality. The principles that guided subspace communication were pretty much universal, in her experience.

Nodding, Murgh replied, "I am told you have some experience with our equipment."

True enough, Uhura thought. She had spent several months learning the intricacies of the communications system aboard the Klingon bird-of-prey that Captain Kirk had captured earlier the previous year. Based on that experience, she believed she just might be able to assist her newfound friend. But there were other concerns.

"Won't letting a Starfleet officer aboard your ship upset your captain?" she asked.

The Klingon shook his head. "I have already informed my captain that if you were to do anything suspicious, I would kill you myself."

Even when Murgh's broad smile reappeared and his riotous laughter threatened to drown out the rest of the activity in the conference hall, Uhura was left to wonder just how much of what the Klingon had said was truly intended as humor.

"You can't be serious."

The face that stared out from the small viewscreen in

the office area of Kirk's quarters was tired. Roused from sleep in the middle of the night back on Earth, Admiral Bennett had made no effort to compose himself before taking the high-priority call from the *Enterprise*.

Kirk understood how he felt. Between preparations for the dinner party on Starbase 49 and the bizarre chain of events that had brought Koloth and his information about the *Gagarin* aboard the *Enterprise,* to say nothing about the lengthy discussions that had taken place afterward, he was feeling the first twinges of fatigue himself. The cramped atmosphere of his office didn't help matters, either. Designed primarily as a private workspace, the office was crowded with himself, Spock, McCoy, and Koloth.

He had never liked using the office in his quarters to begin with, preferring instead to conduct business on the bridge or the main briefing room or even the officers' lounge. But as the crew had been informed that he had been confined to sickbay by Dr. McCoy to recover from his "food poisoning," it wouldn't do for him to be seen in any of the ship's public areas.

Listening as Kirk relayed the information provided by Koloth, Bennett shook his head in disgust. *"For years there have been rumors about Starfleet personnel being held captive within the Empire. The Klingons always denied this, of course. As far as our official records indicate, the* Gagarin *was lost with no satisfactory explanation eight years ago."*

"I have come here to help correct that, Admiral," Koloth said with more than a slight air of indignation in his voice.

Kirk cast a look at Koloth that told the Klingon to leave the conversation to him, then turned back to regard the admiral. "Sir, shouldn't we at least investigate? Doesn't the *Gagarin*'s crew deserve that much?"

"Without a doubt," Bennett replied. *"But if what you're telling me is true, then any official inquiries we make could be dangerous for any prisoners the Klingons are holding, whether they're from the* Gagarin *or some other ship we've lost over the years. If we do this, discretion must be our watchword."* He paused for a moment, aware that Koloth was still in the room. *"Jim, have you considered that this is a ploy to lure you into some kind of trap?"*

From behind Kirk, Spock said, "Admiral, I have verified the authenticity of the *Gagarin* log tape, as well as the surveillance records from the prison showing members of the ship's crew interred there. Based on this information, I believe a more detailed investigation is in order."

"Oh, I agree that it's worth a look, Captain Spock," Bennett said, *"but let's cut to the chase. Jim, can you trust him? Are you willing to risk your life on the word of a Klingon?"*

Kirk could feel Koloth bristle at the words, but he was impressed that the Klingon commander held his tongue.

The *Enterprise* captain could understand where Bennett's question came from. Like the admiral, Kirk had been taught at an early age to distrust Klingons, a position that had been reinforced through numerous occasions with the warrior race throughout his career.

It was only much later that he learned he could hate them as well.

He believed those feelings had started on the battle-crippled bridge of the original *Enterprise.* With the smoke of destroyed consoles assaulting his nostrils and stinging his eyes, he had stood powerless as a Klingon ship captain ordered the execution of David Marcus.

Tears generated by the smoke had been overwhelmed

by those of anguish after Lieutenant Saavik's simple report of his son's death. He also remembered how he had channeled that pain into anger directed with unmitigated force upon the Klingon commander who had given the execution order. His body felt the impact of the physical blows he had traded, of his own booted foot against Kruge's head as he lashed out with fury until his opponent fell from the jagged cliffs they had fought upon. He felt the heat of a world on fire licking at his skin as the twisting body of the Klingon plummeting into the roiling lava flows that were the lifeblood of the Genesis planet, bleeding out as the newly created yet unstable world tore itself apart.

Kirk pushed the memories away. This was not the time for personal grief or renewed mourning. Instead, it was an opportunity to take action. Because of this, he wasn't surprised with the ease at which his response to Bennett's question came.

"Yes, sir, I believe him. Between what he's told us and what Spock's been able to confirm, I trust him." He turned to face Koloth, his expression becoming haunted as he thought of young Stephen Garrovick.

"Besides, I can't just leave this alone now. I have to find out what happened, one way or another."

Nodding in understanding, Bennett said, *"Very well. I'm authorizing you to do this, on my own responsibility. I don't suppose there's any chance you'd obey my order to stay on the* Enterprise *and assign this mission to someone else, is there?"*

Kirk smiled slightly at the light teasing tone of Bennett's question. He'd taken quite a bit of flak over the years regarding his infamous propensity to "lead from the front" as he and his crew faced hazardous encounters both in space and on hostile planets. Admirals up and down the chain of command had advised him, cautioned him, even ordered him against the practice, stating how valuable and irreplaceable a starship captain was.

He had listened to it all, but in the end he always exercised what he believed to be his prerogative as a commanding officer to place himself wherever he thought best during a given situation. Until Starfleet issued a standing order preventing him from doing so, he was not prepared to send a member of his crew into danger unless that crew member was following him.

"Bob," he said, "if I'm captured in Klingon space, Starfleet will have to deny any knowledge of my mission for the good of the Federation, especially now. I can't ask anyone to do that while I sit here."

Bennett conceded the point, knowing that Kirk was right on several counts. For all intents and purposes, the Klingon Empire was still the enemy, even if peace negotiations were ongoing. The Federation Council wouldn't allow anything to jeopardize the chances of reaching some kind of truce with their longtime enemies, even if it meant disavowing the reckless actions of a single starship captain.

"Don't worry, Jim. If that happens, I'll steal a ship and come after you myself."

Kirk drew comfort from the conviction with which his friend spoke. "Thanks, Bob. I won't forget this."

"Don't worry about it. We've got a lot of people listed as missing in action over the years, Jim. If this helps us find out what happened to some of them, then we have to try. It's the least we can do for them and their families. As for you, I can't let you take the Enterprise *over the border, of course, but I imagine you've already got some kind of plan in the works to get around that. Care to share some of that with me?"*

Before he could reply, the chime for the door to his quarters sounded. "Come," he called out, and the doors parted to admit Sulu.

"Captain?" the helmsman said as he entered the room, startled by what he was seeing. "Dr. McCoy told me earlier that you were in sickbay, recuperating from some kind of food poisoning." Then he saw Spock and Koloth standing to either side of the console, along with the activated communications screen and the face of Admiral Bennett on it, and he knew that things were not what they appeared to be.

A thin smile graced Kirk's lips. "Come in, Commander. You're just in time."

Chapter Eleven

As THE OTHER MEMBERS filtered out of the Great Hall that was the meeting place for the High Council of the Klingon Empire, Komor allowed his gaze to drift upward. His eyes beheld the high slanting walls of the hallowed chamber, once again reflecting on the history they must have been silent witness to.

Nearly every decision governing the Empire for centuries had been made within the confines of this hall. Even after the inception of the Council itself, the Emperor had contemplated and forged the future of his people from here. Following the death of the last Emperor, more than two centuries ago, the Council had begun presiding from this chamber. However, the influence of the single mind charged with such great responsibility could still be felt here, embodied in the massive throne at the head of the Hall. Still the seat of power, the throne was now the ceremonial position for the Chancellor of the High Council.

Komor eyed the throne symbolizing the gleaming edge

of the warrior's blade ruling the Empire. Would he ever occupy that seat himself? He thought it unlikely. New ideas and views were making their way into the Council and by extension the rest of the Empire, many of which were in conflict with beliefs Komor held sacred. Change was on the horizon, he had come to realize.

And that change involved humans. This he knew as well.

"Something troubles you, Komor?" a voice called from behind him. He turned to see a figure emerge from the shadowy perimeter of the Great Hall. It was K'lotek, his longtime friend and fellow member of the High Council.

"Our brothers on the Council seem quite happy to throw away everything the Empire has been built upon in order to ally us with the Federation." Komor spat the words, and with good reason. He had spent a number of years as an officer aboard a battle cruiser, serving for the glory of the Empire. Had that all been for naught? Were the values he had held sacred for his entire life, the traditions and beliefs instilled into him from his earliest days, to be so casually thrown away?

"I do not think the situation is as drastic as that," K'lotek told his friend. "We are not kneeling before the Federation, after all. Instead, the Empire would be taking advantage of the prosperity such an alliance would bring us. You know that if we were to go to war with the Federation today, we would be vastly outnumbered, in both ships and warriors."

"Statistics are the defense of cowards," Komor replied harshly, though their friendship was such that K'lotek was incapable of taking offense. "We are Klingons. We are the stronger. The Federation is weak, a chorus of diplomats more comfortable talking than with taking action. They cannot conceive of battle as bloody as that which the Empire can bring."

K'lotek smiled grimly. "The Federation is made up of many races, my friend, some of whom have pasts as glorious and enriched by battle as the Empire. The humans, though their notions of honor may be laughable, have one of the most violent histories of all. Some of their present-day ship commanders can also be shrewd and cunning in combat. They haven't forgotten their bloody heritage as completely as they would have others believe. They should never be underestimated, Komor."

"I do not underestimate them," Komor replied. "On the contrary, I distrust them with every fiber of my being. I agree that we should seek peace with the Federation, but only because doing so will place us in a better position to dictate our destiny in the years ahead. After all, who is to say that, after negotiating a peace treaty with the Federation, we will not have left ourselves open to attack once Starfleet vessels are allowed into our space?"

"I do not believe we are so foolish and shortsighted as to allow such a thing," K'lotek countered. "Chancellor Kesh is no fool, nor are the other members of the Council, even those who have only recently been seated."

Komor turned, leveling a stern gaze at his companion. "Even Gorkon?"

Smiling, K'lotek shook his head. "You may not agree with everything Gorkon brings to the Hall, old friend, but it is hard to discount the things he says. He also has many supporters. Kesh knows this, as he knows that Gorkon and those who share his views may well represent the future of the Empire."

Deep in thought, Komor faced the throne, as if trying to draw strength from the centuries-old symbol of Klingon power and purpose. Hearing K'lotek's words, he dismissed them with a wave of his hand.

"It is Gorkon himself who concerns me now. He is up to something, I think, something which he has chosen not to share with the rest of the Council."

The expression on K'lotek's face changed to one of concern. "What makes you say this?"

Reaching into his robe, Komor withdrew a data cartridge and held it up for his friend to see. "This is the record of a subspace communication made by Gorkon to the *Gal'tagh,* one of the escort vessels that took our diplomatic entourage to the Federation starbase for the peace talks. The *Gal'tagh* left the starbase several hours ago in order to return to its normal duties. Ordinarily, Gorkon would have no reason to contact the ship directly."

"You have a record of the transmission?" K'lotek asked.

Komor, having returned the data cartridge to the folds of his robes, had begun pacing the length of the chamber, and K'lotek walked alongside him. "The message was encoded, using a nonstandard encryption scheme. I have assigned its decoding to my staff, but I find this development most unsettling."

K'lotek moved to a computer workstation and punched in a series of commands. The screen filled with lines of harsh red Klingonese text.

"Koloth commands the *Gal'tagh,*" he noted. "So far as I know, Gorkon and Koloth share no past. He is a capable commander who has served the Empire with distinction. I doubt he would be swayed into doing something questionable, even by someone on the High Council."

"He has had an almost flawless career," Komor added.

"The only blemish on his record is that incident on the Federation space station when he commanded the *Gr'oth*." Komor disdainfully remembered the event, where it had been necessary to destroy Koloth's ship and the millions of abhorrent tribbles infesting it. Even after that, the curse of the fuzzy parasites had continued, and they soon began to find their way onto outlying Klingon planets by way of merchant freighters and other independent spacecraft that did not employ Klingons as crew members. Now, twenty years after that initial contact, complaints of tribbles nearly overrunning remote colony planets or annexed worlds frequented by heavy merchant traffic were commonplace.

Koloth, for his part, had fared much better than his ship. His good standing with several members of the High Council enabled him, after only a short time, to gain command of another battle cruiser, the *Devisor*.

Deactivating the computer station, K'lotek turned back to face his friend. "What could Gorkon be after that would require Koloth's services?"

"I am already seeking the answer to that question," Komor replied. "Before this diplomatic mission began, I saw to it that we had loyal servants aboard both ships. They answer to the Council above all else, including their captains." It had not been an honorable tactic, Komor admitted silently. The original mission for the covert operatives assigned to the two escort vessels was to conduct simple surveillance and reconnaissance. After all, how often did Klingons get to board a Federation starbase? Even with the heightened security measures they were sure to face during the peace talks, an alert spy could still gather valuable intelligence.

Now it seemed his careful planning would prove even more useful.

"Will you be able to contact your operatives on Koloth's ship?" K'lotek asked.

"We shall soon see," Komor replied. It would take some time to get a covert message through to his agent on the *Gal'tagh*.

No matter, though. There was much work to be accomplished here in the meantime. Chief among his concerns was to learn just what activities had been consuming Gorkon's time of late. His thoughts wrestled with what he might find.

What have you done, Gorkon, and what does it mean for the Empire?

Chapter Twelve

IT WAS ALMOST MIDNIGHT by the ship's clock, and as she sat in the *Enterprise*'s command chair, Uhura was thankful for the quiet atmosphere permeating the bridge of the mighty starship at this late hour.

During this new vessel's shakedown cruise several months earlier, she had begun volunteering to take the conn during gamma shift. Earlier in her career, she had become proficient enough in the navigator's position that she could take over in a crunch situation, but it hadn't been until recently that Uhura had felt the need to expand her horizons to other shipboard duties. Taking the conn, in effect taking command of the ship while the captain and the first officer were otherwise occupied, was a satisfying change of pace from her regular duties as communications officer. Besides, the relative peace offered by the overnight shift permitted her plenty of time and little pressure to learn the various other systems controlled from the bridge.

It also gave her a lot of time to think.

And right now, she was thinking that something odd was going on.

At first she had been concerned when she heard that Captain Kirk had fallen ill from food poisoning while at the formal dinner on Starbase 49. She'd felt better, of course, when she'd learned that Dr. McCoy had been able to treat his condition, after which Kirk had been ordered to remain in sickbay for observation. While Kirk was recovering, Spock would take temporary command.

And then things started to get suspicious.

The captain was out of touch, for one thing. Uhura had served with Kirk for over twenty years and had seen him injured on numerous occasions. While recovering from all of those instances and as long as he was conscious, Kirk had always kept in close contact with the bridge. It was out of character for him not to have contacted the duty officer at some point, regardless of the current work shift.

On top of that, one of the Klingon ships had left the starbase, heading back into Klingon space at high warp. There had been no notice of their plans to depart, not that Uhura would have expected an explanation from the commander of a Klingon battle cruiser. Still, she couldn't imagine not having picked up some kind of information on the new development.

Her thoughts were distracted by the sound of turbolift doors opening. Swiveling the command chair around, she saw Chekov stepping onto the bridge. He remained standing in the turbolift alcove, the lines of concern on his face deepened by the shadows created by suppressed lighting helping to simulate ship's night. Seeing his expression, Uhura rose from her chair and moved to join him.

"Something's going on," he said in a low voice as she

joined him. "Sulu and I had plans for a light workout tonight after dinner, but when I went to meet him, he wasn't in his quarters. He's not in the gym, or anywhere on the ship so far as I can tell."

Uhura nodded, grateful for the opportunity to discuss her uneasy feelings with someone she knew she could trust. "Sulu was with me after dinner tonight when he was ordered to return to the ship by Spock. That's the last time I saw him. When I asked Spock about it, he told me that Sulu had been given some kind of special classified assignment."

Her expression melted into a frown as she added, "The thing is, there's no record of any command orders being received, just a scrambled subspace communiqué that Spock requested, even though the call originated from Captain Kirk's quarters." Who had they talked to back at Starfleet Command? That message was obviously at the heart of the unusual orders Sulu had received.

She told Chekov about the abrupt departure of the Klingon vessel. An idea was working its way up from the depths of her mind, and she didn't like what it had to say.

"You don't think Sulu might be on that ship, do you?" Chekov wondered aloud, echoing Uhura's unspoken theory. "No, that doesn't make any sense."

Uhura shook her head. "No more than the idea of Captain Kirk not checking in, even from sickbay."

A sudden thought begged for her attention.

Could Sulu *and* the captain *both* be on the Klingon ship? Uhura's mind swam with the possibilities. What kind of secret mission into Klingon space would require the *help* of Klingons?

It was a crazy notion. Almost.

She rubbed her eyes in an effort to relieve some of the tension she was beginning to feel. The soothing sounds of the bridge and her nice quiet graveyard shift with its low stress level was fading under the gentle yet persistent onslaught of their joint brainstorming. They'd seen too much over the years to accept anything unusual at face value.

"I'm starting to get that red alert at the back of my neck."

She'd heard the captain speak of that peculiar sense on occasion, the instinctive feeling that something alarming was going on, somewhere. Uhura had always figured the trait was either something one was born with, as Uhura believed Captain Kirk had been, or else it was something one learned to develop, along with the numerous other talents and abilities one needed to command a starship.

"You and me both," Chekov agreed. Then, with a slight chuckle, he added, "If you're starting to get those extra senses the captain seems to have, maybe it's finally time you thought about pursuing the command track."

Smiling at that, Uhura glanced around the bridge once more. She had never seriously given thought to commanding her own ship, but sitting in the center seat on occasion, with the comforting embrace of the ship's nerve center surrounding her, provided her a sense of power and responsibility she had rarely felt elsewhere. Experiencing it helped her understand what drove someone like James Kirk, and even her friend Hikaru Sulu, to command. The captain made it seem effortless, and even Sulu's own abilities had progressed rapidly. Uhura had no doubts that a starship command was in his future.

As for her?

It really didn't sound like such a bad idea.

Chapter Thirteen

"Mmmmmmmm. There's nothing like home cooking to warm the stomach and let you know you're loved."

Garrovick took a seat on the unyielding rock floor of the mining cavern, chuckling at Sydney Elliot's dry verbal attack on their lunch just as he had at some variation of the joke countless times during their captivity. As he peered into the metal cup and examined his own meager portion of the bland, pale gruel serving as their midday meal, he tried once again to imagine it was oatmeal.

Once again, he failed.

He shrugged, knowing the tasteless concoction wouldn't kill him. On the contrary, it succeeded quite well at providing needed nutrients and vitamins that kept him healthy and able to remain productive in the mines.

As he ate, he once again felt the throbbing in one of his teeth. The dull ache that had started a few days earlier had grown to the point that he was almost constantly aware of it. Garrovick suspected a cavity was forming in one of his molars, the latest casualty of his deficient diet. Sooner or later he'd have to request permission to visit the camp doctor and see about getting the tooth removed. Having experienced Klingon dentistry three times before over the course of his captivity, he did not relish the prospect, but he couldn't risk infection. In this stark place they called home and given the prisoners' generally weakened condition, even the most minor infection could be fatal.

"Look on the bright side, at least it's not moving."

The group looked up as Chief Robert Kawaguchi joined them. As he sat down next to Sinak, the Vulcan replied, "Mr. Kawaguchi, we have had some variation of this conversation at regular intervals since arriving here. One would think that a different observation might present itself to you at some point."

"When the menu improves," Kawaguchi shot back, "so will my observational skills."

Garrovick smiled slightly as Sinak nodded thoughtfully in his direction, a wry expression playing on the Vulcan's otherwise impassive features. Sinak had told him once before that he had long ago accepted the human penchant to invoke humor in nearly every conceivable situation. Though he doubted he would ever fully understand this, he had seen its positive contribution to their present situation. Logic dictated that any method which could bolster morale among his companions should be utilized to the most efficient extent possible. The Vulcan therefore continued to provide the openings from which Kawaguchi could pursue this odd compulsion.

Whereas Sinak was an almost stereotypical Vulcan, always calm and controlled, Kawaguchi was much more animated both in voice and movement, the type of person one would expect to be the center of attention at a party or a bar fight. An enlisted man, the chief had been one of the crewmen charged with overseeing the *Gagarin*'s vast array of sensors, while Sinak had been one of the ship's communications officers. During any normal voyage, meetings between Sinak and Kawaguchi might have been limited to chance encounters in the mess hall or passing by one another in a corridor. Fate had nevertheless cast them together, their shared experiences during the past several years and the fact they had shared a prison cell for most of them forging an unbreakable bond between the two men.

"I heard the guards talking," Ra Mhvlovi said from where he sat leaning against the rock wall of the massive tunnel with the remnants of his paltry meal. "They're probably going to move us to another section of the mine tomorrow. Looks like a new vein's been discovered."

To his right, Ensign Cheryl Flodin looked up in response to Mhvlovi's words. "That'll mean we probably have a chance to exceed the quota, and that means Korax will be happy." Absently she rubbed her bald head, having long ago forgotten how her shoulder-length auburn hair felt when she ran her fingers through it. Like the work details and the bland food, the lack of hair was just one more prison reality she had long since come to accept.

In those rare moments of quiet that presented themselves in the middle of the night, locked in her cell with Mhvlovi, Flodin allowed her guard to drop and let the cascade of feelings she normally kept in check to wash over her. She dreamt of performing her duties aboard the *Gagarin* as part of the ship's engineering staff. She wondered about the man she had been destined to marry and what might have become of him. She worried about her father, a widower only a few short months prior to the *Gagarin*'s departure on its ill-fated last mission. Had the crew been presumed dead? Her father's health had not been good before she'd left. How had he handled the news of his only daughter's disappearance? Thoughts like these had threatened to consume her on many occasions, and it was only the support of her closest friend and cellmate, Ra Mhvlovi, that got her through the rough times.

Sitting next to her as he often did, Mhvlovi was the emotional rock she had clung to over the years of their captivity. The friendship they had cultivated had enabled her to withstand the worst that life as a prisoner could offer. Mhvlovi was a typical Efrosian, with skin a deeply hued orange and piercing cobalt blue eyes that looked as if they could penetrate cast rodinium. Flodin remembered how, on the *Gagarin*, Mhvlovi had looked almost regal in his uniform and with his mane of flowing white hair and matching mustache. The hair and mustache were gone, of course, and his uniform had been replaced long ago with the standard gray one-piece garment that all prisoners wore. Still, despite everything that had happened to him during the past years, Mhvlovi managed to retain some of his dignity and poise.

"Here," Garrovick said to Flodin as he handed his cup and the remainder of his meal to the ensign. "Eat this. You're starting to look thin." Flodin, who had been a computer specialist aboard the *Gagarin*, had always been slight of build, a condition that had been compounded by the substandard nutrition she and the others had received during the initial years of their imprisonment. Though conditions were better now than they had been originally, the rest of the group still periodically supplemented Flodin's diet with portions of their own meals to help her maintain her health.

Appraising the contents of the cup as well as her own, Flodin frowned. "I think they call this type of action 'cruel and unusual,' Commander."

"It's still better than the stuff they'll pump into you if you keel over on a work detail from not eating." Garrovick had nearly succumbed to malnutrition during the previous year. The dietary supplement the camp physician had inflicted upon him had been near torture, with his insides feeling as though they were fighting to turn themselves inside out. Trips to what passed for the prisoners' lavatory facilities had been both frequent and painful. Garrovick swore he'd never come near the vile "nutrients" ever again and his companions, having witnessed his ordeal, seemed to take a greater interest in the prison menu after that.

Wiping his brow, Garrovick's hand came away damp with perspiration. The hot season would come early this year, all right. Humidity covered everything and everyone like a thick blanket. Breathing was difficult, especially during physical labor such as mining. Even down here, several hundred meters below the surface, the temperature was still uncomfortably high, and the heat generated by the portable laser drills exacerbated the problem. Though they were allowed plenty of water to drink and were given rest periods throughout the day, it did little to alleviate the long-term effects of the exertion composing the bulk of a prisoner's existence.

A horn sounded several dozen meters away at the small portable workstation for the Klingon in charge of the work detail, signaling the end of the meal period. All around the *Gagarin* officers, prisoners began to rise and shuffle into columns to be marched back to the area of the mine being worked today.

"I distinctly remember seeing the clause about rest breaks in my contract when I signed on for this job," Elliot said as she stood up. "I think they're shortchanging us."

* * *

By midafternoon, the temperature in the tunnels had risen to the point that sweat poured from the faces and bodies of the hundreds of prisoners working in this section of the mine. The fact that the region's hot season was still weeks away was not lost on any of the workers. Even underground, soaring temperatures combined with oppressive humidity would soon create a stifling atmosphere where heat-related injuries would become commonplace.

The prisoners also knew that steps would be taken to preserve their health. With dilithium production a high priority regardless of the time of year, Korax would allow increased water rations for the workers. He would also authorize the activation of the mine's air-circulation system, which, while beneficial to the workers toiling hundreds of meters below the planet's surface, was costly in the amount of energy it required from the compound's power generators. Though it was somewhat efficient when it had first been installed, the ventilation system's power and flow regulators could no longer keep pace with the mine, which had grown far faster than originally envisioned.

The mining shaft echoed with the sounds of laser drills boring into the dense rock of the tunnel, as well as pick axes and other tools breaking larger boulders into smaller sizes that could then be loaded onto carts and removed from the work area. The operation was a fluid one, its efficiency having been perfected over years of practice. Indeed, the mine's production quota had been a source of pride for Korax since his arrival at the prison. His appreciation for the prisoners' output came in many forms, most notably in the food rations they received and in the camp commander's policies regarding the guards' treatment of the inmates. So long as the prisoners worked hard and made no trouble, Korax was content to treat them fairly. It was a symbiotic relationship that all parties had come to accept.

Working alongside Lieutenant Sinak, Sydney Elliot deactivated her laser drill and lowered its still-glowing muzzle to the ground. She lifted her protective visor and wiped a gloved hand across her sweat-drenched face. Appraising the piles of rock she had created, Elliot nodded in satisfaction.

The tunnel she and her fellow prisoners had been working in during the previous month had been widened into a larger cavern after geological surveyors had determined that a sizable dilithium deposit had been tapped. As was standard practice now, the prisoners would continue to work here, widening the underground chamber and extracting the precious mineral until the cache ran dry. Afterward, the work detail would cut another tunnel and begin the process anew.

Elliot set her laser drill on the dusty rock floor of the cavern. Reaching behind her, she retrieved the canteen attached to the belt she wore over her coveralls, only to discover that it was almost empty. Finding water wasn't a problem, though. She simply had to ask a guard for permission to fill her canteen from the water drums staged near a connecting tunnel at the rear of the cavern.

Turning away from the wall to look for a guard, Elliot's blood ran cold as she caught sight of Khulr.

The head guard hadn't seen her and Elliot quickly turned away, lowering her visor back into place. The protective gear, along with the layers of dirt and grime caked to her clothing and skin, made her indistinguishable from the other prisoners working in the cavern.

"Damn," she said in a low voice, unheard by anyone else save for Sinak, who was working to her left. The Vulcan deactivated his own drill and lifted his visor.

"Sydney?" he prompted. "Are you experiencing difficulty?"

Elliot held up her canteen. "I'm out of water, but it's not worth bringing Khulr down on me." She had managed to avoid attracting the guard's attention, and his wrath, since being released from punitive isolation the previous day. It was only a matter of time before she did something, however inconsequential it might be, that the Klingon could use against her.

Sinak reached for his own canteen and handed it to her, exchanging it for her empty one. "Perhaps it would be more prudent for me to retrieve the water." Through her visor he could see Elliot smile gratefully. The Vulcan nodded, understanding that his friend's strong personality and sense of pride chafed at the notion of needing assistance to perform a task as basic as obtaining water. Sinak thought nothing of it, mindful of Khulr's peculiar, almost sadistic obsession with antagonizing the young security officer. Breaking her seemingly indomitable spirit had become a hobby for the Klingon, with Sinak and the other *Gagarin* crew members constantly working to protect her.

The ongoing battle of wills had not been kind to Elliot, either. Garrovick had confided to the rest of them about her bouts with insomnia as well as the nights she had awakened screaming, her subconscious in the grips of a violent nightmare. All of them believed that Elliot's mental condition was deteriorating, despite the courageous front she continued to project and the fact that she had not allowed her work output to be affected.

Acting on this, Sinak had endeavored to impart to Elliot a series of basic mental exercises designed to focus the mind and relieve any turmoil she was experiencing from the constant stress. She had accepted the assistance, grudgingly at first but later with greater enthusiasm. The exercises had worked for a time, but Garrovick soon reported that Elliot had given them up, preferring instead to channel her anxiety into anger and direct it at the defenseless rock of the mining tunnels. Though her output had increased and still continued at a high level, none of her friends were taken in by the ruse. Elliot might be handling her personal demons for now, but how long could she keep it up?

Sinak set off toward Khulr and the water drums. As he moved away, Elliot retrieved her laser drill and, taking aim at a crack in the wall before her, activated the unit. Intense red energy erupted from the drill as the beam bored into the dense rock, widening the tiny crevice. Once again she heard the almost comforting sound of disintegrating rock over the high-pitched whine of the drill.

Then the rumbling got louder.

If she'd still had hair on the back of her neck, Elliot knew it would have stood straight up.

"What the hell . . . ?"

Her instincts screamed at her, telling her that something else was wrong. She deactivated her drill as the sound of the rumbling continued to increase, and that's when she felt the first vibrations in the soles of her feet. They had started out gently but she could already sense their intensity beginning to increase. Looking around, Elliot saw that other prisoners had stopped their digging and were turning in reaction to the growing cacophony. Everyone in the massive underground chamber knew what the sounds meant.

Chapter Fourteen

EARTHQUAKES HAD BEEN an infrequent but not unknown occurrence on this world. The last one was a minor tremble that had happened almost two years ago. Elliot had been working in the mines on that day and she remembered the tremors that had shaken the entire tunnel, with the prisoners and guards helpless to do anything except dive for cover and pray.

This quake was a lot worse.

"Watch out!"

Elliot didn't know where the warning had come from and didn't care. All she knew was that within an underground cavern, such a danger cry could only mean one thing.

Cave-in!

She sensed rather than saw the first rocks falling from the ceiling, which had been expanded by the mining operation to at least a dozen meters over the heads of the workers. All along the wall, prisoners working from crudely cut ledges scrambled for any cover they could find as chunks of overhead rock began to break away.

Elliot herself dove into the area she had carved out of the wall during her morning's work, the opening more than large enough to hold her compact form. Now protected from falling debris, she could watch as pieces of rock, varying from the size of a fist to that of one of the mining carts, rained down from the ceiling. Those caught without some form of cover were at the mercy of the cavern. Elliot watched in horror as a particularly large piece of rock crashed down atop one prisoner, a Rigelian, crushing him under its massive weight.

She scanned the chamber, looking for her companions. In addition to Sinak, Garrovick and Ra Mhvlovi had been assigned to this work detail, but there was no way to make out any specific individual, prisoner or guard, through the thick clouds of dust.

Gradually, the rumblings of the earthquake began to subside. Still tucked safely inside the small crevice she had created, Elliot coughed and covered her face with her glove, trying to breathe in the dust-polluted air of the cavern. The thick dust had reduced visibility, though she could still make out the rock walls and the obscured figures moving about. Here and there, she saw beams of light cutting through the fog as guards found the portable lamps they carried on their own belts.

Elliot registered the cries of pain coming from people wounded during the quake. She had no idea whether those injured were prisoners, guards, or both. Falling rocks would not have been particular in that regard. Elliot wondered about her fellow crewmates. What about Sinak? He had been in the open when the quake had begun. He would have been among the most vulnerable to anything falling from the ceiling.

The dust had started to settle and visibility was beginning to improve. Elliot pulled herself from her protective alcove, pulling off her visor and gloves and opening the front of her coveralls in an attempt to cool her body.

"Sinak?" she called out. How far would he have gotten before the tremors had started? She guessed he was still somewhere close by, having turned and headed for the relative safety of the cavern walls when debris began to fall.

Then she heard his voice, calling out in reply. "Sydney." It was a weak response. "I am approximately ten meters in front of you."

Following the sound of his voice, Elliot was able to pick Sinak out from the droves of other prisoners moving about the cavern. He lay on his back, with chunks of rock littered about his body. One piece, nearly the size of a large suitcase, rested partially on his left leg.

"Oh my god," she breathed as she rushed to him. Placing a hand on his arm, she looked down at the rock and his leg pinned beneath it. "Is it broken?"

The Vulcan shook his head. "I do not think so. It did not fall directly on me, but rather rolled atop my leg as I fell. I was quite fortunate, given the circumstances."

Elliot almost chuckled at the understatement. Moving down to where she could put her hands on the rock, she said, "Think we can move it? We only need to lift it a little bit to get your leg out."

Sinak pulled himself to a sitting position. "I believe so." He put his own hands under the jagged edge of the rock as Elliot set her legs and braced herself for the effort she would have to make. Were Sinak at his normal level of fitness, his Vulcan strength alone would have been more than enough to lift the rock. Unfortunately, their depleted condition made it necessary for both of them to work together.

They heaved upward, the rock lifted several centimeters away from Sinak's leg, and he quickly extracted it. They let the rock fall back to the earth and Elliot moved to examine the Vulcan's injury.

"It's cut pretty bad," she said, also noting the dirt that had worked its way into the open wound, mixing with the bright green hue of Sinak's blood. "We should wash it out." She reached for her canteen, only to discover it not hanging from her belt. She must have dropped it when the earthquake had started. A quick check revealed that Sinak's canteen was nowhere to be found, either.

"No problem," Elliot said. "I'll fetch some and be right back." Getting her bearings, she saw where the water drums still sat near the entrance to the small connecting tunnel. One of the six metallic containers had been crushed by an enormous rock, but the others looked to be undamaged.

As she moved toward the water tanks she looked around for Garrovick and Mhvlovi, but it was impossible to make out any particular individual. She called their names, but heard no response.

Five of the six water drums were still intact as she had first seen. She had no canteen to carry water, though, so the pouch it normally rested in would have to do. Stripping the belt from her waist, she grabbed the pouch and held it to the faucet on the nearest drum, her hand reaching out to turn the valve and allow the water to flow.

A hand closed over her mouth.

Shocked at the sudden movement, her body froze before she felt herself forced upright and then completely off her feet. She couldn't scream, couldn't even bite through the leather glove that covered the lower half of her face.

Her attacker moved quickly, possessing great strength

as he carried her into the small tunnel behind the water drums. The passageway was only a few meters wide and not even as high, lit dimly with portable lamps hanging from the walls on metal pins.

"We only have a few minutes," a voice hissed into her ear, and she immediately realized it was Khulr. "The quake sealed the main entrance to the tunnel. They are already digging us out, but it will take time. Not much, but enough for you and I to finish our business."

The hand came away from her mouth and then Elliot was flying through the air, just barely able to throw out her arms for protection before she hit the ground. She struck the hard rock floor of the tunnel, only partially able to roll and absorb the impact as the air was forced from her lungs.

You're out of practice, her mind scolded her.

Far slower than when she had been in prime fighting form, she regained her footing and assumed a defensive stance as she stared down her attacker.

Khulr, for his part, was grinning devilishly. "You want to fight," he taunted. "That's good. You've earned a bit of respect, Earther. Perhaps when I'm finished with you, I'll let you die quickly."

Elliot's eyes scanned the cramped tunnel for anything she could use as a weapon. The only thing available was the stun baton in Khulr's hand.

Okay, she thought, *so that's how it has to be.*

"Quit talking, Klingon. You're wasting time."

Khulr charged, a move Elliot didn't think he would be stupid enough to try despite her taunt. The baton in his right hand was raised high, his intention clear: this wasn't about punishment. This was a fight to the death.

If he got close enough.

Seeing the charge for what it was, Elliot stepped forward and into the attack. Khulr's aim was spoiled as she blocked the Klingon's swing enough to allow her an opening. His momentum carried him nearly over Elliot's shoulder as the security officer pivoted and twisted her body, spinning the guard off her hip and using the force of his own attack to throw him to the ground. He struck the hard floor heavily, face first.

Before Khulr could react, Elliot was on him again, this time lashing out with a vicious kick that connected with the Klingon's hand and dislodged his baton. The weapon flew from his grasp toward the mouth of the tunnel.

Elliot moved to retrieve the baton when she felt the hand on her foot, tripping her up. She crashed to the ground again but this time was able to absorb the impact of the fall and regain her feet. She was already breathing hard, though, further evidence that her physical condition was nothing like it had once been.

She turned to face her attacker again, noting with satisfaction the streams of thick purplish-pink blood that flowed from the Klingon's nostrils. His nose was bent to the left, broken by its encounter with the tunnel floor.

Khulr brought a hand to his face and wiped at his broken nose. Seeing the blood on his gloved fingers, his expression turned murderous, though he was still grinning madly. If his nose was causing him pain, he didn't show it.

"Excellent, human. I didn't think you capable of such a ferocious counterattack."

Elliot knew the Klingon would kill her, now, if given the chance. There was no way he could allow her to live, could not risk her going back to tell anyone else of their personal combat and how she had bested him so easily in his opening attack.

It's him or you, her mind screamed at her. *So don't let the bastard win.*

This time, she didn't wait for his attack. Instead she charged him, letting loose a war cry with ferocity born of years of captivity and harassment at the hands of this loathsome Klingon. If she was going to die, then she would die fighting.

Khulr tried to mimic her earlier move, stepping forward and into her charge. Unlike the guard, Elliot had anticipated such a response and adjusted her attack, feinting first one way and then another. She spun, planting her left foot and lashing out with her right, catching the Klingon in the stomach with all the force she could muster.

There was a gratifying grunt of pain, though the guard's brute strength enabled him to keep going. As Elliot pulled back for another blow, Khulr's arm darted out toward her head. She ducked and escaped the Klingon's massive open hand, grateful for the first time since arriving at this prison for the lack of hair on her head. She spun away from the attack and lashed out again, her foot connecting this time with a muscled thigh.

Elliot was off-balance though and the kick was a weak one, inflicting little if any appreciable damage. More important, the attack had caused her to lose what little stability she'd had, and she fell to the ground.

She rolled to regain her footing but she wasn't fast enough as Khulr fell across her body with his full weight, pinning her to the rock floor. Elliot lashed out with a free hand but missed the Klingon's face. She tried again, but this time Khulr grabbed her arm and forced it to the ground behind her head, then struck out with his other hand.

Elliot's vision blurred from the force of the blow before the nerves in her face registered the pain. She tasted blood, realizing that she had bitten the inside of her cheek. Then the pain was almost forgotten as Khulr leaned in close to her face, the foul odor of his hot breath filling her nostrils.

"Enough games, human," he hissed. "You fought well, but it is time to end this."

That was when Elliot, and Khulr, heard the telltale whine of an activated stun baton.

The Klingon's body suddenly went rigid and he thrashed in pain, the electrical discharge of the baton almost deafening in the cramped confines of the tunnel. Khulr cried out as he twisted away from Elliot.

Standing over the Klingon, baton in hand, was the dirty, disheveled form of Garrovick. Blood ran down the left side of his smooth head from a large gash, no doubt inflicted by falling debris during the earthquake.

"Thought you could use a hand," he said, smiling at her before returning his attention to Khulr. The force of the stun baton had immobilized the guard, indicative of the power setting Garrovick had used.

Khulr looked up at the human prisoner with an expression of undiluted hatred. "Your death is assured now, human," he spat through teeth clenched in pain.

"I wouldn't bet on that," Garrovick replied, waving the baton in front of the guard's face. "That stun will take a while to wear off, at least as long as it will take to report to Korax what you were doing here just now." He indicated Elliot, who's face had already begun to swell from the Klingon's last strike.

Khulr nearly shook with his rage. "You expect Korax to believe the word of a prisoner over that of a fellow Klingon?"

Garrovick leaned in closer to the Klingon. "Korax is no fool, Khulr. He knows all about your little crush on humans, and Sydney in particular. Think about that while you're lying here. Otherwise, I'll just have to see how much damage this thing can do." He tapped the Klingon's shoulder with the now-inert baton for emphasis.

Leaving the guard, Garrovick and Elliot backed out of the tunnel and into the main cavern. All around the chamber, cleanup efforts were already under way. Prisoners were giving their comrades medical assistance, and in some tragic cases mourning the loss of a friend who'd fallen victim to the earthquake.

As they made their way back to where Sinak still lay, now being tended to by Ra Mhvlovi, Garrovick studied Elliot's face. It was swelling and would probably leave a nice bruise. "Are you okay?"

Elliot nodded. She still tasted blood, and her probing tongue had found two loose teeth. "I'll be all right." She placed a hand on Garrovick's arm. "Thanks, Stephen. Really."

Garrovick patted her hand. "No problem. You'd have had him if you hadn't fallen." He smiled as he added, "Didn't look like you'd lost a step to me."

"One thing's for sure," she said as she rubbed a sore spot on her back, exhaling tiredly. "I won't have any trouble sleeping tonight."

Chapter Fifteen

THICK SMOKE HUNG in the air of the tavern, making it appear even more dimly lit than it already was. Kirk could barely make out the walls of the room, which were cluttered with all manner of exotic weapons and assorted hunting trophies, each item doubtless possessing a story about life on this backwater world. On the tavern's back wall hung an intricate and well-used octagonal-shaped target board at which two Klingons were taking turns throwing their large knives. From what Kirk had been able to surmise, the object of whatever game they were playing was to strike small black octagons scattered among a larger red field. He also noticed that neither Klingon appeared to be doing very well, no doubt due to the copious quantities of bloodwine they had consumed.

Kirk brought a hand up to scratch his chin where it had begun to itch again under the coarse facial hair he sported. The beard was just one part of a Klingon disguise he and Sulu had donned prior to boarding the

Gal'tagh for the journey through Klingon space. At Koloth's insistence, Dr. McCoy and the *Enterprise*'s quartermaster had forgone trying to re-create the prominent Klingon cranial ridges. Instead, the two men studied twenty-year-old log excerpts stored in the ship's library computer and had succeeded in fashioning effective disguises for Kirk and Sulu that could be applied and removed without benefit of special tools or accessories. Their human skin was now buried beneath dark makeup that wouldn't wipe or wash off from casual contact or rain or even perspiration. Long flowing hair tied at the base of the neck concealed their human hair, while the beards along with mustaches and thick eyebrows completed the transformation of their human features.

Noticing Kirk stroking his beard, Koloth said, "I still think it's a distinct improvement, all things considered." He grinned as he brought a massive tankard of bloodwine to his lips and drank deeply.

"Your crew didn't seem to share your view, Captain," Kirk countered, recalling the menacing looks and even the handful of growls he and Sulu had encountered upon arriving aboard the *Gal'tagh*. All of the Klingons aboard the vessel resembled their captain: tall, wild hair, jagged teeth and, of course, the forehead ridges. The raw animosity the two Starfleet officers had faced told Kirk there was more to the radical appearance disparity in Klingons than he had first imagined. It was a conundrum that deepened as the next two days passed, with members of the *Gal'tagh* crew continuing to eye Kirk and Sulu warily at every opportunity. Koloth had not revealed the Starfleet officers' true identities, but instead issued orders that they be treated with the same respect reserved for any other superior officer.

"However," Sulu added, glancing around the bar for

emphasis, his Asian features giving him an even more severe expression than Kirk's, "I think we could find a few supporters here."

Soon after beaming down to the Jlinzegh' province of the colony world known as Don'zali IV, Kirk and Sulu had taken note of one important fact: they resembled almost all of the Klingons they encountered. Koloth, along with the handful of Klingons they had seen with pronounced forehead ridges, were in the definite minority. Now it was he who drew the curious and sometimes intimidating looks from other Klingons they passed on the street. Both *Enterprise* officers knew that Koloth was aware of the apparent turning of the tables, but he had said nothing on the subject, focusing instead on their mission.

He did so again here, ignoring Sulu's remark and turning in his seat to survey the tavern and its clientele once more.

"According to his servant," he said, "K'zeq should be returning from his hunt soon after sunset. The sooner he arrives, the better. I grow weary of this den of sloth."

Kirk had to agree with the Klingon captain. What had been intended as a brief detour was becoming an extended layover. A colony world, Don'zali IV made its major contribution to the Klingon Empire in the way of agriculture. Farming communities could be found all over the planet, which had been discovered decades ago to possess lush and fertile lands. The world had proven ideal for cultivating foodstuffs that could be exported to the many worlds within the Empire that did not share such good fortune.

Such operations required spaceport facilities, both on the planet's surface and in orbit. Don'zali IV boasted no small shortage of these, with small towns and in some cases large cities spiraling out from the major farming centers across the planet.

That Don'zali IV played a significant, if rather mundane, function in the vast scheme of the Klingon Empire did not interest Kirk. What did matter to him was that it held the key to finding survivors of the *Gagarin*.

"Koloth," Kirk said, leaning across the table and speaking in a low voice, "I know you said this K'zeq could help us, but what exactly is his connection with all of this?" Indeed, the Klingon captain had proven tight-lipped during their voyage from Starbase 49.

Turning back to face Kirk and Sulu, Koloth leaned forward, still clasping one massive hand around his tankard of bloodwine.

"You're correct, and I apologize for not sharing this information with you aboard ship. I received the latest message from Gorkon while we were in transit, and I didn't want to take the chance of anyone else learning its contents." His eyes narrowed and he smiled slightly. "One never knows where spies may lurk, my dear Captain."

Kirk instinctively looked up and scanned the bar, but saw that other than the occasional stares from other customers, no one in the tavern appeared to be interested in them. The mood in the room was festive, even raucous at times, with the various patrons absorbed with their own activities. If they were being observed, he decided, it could only be from a distance.

"I think we're safe here, at least for a little while," he said.

Nodding, Koloth continued. "The problem we face is rather simple, gentlemen. Gorkon believes your officers are being held deep within Klingon space, but the actual location of the prison itself is not known. He has been unable to find any record of the facility, as though it does not exist. But that is impossible, because of other information he has uncovered."

Sulu said, "K'zeq is our point of contact, then, because he either worked at the prison or knows someone who did."

They paused in their conversation as a server stopped at their table, a large Klingon woman with long hair falling across her broad shoulders. As she refilled the three men's tankards with bloodwine, she smiled at Kirk with a mouthful of jagged, uneven teeth. She lingered at the table longer than should have been necessary to complete her task, frankly appraising Kirk until the *Enterprise* captain finally returned her smile with a meek one of his own.

As she walked away to tend to customers at a nearby table, she continued to cast furtive glances in Kirk's direction. Koloth watched the episode with unrestrained amusement, making no attempt to stifle his laughter.

"Take caution, Kirk," he said. "Even your supposed prowess with females would be sorely tested in the arms of a Klingon woman."

Though he thought he detected a smirk on Sulu's face, the helmsman's expression was composed when Kirk looked over at him. Sighing in resignation, he returned his attention to Koloth. "What about K'zeq?"

"He was once the commander of the prison I believe we are looking for," the Klingon replied. "Gorkon found archived communiqués from K'zeq to another member of the Council, Komor, reporting regularly on a small group of prisoners in his charge. Though the location of the prison was not revealed in the messages and no names of prisoners are mentioned, there were sporadic references to the dietary or medical needs of humans, Vulcans, and Efrosians. There was also one particular entry where the commander references an 'Andorian captain.' This Andorian, a female, was executed as an example to her subordinates."

Sulu turned to look at Kirk. "The *Gagarin*'s captain was a female Andorian."

Anger clouded Kirk's vision at the thought of Captain Gralev, an accomplished starship commander, dying a hideous death far away from home where no one would ever know what had happened to her. Had she been a wife or a mother? Surely she had loved ones who had agonized over her fate when they had learned of the *Gagarin*'s disappearance.

Another thought troubled him. Though he had undertaken this mission to determine the ultimate fate of the *Gagarin,* the very real fact here was that there could be any number of Federation and Starfleet personnel being held in captivity by the Empire. It would make sense for them to be scattered across Klingon space at any number of remote prisons and other places that benefited from slave labor. How many were there? What sort of godforsaken existence greeted them each day? The very thought added fuel to Kirk's rage, and he struggled until the anger was once again under control.

"So now K'zeq lives here, on a farming colony?" he asked, his jaw tight as he spoke. It seemed incongruous to him that a soldier of the Empire could find contentment in a place as devoid of excitement as this planet appeared to be.

Koloth nodded. "Gorkon was able to determine that he had relocated here after retiring from the military." The words came out of the Klingon's mouth wrapped in an air of mild disgust, the very notion of retiring from military service appearing to offend him. "Rather than risk exposure of his activities by trying to contact K'zeq over subspace, Gorkon has ordered me to contact him personally."

Finding out where K'zeq lived had been a simple affair. According to local law enforcement, he lived in a small domicile within a group of large multi-residence buildings on the edge of town. However, the Klingon had not been at home when they had called, and an aged and crotchety woman who acted as his servant informed them that K'zeq was on a hunting excursion and would return the following day. Before ordering them to leave the vicinity and slamming the door in their faces, she also said that K'zeq's usual habit called for him to stop at his favorite tavern before returning home from a hunt.

Upon arriving at the tavern, the bartender had reacted first with recognition and then near disgust when shown K'zeq's likeness, which Koloth had reproduced from the Klingon's service record. The image was of a fierce-looking soldier, with cold, cruel eyes glaring out from beneath a heavy brow and a sinister expression made more so by the long thin mustache drooping along either side of his mouth. Except for the darker skin tone, K'zeq reminded Kirk in many ways of Koloth as he had first encountered him all those years ago at the K-7 space station.

"I know who he is," the barkeep said, making no attempt to hide the loathing in his voice. "He should return this evening. He usually drinks a tankard of bloodwine before returning home." Then the bartender had turned his back on them and returned to whatever it was he had been doing, nearly inciting Koloth to violence at such a casual dismissal. Kirk and Sulu were able to restrain the Klingon captain and push him to a table in a far corner of the tavern where they could keep an eye on the door. For the next few hours, though the three of them were able to get grudging service from the bar, Koloth continued to earn hard stares from the bartender as well as many of the other patrons.

"I hope he shows up soon," Sulu said to Kirk as he sipped his drink. "The longer we sit here, the more some of these people seem to dislike Koloth."

Kirk nodded in agreement. He had almost suggested waiting outside for K'zeq to appear, but had thought better of it. At least in here, energy weapons were checked at the door, and with his back to the rear wall Kirk didn't have to worry about trouble coming from behind him. He knew that Koloth was also aware of the tension in the room, though the Klingon gave no indication of it. Instead, he continued to sip his drink as though he had not a care in the world.

"Uh-oh," Sulu whispered, nudging Kirk's elbow.

Even as he started to look up from his own drink, the *Enterprise* captain knew what he would see. For over half an hour, the two Klingons playing the strange game with the knives and the target board had been giving Koloth, as well as Kirk and Sulu, looks of unconcealed disdain. As their bloodwine consumption and boisterous behavior increased, Kirk knew that some sort of confrontation was inevitable.

He decided against patting himself on the back for his deduction as he watched the two Klingons begin to move in their direction. Besides, what he had failed to consider was that two of their friends would join them as they crossed the floor of the bar, weaving their way around tables and chairs and heading for them, the expressions on their faces making their intentions clear.

Chapter Sixteen

"KOLOTH," Kirk hissed.

In response, the Klingon captain took a long pull of his drink before setting the tankard on the table and wiping his mouth with the back of his gloved hand.

"I was wondering what was taking so long," he said at last. "I was beginning to get bored and I can think of no better way to pass the time." With that, he rose from his chair and turned to face the approaching Klingons.

Kirk and Sulu exchanged matching looks of alarm.

"I just knew he was going to say something like that," Sulu said as he followed Kirk's lead, standing up and moving around the table to join Koloth. The four Klingons, walking with a confidence Kirk was sure had been augmented by bloodwine, closed the distance until the groups stood barely two meters apart.

"You," the supposed leader of the group said as he pointed at Koloth. "You are not welcome here. Leave now, or face me."

Koloth regarded his opponent with a bemused expression. "The barkeep seems to welcome my patronage, so far as my money is concerned. He hasn't asked me to leave, so I believe I shall stay a while longer. Accept that, or face *me*."

Kirk knew that diplomacy in this instance was not an option. Koloth had explained earlier that trying to talk oneself out of a situation like this would be considered offensive to the other party and no doubt result in an invitation to personal combat. Showing weakness or indecision was likewise out of the question, as Kirk himself had learned from his many encounters with Klingons and other races with similar values and traditions. The lone choice here was to maintain a strong, aggressive front and follow the path it trod from there.

It's days like these that make me wish I'd gone to raise horses with my uncle.

The face of the quartet's leader broke into a sinister grin. "A challenge? Excellent. I like that." He turned his gaze to Kirk. "And you befriend this outsider? Do you share his . . . beliefs?" There was no mistaking the disgust enveloping the final word.

He wobbled slightly, and Kirk might have thought that an advantage had he been a reckless cadet. Instead, his eyes moved from one Klingon to the next, assessing each one's threat potential. He didn't have to look at Sulu to know the helmsman was doing the same thing.

The Klingon's words puzzled Kirk. What "beliefs" was he talking about? It was yet another question he was sure Koloth would evade answering when Kirk asked him later.

If we get out of this, he reminded himself.

"Their association to me is not your concern," Koloth said. "But I suggest you choose your next actions carefully, for they will stand beside me in battle."

Koloth was a blur of motion as he closed the gap between himself and the Klingon facing off against him. His left arm exploded outward, catching his opponent in the face with the heel of his hand. The strike forced the drunken Klingon backward and into one of his companions.

The other two Klingons responded quickly, each moving to avoid their stumbling friends. The menace in their eyes was unmistakable as they closed on Koloth.

"Here we go," Sulu said as he moved to assist, but the helmsman need not have bothered. Koloth rushed the two oncoming opponents, driving into them with bone-jarring force that lifted both Klingons off their feet and sent them tumbling into a nearby table.

By this time the first two Klingons had regained their balance and were moving to enter the fray. Sulu saw that Koloth was facing away from the new threat and charged ahead. Ducking under the arm swing of the first Klingon, he lashed out with his leg toward his companion. The kick took the Klingon in the chest, forcing the air from his lungs with a loud grunt.

The Klingon who had missed Sulu turned to try again and was greeted by Kirk, taking advantage of his opponent's momentary disorientation to deliver a roundhouse punch to the side of the attacker's head. Pain erupted in his hand as it made contact with the dense bone of the Klingon's skull, but he had no time to be distracted by it.

"Captain! Watch out!"

Kirk saw the Klingon's arm sweeping toward him at the same time he heard Sulu's shout of alarm. Instinct took over and he pivoted away from the attack, causing the Klingon to overextend himself and fall forward. Kirk seized the opportunity and kicked out, striking the Klingon in the face with the toe of his boot and sending his opponent crashing to the floor.

Koloth in the meantime had dispatched one of the two Klingons he had charged. The fallen Klingon lay in a disjointed heap across one of the tables as his partner stepped forward, light gleaming off the polished blade of the knife he now wielded in his right hand.

"You have invited your death today, outsider," the Klingon hissed, waving the knife and describing an intricate pattern in the air before him. "Your blood will feed the insects that cower beneath the floorboards."

Staring down his adversary with the same expression of near amusement on his face, Koloth replied, "Today is as good a day to die as any. Show me your warrior's rage if you can."

The Klingon snarled something unintelligible before raising his knife above his head and uttering a gut-wrenching war cry. As he charged toward him, Koloth did not tense up in readiness to defend himself. Instead he almost serenely stepped to one side at the last possible second and as his attacker's momentum began to carry him past, Koloth drove his right knee with merciless force into the Klingon's abdomen. At the same instant he delivered a chop to the back of his opponent's neck with the edge of his left hand. The vicious double attack was devastating, driving the Klingon to unconsciousness even before he struck the floor.

Sulu backpedaled to avoid the sharp blade of his opponent's knife and abruptly struck the wall behind him with the heel of his boot. He dodged to his right as the Klingon swung his knife toward his head. His attacker swore as his blade stuck in the aged wood of the tavern wall. Sulu took advantage of the distraction and leapt forward, striking out with a savage kick that sent his opponent flailing into a group of unused chairs. The Klingon tried to grab one of the chairs for balance but his weight was too much and he tumbled to the floor, striking his head on the edge of a table as he fell.

Elsewhere in the tavern, Kirk was still dealing with his rival, who had regained his feet and was closing the distance between them once more. Seeing a tankard lying atop a nearby table, Kirk grabbed it and swung it in a high arc just as he felt the brush of the Klingon's fingers on his shirt. His opponent saw the attack coming and was able to defend against it, grabbing Kirk's wrist and pulling the *Enterprise* captain off balance. Kirk crashed to the floor, the impact forcing the air from his lungs.

Okay, this is not going well at all.

He saw the knife in the corner of his eye just as the Klingon swung the blade downward. Kirk rolled away from the attack and tried to stand, but a wayward chair that he should have noticed before foiled his efforts. As he tripped and fell back to the floor of the tavern he saw the Klingon looming closer, his knife searching for a target.

The attack never came as another shadow fell across Kirk's face. A dark, hooded figure in soiled robes rushed forward, catching the Klingon by surprise. The new arrival carried what looked to Kirk to be a canvas knapsack, stuffed to near bursting, which he drove with unrestrained force into the stomach of Kirk's opponent. The Klingon grunted in both surprise and pain at the unexpected attack, dropping his knife in the process. The blade fell to the tavern floor and the new arrival kicked it out of its owner's reach as he brought the knapsack around for another strike. This one caught the Klingon in the side of the head and he fell to the floor and stayed there.

Kirk watched in amazement as the new arrival turned

to face him and offered his hand. The *Enterprise* captain took hold and allowed himself to be pulled to his feet.

"Thank you," he said. "I thought he might have had me there for a moment." He indicated Sulu and Koloth, who were working their way toward him. "Perhaps my companions and I might buy you a drink, to express our appreciation."

"Just as well," the robed figure replied as he reached for his hood. "The barkeep tells me you and your friends have been looking for me."

His free hand pulled the hood of his ragged robe away from his head, and for the first time the dim lighting of the tavern cast itself across the new arrival's face. Despite the thicker beard, longer hair smattered with more than a touch of gray, and the large eminent cranial ridges, Kirk realized he was looking into the face of K'zeq.

Chapter Seventeen

"CAPTAIN? Are you all right?"

Kirk managed to stop staring at K'zeq long enough to nod to Sulu as the helmsman moved toward him. "I think so." He rubbed his arm and grimaced in both the pain he felt now and the bone-numbing ache he knew would greet him in the morning. Smiling ruefully at Sulu, he added, "I think I'm starting to get too old for this sort of thing, but if you say anything to McCoy, I'll deny it."

"It's not the years, sir," Sulu said with a grin, "it's the mileage."

Koloth strolled toward them, and Kirk noted that the Klingon had retrieved his bloodwine. "An engaging way to spend a few minutes, but ultimately dissatisfying, wouldn't you say, Kirk?" The Klingon punctuated his sentence by downing his tankard's contents and tossing the empty vessel over his shoulder.

Sulu, who, like Koloth, was not even breathing hard, nodded in the direction of the two Klingons Koloth had dispatched with relative ease. "That was some show you put on. I'd be interested in learning some of those techniques."

Snorting in derision, Koloth dismissed their now unconscious opponents with a wave of his hand. "They are undisciplined and clumsy, the result of too many years spent drinking and rotting away on this backwater mudball and not enough time honing their skills as warriors. I could have killed them all easily, but there would have been no honor in it."

Kirk directed Koloth's attention to his unexpected benefactor. "May I introduce K'zeq, to whom I owe my thanks, by the way."

Ignoring Kirk and his offer of gratitude, K'zeq instead focused his attention on Koloth. "Who are you and why are you looking for me?"

"I am Koloth, and my companions and I require information that you possess."

Nodding, K'zeq said, "I have heard of Koloth. You have long been known as a formidable military commander with many glorious victories to your credit. You honor me with your presence."

Koloth waved the platitudes away. "There is no time for that. You once commanded a prison facility. I require information about it."

Shaking his head, K'zeq replied, "You have sought out the wrong person. Your information is incorrect."

In response, Koloth produced the small datapad from beneath his robes and activated it. Still stored in the device's memory core, the service record he had received from Gorkon appeared on its miniature screen. He held it up for K'zeq to see, and once again Kirk saw the picture of the Klingon that Koloth had shown them earlier and noted the resemblance between the picture and the

Klingon now standing before them. As he had noticed in Koloth before, the telltale clues came with the eyes. K'zeq's burned with the same fire as the severe-looking soldier in the picture.

Kirk watched as K'zeq stared at the image, recognition registering on his face even though he almost managed to keep his facial features under control. His eyes betrayed him, though, and Kirk imagined the memories that must be reliving themselves in K'zeq's mind.

"Do you deny that this is you?" Koloth pressed.

Finally, K'zeq shook his head and Kirk breathed a small sigh of relief. Maybe this detour would prove beneficial after all.

"That was me," K'zeq said. "But it is a part of my life I choose to forget. I was a different person then, young and misguided. I have since moved beyond the weakness of my youth and have attempted to strive toward a higher ideal." He paused, eyes locking with Koloth's for several seconds before adding, "Surely you understand that?"

To Kirk's surprise, Koloth nodded in agreement. "I do indeed understand. Like you, I too have a past that I would like to forget, and were this any other occasion I would respect your wishes. However, the situation I now face requires that I impose upon you this one time."

Watching the two Klingons, Kirk got the sudden feeling that their conversation was taking place on two separate levels. There was the obvious communication, with simple answers being given to straightforward questions. However, the ambiguous statements Koloth was using appeared to convey a great deal to the other Klingon, because Kirk could see K'zeq relax somewhat as Koloth spoke.

K'zeq nodded to himself as if arriving at some decision. "State your request."

"Tell us about the Starfleet personnel who were interred at your prison."

K'zeq's eyes widened, the Klingon obviously not expecting anything like that. He recovered quickly though and shrugged.

"A group of Starfleet spies was brought to my prison several years ago. Their ship had been captured in Klingon space while conducting espionage."

"Espionage?" Sulu repeated. For a frantic moment Kirk was worried that they might blow their cover, but K'zeq didn't seem to take notice at Sulu's reaction.

Instead, he nodded in confirmation to the question. "Their ship was destroyed when they attempted to escape back into Federation territory. Many of the crew were killed in the battle, but the survivors were brought to me, including their captain." The Klingon's mouth curled into a snarl. "She was an Andorian, and she was executed for her role in ordering an attack on a Klingon vessel."

Kirk's gut told him that K'zeq was telling the truth, at least as he understood it to be, but it didn't make the blunt statement of Captain Gralev's fate any easier to swallow.

"Who told you about espionage?" Sulu asked, once again acting the role of a Klingon.

This time, K'zeq glared at the *Enterprise* helmsman for a moment before replying, a strange suspicious look on his face mixing with an expression which conveyed that he did not appreciate Sulu addressing him. Rather than responding to Sulu, he instead directed his answer to Koloth.

"I was informed by the captain of the vessel who delivered the prisoners to me. They remained in my charge until their trial, which was held several months later. Afterward, some of the prisoners were returned to me. I don't know what happened to the others, but at the time I assumed they were either returned to the Federation or executed for their crimes."

"There was no trial," Kirk said.

With eyes boring into Kirk in the same manner that had skewered Sulu, K'zeq snapped, "Do you call me a liar?"

Kirk shook his head. "No, of course not. It's just that according to interstellar law, the government of the accused person must be notified prior to the commencement of legal proceedings. The Federation was never informed of any trial."

"I know only what I was told," K'zeq replied. "The High Council informed me of the trial and had me prepare the prisoners for transport. They were taken from my prison and some were returned three weeks later." Turning his attention back to Koloth, he added, "Why do you consort with these dogs who insult me and accuse the High Council of wrongdoing?"

"He is right," Koloth replied. "If there was a trial, then it was for appearances only."

K'zeq's mouth opened in profound shock and remained that way, the succinct indictment catching him without warning. Such a statement would be perceived as treasonous in some circles.

"What would lead you to such a conclusion?" he asked.

Again, Koloth produced the datapad and, using the information Gorkon had delivered to him, described the details of the surprise attack on the *Gagarin* and the seizure of at least part of its crew. As he listened, K'zeq's expression grew more alarmed with each passing second.

"Are you saying that a Klingon vessel crossed into Federation space without the authority of the High Council, attacked a Starfleet vessel, and took prisoners for no valid military reason?"

Koloth said, "The Council as a whole had no knowledge of the attack. However, there were members of the Council who were aware of the incident but chose to cover it up. Peace talks with the Federation were beginning, and the Empire was in dire need of some sort of agreement allowing it to expand its borders into territory possessing resource-rich planets such as those on the Federation side of the Neutral Zone."

K'zeq nodded. "The prisoners could have proven valuable if negotiations stalled."

"Exactly," Koloth replied. "And for whatever reason, the talks did fail, and even though the prisoners did not prove useful then, there were those on the Council who thought they might be needed at some later point. So they were sent to various prisons, including yours, where their commanders were fed lies about them and where they were eventually forgotten by all except those few who might one day have use for them."

K'zeq appeared almost dumbstruck with disbelief. "Can the Council itself be susceptible to such corruption?" He shook his head. "I cannot accept that. There is no honor in such deceitful action."

"And it is something that we seek to correct," Koloth replied. "Negotiations are once more under way with the Federation. There is real hope that they will succeed, at least in some measure. Some members of the Council believe that cannot happen until this affront to our honor is dealt with. However, there are those who would rather pretend the incident never occurred rather than do the honorable thing and admit their misdeeds."

Koloth locked eyes with the other Klingon. "As a warrior pledged to uphold the teachings of Kahless, I cannot stand by and allow that to happen. You appear to value honor, K'zeq, or is that merely a facade? Do you embrace Kahless, or merely defile his image for your own gain?"

K'zeq stiffened at the challenge. "I strive to live by the standards forged by Kahless each day of my life. To stand and do nothing in the face of this dishonor is as much an insult to Kahless as any direct action I might take. What do you mean to do?"

Stepping forward, Sulu answered, "The prisoners will be returned to the Federation, hopefully in a manner that prevents a volatile incident between them and the Empire."

K'zeq abruptly let loose with a hearty laugh before leaning close to Sulu. In a low voice he said, "I knew that if I was patient, one of you would reveal your true nature." He indicated Kirk with a wave of his hand. "You two are not Klingons, and I suspect you are Earthers, probably Starfleet."

He held up a hand at Kirk's visible expression of alarm. "Worry not, friends. While a warrior of Koloth's stature would most likely not keep the company of Klingons such as those you pretend to be, I can imagine him allying himself with Federation officials trying to secure the safe return of comrades taken in a pathetic act of cowardice." Turning once more to Koloth, he said, "I will assist you in any way that I am able."

Koloth nodded to the other Klingon. "I shall not forget this. You bring honor to Kahless and your house this day, my friend."

Still puzzled, Kirk looked to K'zeq and asked, "When did you first suspect that we might not be Klingons?"

Chuckling again, K'zeq slapped Kirk on the back so hard that he nearly separated the captain's shoulder.

"During the fight. You hit like a human."

On the other side of the tavern, a lone figure sat at a table, a forgotten tankard of bloodwine sitting next to one large hand. Like other patrons in the bar, he wore a long flowing cloak over soiled clothing. He would have preferred to wear the cloak's hood up in order to conceal his face, but that would have invited unwanted curiosity. Instead, he had taken up a position in a far corner of the tavern so as not to risk Koloth seeing and recognizing him. The *Gal'tagh* captain had not authorized any of his crew to transport to the planet's surface, so to be seen here now would arouse immediate suspicion.

J'rgan's original mission, to obtain any valuable information that might make itself available at Starbase 49 during the peace talks, had been interrupted when Koloth abruptly ordered the *Gal'tagh*'s departure. The action had prompted a new assignment, this one given to him by Council member Komor himself. Komor had learned of Koloth's actions, which had been undertaken at Gorkon's request, but not the reasons behind them. It had therefore fallen to J'rgan to find out.

The assignment had not been easy. Koloth had offered no explanations to the crew for the sudden change in orders, instead citing the need for the strictest operational security. That was his prerogative, of course, but it tended to make a spy's job that much more difficult.

A spy.

There was a time when J'rgan would have been ashamed to have such a loathsome title attached to his name. That, of course, was before he had been offered substantial compensation for his services. Honor was one thing, but it lost some of its luster when placed beside the comforts of life that could be had if one could only afford the purchase price.

Somewhere in the back of his mind, J'rgan knew his father, were he still alive, would be furious at having the lessons he had labored to teach discarded by his only son.

J'rgan, however, had long since rid himself of any pressing guilt about that. His father had been an old man, out of step with the times and content to rest on the laurels of long-forgotten battles while pledging his steadfast devotion to principles that at the time were overwhelmingly unpopular. Even in the years after his father's death, as the teachings of Kahless began to experience a resurgence of acceptance, J'rgan held to his own views. Honor could get you many things, but money could get them a lot faster and with a lot less effort.

He had shadowed Koloth and the two unknown Klingons since making planetfall, having arranged to be transported down from the *Gal'tagh* without alerting the ship's security officer. It had been a simple task, given his training and the tools at his disposal.

The two strangers troubled him, boarding *Gal'tagh* as they had at Starbase 49. Where had they come from? No Klingons matching their description were assigned to the *Terthos*. In fact, very few were assigned to ships in the fleet these days at all. J'rgan knew that many such Klingons still served the Empire, but most had been relegated to low-priority or unglamorous assignments. Such was their reward, after all, for the choices they had made.

At first he had considered the possibility that the two newcomers were defectors or undercover agents that had been repatriated. Those theories died quickly, though, when the *Gal'tagh* arrived at Don'zali IV. Now he was almost certain they were spies just as he was, working with Koloth toward some dark purpose on Gorkon's behalf.

As Koloth and the others moved toward the door of the tavern, J'rgan resisted the urge to follow them. They would be on the alert for anything suspicious, just as they had been the entire time he had been observing them. He knew he wouldn't be able to get close enough to learn anything else of value.

Instead, he decided the best course of action was to return to the ship and get his report to Komor. J'rgan himself had no idea as to the Council member's reasons for this assignment, and didn't particularly care. Let Kesh and Komor and his bureaucratic ilk play their political cloak and dagger games. Perhaps whatever they were after had potentially disastrous potential for their continued presence on the High Council, if not their very lives. None of this concerned J'rgan beyond the impact it might have on his receiving payment for his services.

Chapter Eighteen

SULU MOVED ABOUT the room in a slow, deliberate circle, the weight of the curved, bladed weapon comfortable in his hands. It had taken a few hours to get used to the feel of the *bat'leth,* but after practicing with it under Koloth's watchful eye, he was beginning to understand the weapon's elegance.

Like the use of the swords he had mastered in his youth, the employment of a *bat'leth* was as much an art as it was a skill. It required keen balance as well as hand and eye coordination, even more so for a human, whose strength and body mass were smaller than that of the average Klingon.

"Excellent!" Koloth said, he too wielding a *bat'leth* and circling in a similar fashion to Sulu, moving to keep the *Enterprise* helmsman in front of him. A huge grin broke out on the Klingon's face as he twirled his weapon in his massive hands. "You move with the ease of a seasoned warrior. Except for that hideous makeup, you could almost pass for a real Klingon."

Sulu had no time to ponder the remark in depth, for at that moment Koloth stopped circling and charged. In fluid motion he set his feet and brought the blade over his head, slashing downward viciously. Sulu managed to get his own weapon up in time to parry the attack. The sound of the two blades striking was nearly deafening in the enclosed space.

Twisting away from his opponent, Sulu pivoted on his left foot and brought his own *bat'leth* around, the weapon slicing through the air at chest level. Koloth spun his blade, countering the strike but not without being forced backward a step.

Following with another attack, Sulu twirled his blade in an effort to side step Koloth's defensive parry. He would have succeeded but for the Klingon's own startling speed. His own weapon seemed to move of its own accord as if anticipating Sulu's strike. The clash of metal on metal sang in the room once more.

"Most impressive!" Koloth said, stepping backward and disengaging from the battle. "You are a remarkably quick study. Though you still have a long way to go to achieve true mastery of the *bat'leth*, I would rate your performance so far to be among the finest cadets at the military academy who've completed their first month's training."

Sulu couldn't help chuckling at Koloth's deadpan delivery. The Klingon was ultimately unable to maintain a serious expression, laughing at his own joke.

The doors of the exercise room parted, and Sulu and Koloth turned to see a visibly uncomfortable Kirk enter. Like Sulu, he was still dressed in his Klingon ensemble. Rubbing the small of his back, the *Enterprise* captain grimaced in pain.

"I don't know what's worse, getting beaten up by a bar full of Klingons, or sleeping on a Klingon bed."

Sulu raised the Klingon weapon he still carried. "Some

exercise will help stretch out the muscles, sir. I recommend the *bat'leth* drills. They'll definitely get the blood pumping."

"Indeed," Koloth added. "Mr. Sulu's innate personal combat skills make him adept at learning the *bat'leth*. I must warn you, Captain, that at the rate he's progressing, I may offer him a position among my crew by the time we reach Pao'la."

Kirk eyed Sulu, a mischievous grin playing at his lips. "I always knew you were ambitious, Commander. Being the first human to serve in the Klingon fleet would certainly get you noticed. I knew all that time you spent flying a Klingon ship would pay off one day."

Spinning the *bat'leth* in his hands, Sulu laughed again. "But we both know that's not what I'm after."

Kirk nodded. Sulu was past due for promotion, of that the captain had been certain for quite some time. He also knew the helmsman possessed all of the qualities he would need to thrive as a starship captain. Kirk had recommended Sulu for his own command once already and had received enthusiastic endorsement from Starfleet. Much to his surprise, Sulu had declined. Kirk hadn't been able to understand his helmsman's reluctance to accept promotion, until he heard the reason.

Excelsior.

Since first laying eyes on the vessel nearly two years ago, Sulu had been enraptured by it. Larger and, in Kirk's eyes at least, possessing none of the elegant lines of his own *Enterprise,* the *Excelsior* had been the first in a new design of deep-exploration starships. Kirk knew the more modern vessels were intended to replace the *Enterprise* and the other Constitution-class ships. They were designed to last longer, and engineers were predicting the longevity of their spaceframes at nearly a century.

The ships would open up a whole new era of exploration, and the adventurer in Sulu wanted to be a part of that. *Excelsior* called to him in much the same way the *Enterprise* had enticed a young James Kirk. For that reason, the helmsman had opted to wait until the *Excelsior* became available before assuming the mantle of command, and Starfleet had grudgingly accepted, thanks in no small part to an appeal from Kirk himself on Sulu's behalf.

The *Enterprise* captain was therefore certain that Koloth would not succeed in wooing his helmsman away from Starfleet by the time they reached their destination.

Pao'la, the remote jungle-covered planet that was the location of the prison K'zeq had once overseen. The Klingon had been a wealth of information regarding the prison once Koloth had convinced him to assist them. In addition to its location, they now knew what to expect in the way of personnel and defenses on both the exterior and interior of the prison, at least as they were during the time K'zeq had served there. They would still need to supplement their information with an on-site reconnoiter before they could begin to formulate a plan, but it was a start.

Kirk looked around the room, examining the collection of weapons, armor, plaques, and other assorted items. Every vessel he had ever traveled aboard had a room like this one, with prizes that spoke of glorious campaigns the vessel and its crew had taken part in.

A statue situated in a lighted alcove caught his eye, depicting two figures locked in unarmed battle. The polished sculpture highlighted the straining muscles of each combatant, as though the fighters were embroiled in a great struggle of life and death.

"Koloth, what is this?" Kirk asked.

Seeing what Kirk was looking at, Koloth replied, "That is Kahless and his brother, Morath. According to legend, Morath brought shame to their family and Kahless opposed him. They fought for twelve days and twelve nights." He added with a smile, "Kahless won, of course."

"You spoke of Kahless to K'zeq, back on Don'zali IV," Kirk said. "Why is he significant?"

Koloth was studying his *bat'leth,* noting scratches and blemishes in the gleaming surface of the blade. At first Kirk thought his question, like so many others he had asked since undertaking this mission, would go unanswered. But then the Klingon lowered the blade and slowly crossed the floor of the exercise room, his footsteps echoing on the bare metal of the deck plating. Walking up to the statue, he studied the figures embroiled in mortal combat for several seconds before finally responding.

"Kahless the Unforgettable, the greatest Klingon warrior who ever lived. He united my people, single-handedly forging what would become the Klingon Empire. It is he who tells us of honor and courage and commitment, and how we must strive each day to live by the example he set for us." Holding up the *bat'leth,* he continued, "Kahless defeated the tyrannical overlord Molor in mortal combat, using the first *bat'leth,* which he forged from fire with his own hands. Any Klingon with any shred of honor owes what he is to Kahless. Even now, fifteen hundred years after his death, Kahless guides us, so long as we are willing to listen. He is there when we go into battle and if we should fall honorably, we will join him in *Sto-Vo-Kor.*"

Sulu nodded, awestruck with the intensity Koloth displayed as he spoke. "That's some story."

"It is no story," Koloth snapped as he moved to a weapons rack adorning one wall of the room and placed his *bat'leth* on an unused pair of pegs. Kirk noted the care with which the Klingon treated the weapon, as though he were a collector handling a prized possession.

No, he decided, it was altogether different from that. Koloth had treated the formidable blade with an almost reverent touch. That made more sense, Kirk decided. Considering what Koloth had told them, after all, the *bat'leth* occupied a central point in Klingon culture, a symbol of strength and conviction in the face of chaos and tyranny.

"The legend of Kahless," Koloth continued, "is the foundation upon which the Empire stands. Without his guidance, we are doomed to a fate of self-destruction. For a time, that was forgotten by many Klingons. Other, selfish concerns blinded us to Kahless' teachings, but that is beginning to change. His wisdom is being rediscovered and in time the Empire will return to its former glory."

When he had first heard Koloth refer to Kahless, Kirk remembered reading the name during Academy classes on Klingon culture. But he'd just spent the last sleepless night, lying atop one of the unyielding metal slates that served as beds aboard the *Gal'tagh,* reviewing the memories of when he'd heard the name before.

"I met a Klingon named Kahless, almost twenty years ago." The statement drew a derisive snort from Koloth.

"Impossible. Kahless has been dead for centuries, and no other Klingon has ever borne the name."

Kirk frowned, remembering once more the odd circumstances that had brought him into contact with the Klingon warrior, along with other noted and notorious historical figures including the revered Surak of Vulcan and one of his own childhood heroes, Abraham Lincoln. Kirk still remembered the disbelief that he and the rest of the crew had shared when they had first seen Lincoln, floating in space without benefit of spacecraft or environmental suit.

"It wasn't real," Kirk said. "Rather, it was a physical manifestation of him created by a race of aliens who wanted to 'study' us. They were interested in how we dealt with the concepts of 'good' and 'evil.' Kahless was created to represent evil, along with a few unsavory representatives from Earth history. Once they had all the players, we were pitted against one another to see who would win."

Koloth's laugh echoed off the walls of the exercise room. "It sounds as though your testers were a remarkably shortsighted species. Good does not always triumph over evil, my dear Captain, and in fact, the very notion of such clear-cut distinctions is a fallacy. Many of those considered to be evil are not incapable of mercy, while many of those who profess to be pure can commit the most heinous of acts and justify them in the name of what is 'good.' However, I am sure none of this is new to you."

Nodding, Kirk soberly agreed. His travels had introduced him to the best and worst that living beings had to offer, whether they had been born in far-off star systems or on his home planet.

"This aberration of Kahless you met all those years ago," Koloth said. "How was it created?"

Kirk remembered what Yarnek, the leader of the mysterious race who called themselves the Excalbians, had told him. "The representations of Kahless and the others were drawn from images in our minds. That made sense for Lincoln, Surak, and the others, as we had either read about them or seen pictures. But I'd only read stories of Kahless before that incident."

Taking another look at the statue, Kirk almost unconsciously registered the fact that both Klingons depicted in the sculpture bore pronounced forehead ridges, much as Koloth did now. That in itself was not an anomaly, for it was well known that at least two different species of Klingon had been encountered since Earth's initial contact with the warrior race during the previous century.

"More than likely," he continued, "his image was created based on my own experiences and memories of Klingons." He smiled at Koloth. "Needless to say, we know more now than we did then."

"Not that it's a whole lot," Sulu added.

Koloth regarded the helmsman, nodding. "That theory makes sense. The true Kahless would never have aligned himself with those motivated merely by personal gain. Such actions are the very height of dishonor. As for not knowing us, the same could be said for our knowledge of the Federation. Perhaps the peace talks between our peoples will alleviate that."

Their conversation was interrupted by the opening of the exercise room doors for a second time as two Klingons entered. The hands of one Klingon were secured with manacles. As he rose to his feet, Kirk recognized the other Klingon as Toreth, the *Gal'tagh*'s security officer. He marched his restrained charge up to Koloth and saluted.

"My lord, I believe this *petaQ* to be a spy."

Koloth looked the prisoner up and down. "J'rgan? What has he done to warrant such an accusation?"

Toreth replied, "He transported down to Don'zali IV without authorization. The security logs had been tampered with to conceal evidence of this, but I was able to reconstruct the entries. I also uncovered evidence of at least two transmissions encoded within our normal communications traffic. The messages contain information about a Klingon named K'zeq, whom you apparently met on the planet, as well as details of our current course heading to Pao'la."

"So whoever received the transmissions knows everything about our mission," Sulu said.

The menace that appeared in Koloth's eyes was almost matched by the calm, controlled detachment in the eyes of the prisoner. He closed the distance between them until he stood nearly nose to nose with the manacled Klingon.

"J'rgan," he hissed. "You have sacrificed your honor to spy on your fellow shipmates, to say nothing of your treachery to me. Who commands your loyalty?"

J'rgan's relaxed expression broke and the Klingon smiled. "My loyalty is to the Empire, not usurpers seeking to undermine it from within. Whatever it is you seek on Pao'la, there are those who feel it is dangerous to allow you to succeed."

"You mean you don't know what this is all about?" Kirk asked, incredulous.

Regarding Kirk and Sulu with undisguised contempt, J'rgan replied, "I performed my duty. You may have discovered me, but my assignment here is complete. My masters already have the information I was tasked to obtain. What they do with it is their concern, not mine."

Koloth lashed out, his open hand striking J'rgan across the face with such force that the other Klingon staggered backward from the force of the blow. "Do not speak in riddles. No doubt it is Komor who sent you to spy on me. That cowardly parasite has no concept of honor, and I intend to see the day that he is removed from the Council and cast into *Gre'thor* where he will rot for all eternity."

Abruptly, he looked to Toreth. "Release him."

"Koloth, what are you doing?" Kirk asked. He watched as Koloth motioned for Sulu to hand him the *bat'leth* that the helmsman still carried. Toreth unlocked J'rgan's hands from the manacles and Koloth tossed the weapon to the prisoner.

"Granting one opportunity for him to restore some small portion of his honor." Glaring at J'rgan, he added, "That is, if you have the courage to try. Komor cannot protect you here. You must rely on your own warrior spirit, if indeed you possess such a thing."

J'rgan regarded the gleaming blade in his hands, saying nothing.

"Koloth," Kirk began, but was cut off by the Klingon commander.

"This is not something I would expect you to understand, Kirk, nor is it something you need to witness." Nodding to Toreth he said, "Escort them back to their quarters." As Kirk started to step forward, Koloth stopped him with a look and a raised hand. "Do not attempt to interfere in matters of Klingon honor, Kirk. Go. Now."

Kirk caught movement to his left and turned to see J'rgan raising his *bat'leth* in preparation to attack. Letting loose a fierce war cry, the Klingon charged forward, the *bat'leth* flashing in the light.

"Koloth!"

Toreth started to draw his sidearm as Sulu moved forward to intercept the attacking prisoner. Kirk was in front of the helmsman and so was closer to J'rgan, but it didn't matter.

All three of them froze as Koloth stepped boldly into the charge, his left hand grasping J'rgan's right wrist and halting the downward swing of the *bat'leth*. Koloth jerked down on J'rgan's arm, pulling the weapon to the side and drawing the other Klingon off balance, his head and neck now exposed and vulnerable to attack.

Which Koloth delivered.

The strike was so fast, so brutal, that Kirk almost didn't believe it could have happened. It wasn't until J'rgan's lifeless body fell limply to the deck that the realization was driven home.

His mouth open in mute shock, Kirk could say nothing as Koloth calmly straightened his uniform and bent to retrieve the fallen *bat'leth*. Only then did he face his small audience.

While Toreth was smiling in admiration at his captain's impressive display of physical prowess, Kirk and Sulu wore nearly identical stunned expressions. Finally, Kirk was able to summon enough control to speak.

"Was . . . was that really necessary?"

Koloth studied the *Enterprise* captain's face for several seconds before replying. "You may look like a Klingon, my dear Captain, and you may even learn to fight like a Klingon. But do not believe for one moment that any of that gives you any insight into what it means to be Klingon."

Chapter Nineteen

KOMOR READ THE LATEST communications transcript from the *Gal'tagh,* the latest from the deep-cover operative he had stationed aboard Koloth's ship, giving full details as to the *Gal'tagh*'s activities.

"K'zeq," he read aloud from his datapad. Then, in a rare display of his formidable temper, he threw the small device across the room. It slammed against the far wall of his office and shattered into countless pieces of metal and plastic composite shrapnel.

"There can be only one reason for attempting to locate K'zeq," K'lotek said from where he stood near the expansive window dominating his friend's office. "Koloth is looking for the prison on Pao'la."

Komor rose from behind his ornate stone desk. The centerpiece of his office, it had been fashioned from a slab of granite taken from the mountain monastery on Boreth. The remote planet, according to Klingon legend, was where Kahless would one day return from *Sto-Vo-*

Kor to lead the Klingon Empire toward its ultimate destiny. Komor had visited Boreth once many years ago, and had been so taken with the monastery that he desired a souvenir, something that he could look upon each day and which would remind him of the simpler though perhaps more rewarding existence that living on the planet might bring to him. He had possessed the desk that had been carved from the granite since first being elected to the High Council, and it was one of the few items from the office he would take with him when it came time for him to step down.

"Of all the things I thought Gorkon capable, I never imagined this," he said, shaking his head as he paced the office. All around him, the trophies and mementos of a glorious military and political career begged for his attention, but his gaze fell on none of them. Instead, he stared at the worn wooden floor as he walked.

With J'rgan's report stating that the *Gal'tagh* was enroute to Pao'la, it was obvious what Koloth had discussed with K'zeq.

The *Gagarin*.

Komor had long ago relegated the memory of that cursed Federation ship and all the problems it had caused to obscurity. To have it so violently thrown back in his face at this most tenuous of times for the Empire galled him.

He remembered objecting to taking any of the Starfleet crew captive, even if the reason put forth by Chancellor Kesh was to learn of the Federation's plans for the unoccupied planets bordering the Neutral Zone near Klingon space. As he had only recently been elected to the High Council, Komor's voice had not carried the weight of the more seasoned members. So he had sat by and watched as the surviving members of the *Gagarin*'s crew were scattered to various prison facilities across the Empire, including Pao'la, and held in secret.

"Why didn't we simply kill all of them once we'd obtained the information we'd wanted?" he asked, knowing that K'lotek would understand that the question was rhetorical and would not offer an answer. His close friend understood his tendency to ramble, talking and posing questions aloud to himself in the hope that clarity would emerge from whatever confusion might be consuming him.

Komor, as well as a few other Council members, had argued for the execution of the *Gagarin* survivors once their perceived usefulness had come to an end. Once again, though, such thoughts were waylaid as the Empire entered yet another round of negotiations with the Federation. Kesh had believed that Starfleet hostages might prove useful should the talks begin to go against the Klingons. Even when the negotiations ended and both parties came away no better or worse than they had been before, the Council had still not seen fit to dispose of the prisoners.

Now, years later, Kesh, Komor, and K'lotek were the only members of the current Council who had been in office at the time of the incident. They alone shared the secret.

Well, they, along with Gorkon and Koloth, apparently.

Gorkon had only recently been appointed to the Council, but he had wasted no time making his views known. War with the Federation, he espoused, was a waste of time and resources. The Federation, regardless of how differently they viewed the universe they occupied, had at their command far greater reserves of materiel with which to increase their sphere of influence. The Empire, on the other hand, was greatly restricted, territorially speaking. Cosmic Fate had seen fit to position both the Federation and the Romulan Empire in such a manner that Klingon boundaries could only be expanded away from the galactic center and into a desolate region of the Beta Quadrant. Very few suitable star systems had been found in that area of space, with even fewer planets that could be populated or mined for vital resources. Because of this, Gorkon believed the course of action best for the Empire was to seek some kind of peaceful coexistence with the Federation.

"If Gorkon has discovered that the Empire holds Starfleet officers in captivity," K'lotek said, "he will insist on their safe return to the Federation. It's just the sort of goodwill gesture he's been looking for to prove his point."

Komor nodded angrily. "Yes. He's so enamored with establishing peace with the Federation that he's blinded himself to the consequences. With the unrest we face, this will only worsen the problem."

True enough, there was a growing movement within the Empire of Klingons who sought to return to the old ways, to the days when the teachings of Kahless guided the people rather than a group of elected political officials. Many Klingons believed that the High Council had lost sight of the values put forth by the Unforgettable and that they should be made to see the errors of their misguided leadership.

If the swelling ranks of Kahless followers learned of the existence of any *Gagarin* survivors, they would see it as an act of blasphemy in the face of Klingon honor. There would be calls for removal of the Council, an action that could very well plunge the Empire into civil war.

"We must prevent any knowledge of the prisoners from escaping," Komor said. "Gorkon cannot be allowed to take this matter into his own hands, not with the peace talks still underway. Though I prefer the battlefield to a conference table, I am not so dense that I cannot see the greater good being served here. If the Empire can benefit from such an alliance, then so be it. One day, our patience will be rewarded and we will take our place as the supreme rulers of the galaxy."

K'lotek nodded in agreement, knowing as well that his personal beliefs would have to remain subordinate to the needs of the Empire as a whole if it were to continue to thrive.

"What shall we do?"

"Find me a ship," Komor said. "Send it to Pao'la and have it destroy that prison. I want nothing to remain of it."

The look of astonishment was evident on K'lotek's face, and it took several seconds for him to respond. "It will take some time to evacuate our troops."

Komor shook his head. "No. Destroy everything. Make it look like an attack by an outside force. Romulan, Orion, I don't care, but I want nothing to remain."

"Kill our own soldiers to protect this secret?" K'lotek countered. "How is that better than the secret itself?"

"It's their handful of lives against the entire Empire," Komor countered. He indicated the computer terminal on his desk. "We have to purge all information regarding these prisoners. No record of the *Gagarin* can exist anywhere in our archives." He felt his face flush with a fury he hadn't known since he and K'lotek had served together aboard a battle cruiser in their youth.

"Make them disappear."

The desk intercom on Komor's desk chirped for attention. He tapped a control to open the connection and the display screen coalesced into the image of his aide.

"Komor, we have received an incoming transmission from Captain Koloth aboard the Gal'tagh. *He wishes to speak to you."*

At first Komor wondered what Koloth could possibly want with him, but realization dawned and he felt an initial knot of fear well up in his stomach.

"Put him on," he ordered.

A Klingon whom Komor did not immediately recognize replaced the image of his aide. However, he did notice that the Klingon's face was severely bruised on one side, and that his head sat at an odd angle atop his neck. It only took an additional second for Komor to realize that the eyes staring at him from the computer screen were devoid of life.

"J'rgan!" K'lotek gasped, making no attempt to hide his shock.

On the screen, the face of J'rgan fell out of view, to be replaced by that of Koloth himself.

"I'm afraid your spy will not be able to make his next scheduled report, Councilman Komor. If you want any further information about my ship, you'll have to request it from me."

Komor felt his blood beginning to boil. Of all the impudence! Koloth, a mere ship commander, rendering such blatant insulting behavior toward a member of the High Council!

"I will see to it that you and your ship are reduced to atoms," Komor hissed.

Koloth shook his head. *"You are invited to send anyone foolhardy enough to try. In the meantime, I will continue on with my mission."*

"Your mission?" Komor roared. "Your mission to plunge the Empire into chaos?"

"No, Councilman," Koloth replied. *"My mission to see that a hideous blight on the honor of the Empire, which you have helped to perpetuate all these years, is wiped away. And when that is finished, I will come for you."*

The threat meant nothing to Komor. "I know your destination, Koloth. You will be met by Klingon warriors loyal to the Empire, and they will destroy you."

Koloth laughed, embracing the challenge. "*I look forward to that, but my sensors tell me there are no vessels in range to intercept me. We will be away before any resistance can arrive. Besides, I have allies who would not take kindly to my death at the orders of a conniving politician using the power of his office for his own personal gain. Weigh that, Councilman, and remember this: Today may not be a good day to die for you, but one day will be.*"

With that, the computer screen went dark, the transmission severed.

"He's right," K'lotek said. "He has many friends, even on the Council, who would avenge his death."

Komor had begun his pacing again. "So far as we know, the only other Council member who knows what Koloth is doing is Gorkon."

"We cannot take action against Gorkon until we are certain the situation is contained," K'lotek warned. How much knowledge did Gorkon possess? Who had he shared it with? What information still remained cloaked in darkness, perhaps waiting to be revealed in the event of his untimely demise?

"We will address that issue soon enough," he said. "However, we must distract the remainder of the Council long enough to sanitize this entire situation."

And then it struck him.

It was so simple, and it was the perfect method to ensure that no unanticipated loose ends might be dangling.

"The peace talks," he said. "It is possible that someone there is aware of what Koloth is doing. We cannot risk that."

Eyes wide in disbelief, K'lotek stammered, "You're not suggesting . . ."

"What I suggest," Komor said, "is that we deal with all of our problems in the most efficient manner available to us."

"Today may not be a good day to die for you, but one day will be."

On the bridge of the *Gal'tagh,* Koloth severed the connection, then turned to face Kirk and Sulu.

"Are you sure that was the best way to handle that?" Kirk asked.

Smiling wolfishly, Koloth replied, "Komor is angry and perhaps a bit desperate. I saw it in his eyes. That is good. He will be easier to predict that way."

"What if he sends a ship?" Sulu asked. "Are there really none close enough?" The helmsman tried not to look too closely at the prone form of J'rgan. He had to admit, though, that it had been an effective way to initiate communication with Komor.

Koloth consulted the latest report from his sensor officer. "The nearest ship is the *Zan'zi,* but we should be able to retrieve the prisoners and be gone before it arrives. They outgun us, but I know of her captain. He is an inferior tactician." Casting a glance at Kirk that on a human would have been considered mischievous, he added, "Even you could best him in battle, Kirk."

"Thanks for the vote of confidence," Kirk replied, chuckling as he scratched his beard. The adhesive that McCoy had used to affix the prosthetic to his face had begun to irritate his skin, a condition worsened by the warm temperature aboard the *Gal'tagh* which the Klingons found comfortable. He would be glad when he could rid himself of the Klingon disguise.

Turning away from the communications station, Koloth

made his way across the cramped bridge deck to his command chair even as two subordinates moved to carry the lifeless body of J'rgan away.

"Komor won't only be concerned with us, however. He will be trying to cover up all knowledge of our activities. That means the peace negotiations could be in danger."

"They wouldn't try to attack the starbase," Sulu countered. "It's too far inside Federation space, for one thing. There's no way they could get a ship close enough without being detected, could they?"

Kirk shook his head. "No, it doesn't seem likely, but we'll alert Spock to the possibility." For the first time since leaving the *Enterprise,* Kirk found himself wondering how his first officer was coping with the extended deception that had been enacted to cover his absence. He knew that McCoy or Scotty would be there to help him; either man was fully capable of selling sand to a Vulcan.

"No," he continued, "the real problem might be sabotage from within. If they could put a spy aboard the *Gal'tagh,* then they could have one aboard the other ship just as easily."

Koloth slapped the arm of his chair. "It matters not. We will complete our mission and restore the honor of the Empire, regardless of the obstacles we face."

Kirk exchanged looks with Sulu, wondering if the helmsman shared his concern about the trouble that the Klingon captain's convictions was sure to land them in.

Chapter Twenty

THE LASER DRILL was not heavy, nor did it vibrate or kick as he wielded it, but Garrovick hated the tool just the same. Its intense heat wrapped around him like a cocoon, suffocating him and drenching him in sweat. He could feel the rivers of perspiration coursing down his body inside his coveralls, which in turn caused abrasive rubbing against his skin. The one-piece undergarment he wore, also soaked, only compounded the situation.

It had taken less than a day for the guards to return the prisoners to something resembling their normal routine following the earthquake. While eighteen inmates had been killed and dozens more had suffered injuries, Sinak was the only one of the *Gagarin* officers to be wounded. Garrovick once again gave silent thanks to the deity or deities watching over them all these years. How much longer would he and his friends continue to benefit from their divine influence? It was a question he asked frequently, waiting for an answer that he was sure would never come.

He tried to keep his full attention on the work before him, but it was difficult. Garrovick had not yet seen Khulr today, and that worried him. He would much rather have the Klingon where he could see him instead of lurking about in the shadows, waiting for an opportunity to strike. After the incident during the earthquake two days earlier, the *Gagarin* first officer knew that he would be a target now, possibly even more so than Sydney. The Klingon's pride had been damaged, which was far more harmful than any physical injury Garrovick could have inflicted. Khulr was no fool, however, and would not risk having the details of his last encounter with the humans brought to the attention of Korax. Instead he would bide his time, waiting for the right moment to seek revenge.

In front of him, the drill's focused beam of energy continued to bore into the dense rock of the mining cavern. Sensors built into the unit were programmed to cut around any dilithium contained within the bedrock of the mine, freeing the precious mineral from its underground prison and allowing the irregular-sized specimens to fall to the ground. Periodically, the worker manning the drill would have to cease digging long enough to transfer the extracted dilithium into portable containers, which were then transported by hand to remotely controlled collection vehicles. At the moment, a male Gallamite whom Garrovick did not know was performing this task.

As he deactivated his laser drill and set it on the ground to help gather the dilithium, he couldn't help but stare at the Gallamite's transparent skull. Nearly twice the size of the average human's, the prisoner's brain was visible without skin or muscle tissue or blood surrounding it. Only a semi-clear fluid could be seen, surrounding the

Gallamite's brain. Almost every detail of the brain itself was visible, in some ways reminding Garrovick of the holographic representations of the human anatomy he had studied in otherwise long-forgotten biology classes.

"Hello," he offered cordially.

The Gallamite responded at first with a simple nod as he bent to the process of collecting the dilithium. "Your efforts produce much ore," he said as he placed some of the larger pieces into one of two collection containers he had brought with him. "Our masters will be pleased."

Blanching at the reference to the Klingon guards, Garrovick said, perhaps a bit too sharply, "They're not our masters. All I'm doing is making sure they stay happy and treat us decently. That's as far as it goes."

"Amen to that, Commander," Kawaguchi said from his right, deactivating his own laser drill and wiping the sweat from his face with the back of one gloved hand. "If it keeps them off my back, then I'll dig a hole all the way to the other side of this planet. Besides, it's not as if there's much else to do around here. Beats rotting away in a cell, that's for sure."

Garrovick was forced to agree with the sentiment. Without activity to consume their pent-up energy and occupy their minds, he figured he might very well have lost his sanity by now. For that reason, he hated the isolation chambers that Korax had sentenced him and Sydney to just days before. Cut off from all outside stimuli and forced to do nothing except confront the deepest recesses of one's own mind was an unnerving experience to say the least. Trapped inside his tiny cell, thoughts came tumbling forth unbidden. Hopes, fears, dreams, and nightmares all begged for his attention with gut-wrenching clarity, casting him all over the emotional landscape from unfettered joy to stark terror and everything that lie between. The longest amount of time he had spent in one of the isolation cells was ten days. It hadn't sounded like such a stretch at first, but that was before time began to slow and stretch into infinity. He hadn't believed that the experience would be so trying and had come away from the punishment with a harsh respect for the small chambers.

"Stephen! Look out!"

Recognizing the voice as Sydney's, Garrovick spun around to look for his friend. He turned in time to see another prisoner, a Romulan whom Garrovick recognized as Trel and had heard to be a former military engineer, brandishing his laser drill as though it were a heavy phaser cannon.

And he was pointing it *at him.*

Fiery red energy spat from the drill and Garrovick felt the heat of the beam as it passed just to his right. He threw himself to the ground and rolled away from the attack, not comprehending how Trel could have missed him at such close range.

It was simple. *He* wasn't the target.

A cry of pain erupted from somewhere behind him and Garrovick rolled away to see a Klingon cleaved in half at the waist by the force of the beam. As the guard's head and torso came away from the lower portion of his body and fell to the ground with a sickly thud, Garrovick's mind screamed that such an action should be impossible.

The laser drills used by the prison miners were encoded with special programming that prevented the tools from being utilized except as mining implements. If aimed at an organic life-form, even something as small as a rodent foraging for food scraps in the depths of the mine, the drills would not fire. Such measures were prudent, of course, given the number of prisoners working in the mines at any one time compared to the number of guards available to oversee them.

But Trel had overcome these imposed limitations. How? When had he even had the time to try?

The mine erupted into chaos as prisoners dropped their equipment and scrambled for whatever meager concealment they could find. Others, caught out in the open, dropped to the ground and covered their head with their hands.

Garrovick ceased to care about any of that, though, when his eyes fell upon the crumpled form lying slumped against the cavern wall. Kawaguchi.

"Robert!"

The chief had gotten caught in the crossfire as Trel swept the area to hit the Klingon guard he had targeted.

Sprinting across the open space of the mining tunnel, Garrovick knelt over his friend. A ghastly wound desecrated Kawaguchi's midsection, the drill's beam having sliced through the man's coverall garment, skin, muscle tissue, and bone. The sternum had been punctured and Garrovick could see that the liver, a lung, and the heart had been utterly destroyed. Kawaguchi had been dead before he'd fallen to the ground.

"Dammit," Garrovick whispered as he placed a hand on the chief's arm. Kawaguchi had been the first *Gagarin* crew member to die since Ensign Randall Bird, a member of Sydney Elliot's security detachment and a man Garrovick had barely known, had succumbed to a virulent strain of flu during the second year of their captivity. The first officer had been unable to help Bird, and neither had the prison's doctor. The Klingon commanding the camp at that time had refused to take any extra steps to help the ailing ensign, and he had died within days. Several other prisoners throughout the compound had also fallen victim to the flu but none of the other *Gagarin* survivors had contracted it.

The hollow feeling gnawing at the pit of his stomach was one Garrovick had felt on those unwelcome occasions where he had faced the death of a subordinate. It was a pain that never diminished, no matter how many times he confronted it. While he was serving as an ensign aboard the *Enterprise,* many years earlier, Captain Kirk had told him that such pain should never be forgotten. Instead, it should be redirected, focused, channeled into energy that could be used to make the decisions necessary to protect those who remained.

"Take care of your people," Kirk had told him. "No matter the cost."

The words haunted Garrovick as he looked down on the unmoving body of Robert Kawaguchi.

An alarm shrieked in the echoing confines of the cavern. Garrovick knew it meant that reinforcements were already on the way down into the mining cavern. They would be armed this time, having traded their stun batons for disruptors. The Klingons would be anxious to even the score against any rebelling prisoners who had killed their comrades. Tensions would be high, and his priority now was to make sure that neither he nor any of his remaining people fell victim to an overzealous Klingon guard caught up in the excitement.

All around him, prisoners scurried about like animals running from a forest fire as they searched for cover. Except for those who had fallen victim to the laser drill, Garrovick could see no other Klingon guards. What he did see was two other prisoners stooping over the bodies of Klingon guards. As they each bent to retrieve a guard's fallen stun baton, he recognized that they too were Romulan. It confirmed his suspicion that the attack with the laser drill was not a random act of opportunity. It was a coordinated effort. What were they planning? Escape? The very notion was ludicrous.

Indeed, mining tunnels stretched for kilometers in every direction from the prison compound like a giant web. As the years passed and mining increased, cross-connecting tunnels and air shafts had formed an intricate network that could now only be navigated with the use of a portable positioning scanner carried by each guard. Stories and rumors had circulated over the years of prisoners who had escaped their work details and fled into the depths of the mine, never to be seen alive again. Skeletal remains clothed in a deteriorated prison uniform would sometimes be found as work crews were sent from tunnel to tunnel, serving to keep the tales of failed escape attempts thriving.

Looking around the mining cavern, Garrovick saw where Elliot and Ra Mhvlovi had found concealment behind one of the collection carts. Elliot waved to him, the look on her face telling him to quit standing in the open like an idiot and find some cover.

Good idea.

The two Romulans were moving with deliberate purpose toward Trel, striking out at anyone who got in their way. Judging by the results of their attacks, Garrovick guessed that the batons they wielded had been set to near lethal levels.

Garrovick saw a guard emerge from a side tunnel and recognized him as Moqlah, the guard who had gone out of his way to protect he and Elliot from too harsh a punishment at the hands of Korax earlier in the week. Moqlah had risked the wrath of both the camp commander and Khulr because he believed the imprisonment of the *Gagarin* officers was unjust and dishonorable. The action had earned him a measure of respect from Garrovick and the others.

It was this respect that gave Garrovick cause for alarm as Moqlah attempted to approach the drill-wielding Romulan from the side, his stun baton in hand, held high and poised to attack. Garrovick could see the end of the weapon glowing a bright orange, indicating the baton was set to deliver a potentially lethal strike.

Chapter Twenty-one

"MOQLAH!"

Garrovick's warning came too late as Trel sensed the Klingon guard's movements. Moqlah realized he'd been caught just as the Romulan swept the drill around to face him.

Fiery red energy belched forth once again and Moqlah dove to his right, barely able to avoid being sliced in half by the drill's beam. The Klingon still caught a glancing strike, the beam cutting past the heavy material of his uniform tunic and across his back. Moqlah crashed to the ground, writhing in agony.

It took only seconds for Garrovick to reach the fallen guard, the unmistakable stench of burned flesh assaulting his nostrils for a second time as he knelt to inspect the Klingon's wound. The laser drill had burned through Moqlah's uniform and had scorched skin and muscle all the way down to the bones of his rib cage.

His face clouded in pain, Moqlah managed to croak

out a weak question. "What . . . what are you doing, human?"

"Repaying a favor," Garrovick replied as he tore part of his own coverall sleeve loose. Turning the fabric inside out, he hoped it was clean enough to be used as a field-expedient bandage. It was still better than allowing the open wound to remain exposed to contamination in the dust-riddled cavern.

As he applied the makeshift dressing, Garrovick heard footsteps in front of him just before the sound of the laser drill firing came again. Red energy and dirt exploded from the ground in front of him and he fell back, bringing his hands up to protect his face.

When he looked up again, it was to see Trel standing perhaps fifteen meters away, the muzzle of the drill aimed directly at him. The other two Romulans had joined him, still carrying the stun batons they had liberated from owners who would never need them again.

Garrovick recognized one of the newcomers as the one he and his companions had nicknamed "Scarface," due to the prominent crisscross of puckered flesh highlighting his forehead and cheekbones. He was one of several prisoners the *Gagarin* survivors had learned to keep an eye on, due to his propensity for picking fights with other inmates and his professed dislike of humans.

As for the second Romulan, Garrovick knew his face but not his name. Still, there was no mistaking the malevolent grin creasing the prisoner's mouth.

Trel regarded Garrovick for a moment, his dark eyes offering no insight into what he might be thinking. Garrovick became aware of the fact that he was silently counting the seconds that passed as the two men faced off. Was his mind checking off the final moments of his life?

Instead of killing Garrovick, the Romulan turned his attention to Moqlah, who was still a limp, disjointed heap on the ground and who Garrovick saw was beginning to display the initial symptoms of shock.

"The Klingon dog still lives," Trel said. The muzzle of the laser drill moved to aim at Moqlah.

Moqlah sneered back, his expression defiant despite the pain that Garrovick knew must be racking his body. "I have your pathetic aim to thank for that," he hissed through his agony, the tone of his voice deliberately antagonizing. "Perhaps you should find an old blind woman to teach you to shoot with more accuracy."

Anger clouded Trel's face, the first real emotion Garrovick had seen him display, and he knew at that moment that there was no way Moqlah would be allowed to live.

He wasn't holding out much hope for himself, either.

From this distance, he could see where an access panel on the side of the drill had been opened. There were scorch marks along the edges of the panel door, giving credence to Garrovick's theory that Trel had used his engineering expertise to somehow circumvent the mining tool's safety overrides. The work looked to be crude, but there could be no arguing its effectiveness.

"Kill them," Scarface said. "We are wasting time here. The Klingons will return any moment, in greater numbers and with more powerful weapons."

Of course. The cavern extended far underground in this area, where it led to the vast array of tunnels boring through the rock of this godforsaken planet. Garrovick suspected they would use the drill to remove their ankle bracelets and the transceivers embedded in them. He knew, based on what he'd overheard from guards in the past, that the heavy concentration of dilithium and other mineral ores interfered with tricorder and sensor scans.

Only the high-frequency comm signal emitted by the bracelet locators proved effective at penetrating the planet's surface. Once the bracelets were removed, the Romulans would be able to disappear into the network of mining tunnels.

"Yes, we must go," the third Romulan added. "They can still track us until we dispose of the homing devices."

Trel nodded. "You are correct." He regarded Moqlah once more, a cruel smile forming on his lips. "In case you are wondering, Klingon, I will indeed enjoy watching you die."

"Is this really necessary?" Garrovick snapped. "He can't stop you from escaping, and he can't hurt you. What purpose does it serve for you to kill him?"

Smiling, Trel indicated the mining cavern with a wave of his hand. "Consider it sufficient restitution for my having to endure existence under Klingon rule." Locking eyes with Garrovick, he added. "Besides, why do you care so much for the life of a Klingon when you should be concerned with whether or not you will continue to live?"

Garrovick had long ago accepted that he might die in this place, either as the victim of an accident or what might appear to be an accident at the hands of unscrupulous guards such as Khulr. He'd come to accept it, just as he'd come to believe that those who loved him back home had given him up for dead long ago.

But now, for the first time, he felt the cold hand of mortality reaching out to envelop him in its grasp. He was going to die, here and now, not at the hands of nature or the guards, but as an exercise in amusement. Impotent rage boiled in him at the thought. There was no way he could get to his feet or even roll out of the line of fire. He was too close, and the weapon too powerful.

Garrovick looked down at Moqlah. Either the Klingon

refused to respond to the Romulan, or he had fallen far enough into shock that he simply no longer cared.

"Goodbye, human," Trel said as he brought the muzzle of the drill up to point at Garrovick's head. Garrovick imagined he could hear the muscles in the Romulan's finger tightening as he pressed the weapon's firing stud.

Then, all around him, the world exploded.

A hellstorm erupted in the cavern and Garrovick could feel an almost electrical sensation playing across his exposed skin as savage red energy beams sliced through the air. He threw himself across the prone form of Moqlah, who by now had fallen so far into shock that he was oblivious of the explosive firefight raging all around him.

Having answered the alarm siren still sounding throughout the cavern, the Klingons had managed to work their way this far into the tunnel system without being detected by the Romulans. Looking up, Garrovick saw Trel, Scarface, and the other Romulan caught in a vicious, merciless crossfire as Klingons fired on them from several directions. Time seemed to slow down as the unrelenting barrage of disruptor fire dissected the three rebels.

And as quickly as it had begun, the nerve-shattering attack was over, the entire sequence taking only a handful of seconds from start to finish and leaving Garrovick to stare in openmouthed shock at the remains of the Romulans.

There wasn't much to see.

Pulling himself back into a kneeling position, Garrovick saw Sydney and Ra Mhvlovi emerging from behind the collection cart they had been using for cover. Neither of them had been injured in the crossfire. Both officers had their hands held up and away from their bodies to show they were unarmed as Klingon guards began to pour from side tunnels and passageways into the main cavern.

The siren ceased its wailing as Garrovick noticed Korax leading one group of guards from the main tunnel. The camp commander was pointing with both hands, sending subordinates in all directions as the Klingons began to reassert control of the situation. The *Gagarin* first officer then noticed that Korax, along with a small cadre of guards, was marching at a rapid pace toward *him*.

Garrovick rose at Korax's approach, the Klingon's face unreadable as he stopped in front of the prisoner. The human expected some type of angered reaction at the uprising that had disrupted mining production as well as having killed a number of his soldiers and prisoners.

Instead, he turned to face the group of four Klingons who had accompanied him.

"Take Moqlah to the surgeon." As the guards moved to comply with his orders, Korax returned his attention to Garrovick, studying the human as if mentally weighing the events of the last few minutes.

"You came to his assistance," he finally said, indicating Moqlah with a nod of his head as the injured guard was carried away. "Your companions, also, with their distraction tactics. You invited certain death upon yourselves for a Klingon. Why?"

Garrovick replied, "Call it self-preservation, Commander. I didn't want to have your guards coming in here with weapons blazing, cutting down everything and everyone in their way looking for who started this mess."

Korax shook his head. "I know humans better than that. You all have this insatiable need to help others, even if they are your enemy and regardless of the circumstance. I hope you realize that it is a weakness which will be your undoing one day."

"Believe what you want," Garrovick said. "Maybe I should have just let them kill him, or maybe I should have joined in on their escape attempt." He indicated the fallen body of Robert Kawaguchi behind him.

"But they killed one of my people, and the simple fact is that Moqlah has been more humane toward us than we had any right to expect from a Klingon. I helped him out of regard for that. Besides, if I'm going to die as part of a prison revolt, I prefer it to be one I'm leading."

Korax smiled, his respect for the human having just been raised a notch. "Perhaps there is hope for your species, human, if more of them think as you do."

Garrovick remembered the conversation between himself, Sydney Elliot and Moqlah. The Klingon had seemed sincere in his belief that the notions of honor and valor were beginning to reassert themselves within the Empire after having been ignored for so long. For such a crusade to be victorious, it would need people such as Moqlah leading the way.

Garrovick's eyes locked with Korax's. "If more Klingons think the way Moqlah does, there might be hope for you, too."

Chapter Twenty-two

IT WAS A RARE OCCASION that allowed Spock to view the *Enterprise* as she hung in space, and the observation ports in Starbase 49's officer's lounge afforded him an unfettered view of the starship. Without benefit of computer imaging, parts of the vessel were cloaked in shadow, with only portions of her hull exposed by her running lights or from illumination cast off by the starbase itself.

Gazing through the thick plexisteel windows at the ship, he was able to appreciate the efficient blend of form and function that she represented. Though he had served aboard the *Enterprise*-A and her predecessor for most of the past thirty-five years, the vessels themselves had never been more than the sum of their respective parts to him. Logically, there was no other way to view the starships.

Nevertheless, his human traits combined with decades spent living and working with humans had given him a different perspective. He had observed over the years that traveling in space, as commonplace as it was in this day and age, still held a romantic allure for many humans, and the vessel they traveled aboard became their home. More than a simple mode of transportation, the ship was where they felt comfortable, protected, alive. It was where they worked, lived, loved, and, on those unfortunate occasions, it was where they died.

For others, the connection to a ship seemed to exist on a different level, a bond that rivaled even the most passionate of relationships. Spock had observed this odd behavior in a handful of humans, and one in particular.

Though he would never admit it to Dr. McCoy, Spock could understand the emotional attachment that seemed to connect James Kirk to the vessel drifting in space before him. Even if logic could allow for such a bond to an object, it would balk at the idea that Kirk had fostered such affection for this *Enterprise*, which was in fact nothing more than a replacement. Its predecessor, the starship Kirk had commanded into history and perhaps legend, was but a memory now.

The atoms of the original *Enterprise* had been scattered across space along with those of the now-destroyed Genesis planet. Kirk had ordered the scuttling of the ship that had served him faithfully for so many years rather than allow it to fall into enemy hands. Logic told Spock that such an action was the correct thing to have done, given the circumstances. After all, Kirk had prevented sensitive Starfleet technology from being captured and exploited by the Klingons. Federation officials had no choice but to agree.

But because of his relationship with James Kirk, Spock knew that the decision had been painful for his friend. For Kirk, the *Enterprise* had always been more than a simple space vessel. Instead, it was the embodiment of everything he had wanted in life. Freedom and adventure, not power and prestige, Spock knew, though Kirk's detractors would think otherwise.

That ship was gone now, however, and all that remained of her was the history she had helped create. That legacy had been left to the starship Spock now scrutinized. While rationale told Spock that it was an entirely new vessel, he knew that Kirk thought of it as much more. If it gave Kirk comfort to believe that some part of the original *Enterprise* lived on in this new incarnation, then Spock would defy all logic and be content to quietly support his friend.

"A magnificent view."

Hearing Toladal's voice made Spock realize just how engrossed he had been in his observations of the *Enterprise.* It was unlike him to become so focused on something that he could be oblivious of someone's approach, especially a Klingon as large as Ambassador Kaljagh's aide. For a brief moment he thought he might indeed understand the drawing power of the starship, and made a mental note to discuss the odd attraction with Captain Kirk at some point.

Out of earshot of Dr. McCoy, of course.

He turned to see Toladal dressed in dark robes accented with a thick leather belt and sash. Even though the clothing was intended to identify its wearer as part of a diplomatic caste, the military nature of the Klingon Empire could still be seen in its design.

Taking note of the evident fatigue in the ambassadorial aide's face, Spock said, "I trust the negotiations are going well."

Toladal shrugged. "We are in recess for the moment. There is some good, there is some bad. Though we have toiled here for more than a week, there are times I feel we are starting from the beginning."

"There are many obstacles to overcome," Spock agreed. "The Federation and the Empire have been at odds far too long for trust to come easily. Prejudice and misconceptions will continue to cloud judgments until both sides have had sufficient opportunity to see what each might offer the other. That it has not happened after only a week is not surprising. It will take far longer than that, I suspect."

Toladal smiled at the words, a large toothy grin that Spock easily saw reflected in the plexisteel window. "It is a pity that you do not speak on behalf of the Federation," he said. "You possess a wisdom that belies the uniform you wear. If I did not know better, I would think I was addressing Sarek himself." After a pause, the Klingon added, "In fact, it surprises me that your father is not present at these negotiations. Ambassador Kaljagh has spoken highly of him on a number of occasions. I suspect the ambassador fancies the idea of pitting his own political prowess against your father's."

Eyebrow arching, Spock allowed himself a mild expression of amusement. "I believe Ambassador Kaljagh would find Sarek to be a formidable opponent. In any case, my father regrets not being available for this summit, as he is currently holding negotiations with the Legarans."

"Ah, the Legarans," Toladal replied. "Let us hope the Empire and the Federation do not take so long to reconcile our differences."

Spock could not disagree. The Federation had sought a treaty with the Legarans since Starfleet's accidental first contact with the reclusive race fifteen years ago. Initial attempts at negotiations had failed miserably, mostly due to Federation diplomatic representatives committing various political and social gaffes. Perhaps dismissed as minor and understandable transgressions by other races, the Legarans had instead taken these actions as serious affronts against them, their utter devotion to protocol and rigid convention allowing them no other quarter. It was only when Ambassador Sarek of Vulcan undertook the challenge of bringing the Legarans to the negotiating table that the treaty was given any chance of success.

That was fourteen years ago.

The progress Sarek had made during the on-again, mostly off-again negotiations had been small yet significant. Still, the Legarans were a long way from accepting any sort of long-term relationship with the Federation. Spock, however, was certain that if anyone could create a solution that would benefit both the Federation and the Legarans, it was Sarek.

After a few moments spent looking through the observation ports, Toladal turned to Spock. "So, Captain, how does it feel to be in command of a vessel such as the *Enterprise,* no matter how briefly? Does it stir notions and desires of one day commanding a ship of your own?"

As he considered the Klingon's question, Spock allowed his gaze to fall on the *Enterprise* once more. He partly suspected that Toladal, while perhaps genuinely interested in the Vulcan's career aspirations, was more likely fishing for information regarding the whereabouts of Captain Kirk.

"I have never sought a command of my own, though I did captain the *Enterprise* for a short time. It is a position that requires much of the individual charged with the responsibility."

An expression mixed of equal parts mild shock and amusement washed over Toladal's features. "Why, Captain, surely you're not suggesting you are unqualified to hold such a position?"

Shaking his head slightly, Spock replied, "While the technical and administrative duties are well within my scope of abilities, I have found that commanding a starship requires mastery of other intangible skills, subtle nuances and character traits that I confess to finding more difficult in grasping. Though I have improved in these areas as the years have passed, it has been my observation that select individuals display these talents as if possessing an inherent gift for them. Logic dictates that such persons be groomed for the arduous responsibility engendered in starship command."

"You mean people like Captain Kirk," Toladal said. "Speaking of whom, I regret that I was unable to spend any time talking with him. I am most interested in meeting the man behind the stories we hear within the Empire."

Spock nodded, pleased that his initial suspicions about this thread of conversation appeared to have been correct. However, he could not find fault with Toladal for attempting to glean information that could be relayed to his superiors. Were the situation reversed, he was certain he would do the same.

Prior to his departure aboard the *Gal'tagh,* Kirk had surmised that a cover story of him being bedridden in sickbay would not hold up under close scrutiny. Therefore, according to orders sent by Admiral Bennett to Starbase 49, Kirk and Sulu were supposed to have departed with all due haste for Earth to take part in a sensitive mission requiring their expertise. With the help of McCoy to make him look sufficiently haggard from his supposed bout with Klingon food poisoning, Kirk had addressed both the Federation and Klingon delegations about his impending departure and Spock's becoming their liaison aboard the *Enterprise.* Kirk knew it was a weak cover story, but it was the best they could do under the circumstances.

Admiral LeGere had contributed to the illusion by dispatching a long-distance transport shuttle to Earth, which had departed the starbase in a spectacular and very visible demonstration of its warp engines. The two ensigns manning the transport knew only that they had orders to travel to Earth for a classified mission, and would arrive to find that they had been granted two weeks' worth of shore leave, courtesy of the admiral himself.

"Captain Kirk regrets having to leave the conference," Spock said, "but his presence was required elsewhere, and he is first and foremost a man of duty." It was a plotted skirting of the truth, Spock knew, but far enough from an actual lie that he felt comfortable saying it.

Toladal nodded in understanding. "Devotion to duty is a concept Klingons appreciate, as well. Perhaps therein lies a possible bridge between our two peoples."

Spock's reply was interrupted as he felt the floor beneath his feet tremble and heard the plexisteel window ports vibrate in their frames. Beyond the wall to his right he heard what he could only identify as a muffled explosion.

"What was that?" Toladal asked, confusion etched on his face, only to say it to Spock's back. The Vulcan had already moved for the exit.

Spock plunged into the corridor to find it full of members from both the Federation and Klingon delegations as well as Starfleet personnel and soldiers from the Klingon ship. The passageway was also beginning to fill with smoke that Spock could see was coming from the conference hall where the mediated proceedings were taking place.

Cries of fear surrounded him, but Spock saw that *En-*

terprise security personnel were working to reassure others that the situation was under control. For the security detachment to have responded so rapidly could only mean . . .

"Captain Spock!"

He heard Chekov's voice and recognized it as coming from the conference hall, the entrance to which had been cordoned off by two security guards. No one was being allowed into the room and the few remaining people still inside were being escorted into the corridor.

As the guards stepped aside for him to enter the chamber, Spock noticed that the podium at the front of the room as well as the large viewing screen built into the forward wall had been obliterated. Nothing remained but the podium's base, which bore silent testament to the explosion that had occurred here just moments before.

To his left, Spock saw a female security officer tending to one of the Federation diplomats who had suffered a minor injury in the blast. The man was unconscious, but a quick visual inspection told him that the laceration across the wounded man's head was not life threatening.

"Ensign," he said to the security officer, "how many people have sustained injuries?"

Looking up, the ensign replied, "Just this gentleman, sir. I can only find the one cut across his head, but I've already called for a beam-up. Dr. McCoy is standing by to give him the once-over." After glancing back at the slumped form of the diplomat, she said, "We were very lucky, Captain. The room was nearly empty when the bomb went off."

Moving toward the front of the room, Spock was able to examine what remained of the podium's base more closely. The entire top surface of the metal pedestal had been scorched black and was covered with pits and holes where shrapnel from the rest of the podium had been driven downward.

"Mr. Chekov," Spock said as the Russian security chief moved to join him. "My compliments on your team's prompt response to this emergency. What has happened here?"

Chekov indicated the decimated remains of the podium with the tricorder he held. "An explosive was planted here. Whatever it was, it was crudely built, for one thing. There's enough of it here to run a detailed analysis, though, so we should have some answers soon."

He waved his free hand and pointed out where shrapnel from the podium had been blown across the conference chamber, embedding itself into the walls, tables, and chairs. "We were lucky that a recess had been called, otherwise the chairperson or whoever was standing at the podium would have been vaporized, to say nothing of injuries to others in the room."

"Captain Spock?" the distinctive voice of Ambassador Joquel carried across the room from the doorway. Spock turned and, seeing both her and the Klingon ambassador being blocked from entering the conference hall by the security guards, motioned for them to be allowed in.

"Ambassadors," he began, clasping his hands behind his back and adopting his customary relaxed yet alert posture, "it would appear that a terrorist act has been perpetrated on these premises."

Barely contained rage was evident on Kaljagh's face. "Given what I am to understand about the security precautions put in place by both Klingon and Starfleet personnel, how is this possible?"

"It shouldn't be," replied another voice from the other side of the room. Spock recognized its owner as Lorta, the security officer of the *Terthos*. The Klingon's uniform had been tailored to accentuate the musculature of her arms, augmenting the woman's already imposing figure. Her hair was pulled back into a tight bun that made her facial features all the more prominent. She stood taller than Spock and was of course broader across the shoulders and chest. Even with the impressive strength his own Vulcan physique provided him, Spock calculated that she could best him in physical combat.

"Both Commander Chekov and I conduct security sweeps of the chamber prior to the commencement of each session." The tone of Lorta's voice was forceful, crisp, and confident. "No one is allowed entry into the room while a session is under way. Nothing was found in the room before the last session began." Spock had no doubts that the security officer was confident with the report she was giving, having already received the results of the sensor sweep from Chekov when it had first been completed.

"We are therefore left with two possibilities," he said. "Either the explosive was transported into the room after the completion of the security inspection, or one of the individuals in attendance brought the device into the room on their person."

"Surely not," Joquel said, aghast. "Everyone in this room is committed to making this summit succeed."

"Apparently, someone does not share your viewpoint," Lorta said.

Joquel nodded grudgingly. "We were lucky no one was injured," she said as she looked around the room and surveyed the damage. "I wonder if whoever put it in there had a specific target in mind."

"The ambassador has a point," Chekov said. "The morning session proceeded ahead of schedule. None of the issues discussed raised any drawn-out debates or disagreements."

"It was the most productive of the meetings we've had so far," Kaljagh said, the optimism still evident in his voice despite the statement's harsh, gruff delivery.

Nodding in agreement, Chekov continued, "Because of that, things moved along more rapidly, and the midday recess was called early. Ordinarily, they'd probably still be in there for another hour or so."

"Commander Chekov is correct," Lorta said. "The triumph of the morning's discussions may actually have thwarted whatever plan was in motion."

Taking another look at the destroyed podium, Spock said, "It also lends credence to a hypothesis that the explosive operated on a timed delay and was not triggered by a remote signal. That still leaves us with the possibilities of the device having been planted either by means of a transporter or a courier."

"I'll have the *Enterprise* sensor logs reviewed for signs of unauthorized transporter activity," Chekov said.

Lorta added, "As will I with the sensor records of the *Terthos*. Meanwhile, should we not begin interrogating the delegates?"

Seeing the look of utter incredulity on Joquel's face and before the ambassador could respond, Spock cut in. "Lieutenant, given the sensitivity of the current proceedings, that may not be the most prudent course of action. Instead, I believe that you and Commander Chekov should begin an investigation. As you are both seasoned security professionals, we can expect you to address the issue with the required level of urgency and delicacy."

"Delicacy is a concern for humans," Kaljagh said. "But you are correct." The anger on the Klingon's face softened somewhat. "Captain, you speak with the ease of a diplomat. You should quit wasting your time in Starfleet and enter politics. It's certainly a different type of battle than you may be accustomed to, though. Your enemies aren't always visible, but it makes the challenge that much greater."

Spock nodded in acknowledgment of what was, in Klingon parlance at least, intended to be a compliment. Of course, the enemy he faced now was anything but visible. The quarry he sought had no name, no description, and no identity. He, or she, could be anywhere or nowhere. They could be cloaked in shadow, or the next person he talked to.

Perhaps politics would not be so different after all.

Chapter Twenty-three

HANGING LOW on the horizon, the sun cast its last feeble rays through the thick jungle canopy as yet another Pao'lan day readied itself to surrender to the coming darkness. In less than an hour, the stars would be clearly visible in the moonless sky.

But it will still be hotter than hell, Kirk thought.

He and Koloth lay concealed in heavy undergrowth, their elevated position on a hillside giving them an almost unobstructed view of the prison's massive, U-shaped stone wall and the cluster of buildings within it. Inside the wall, Kirk could see the open courtyard but with the exception of the odd Klingon soldier or what looked to him to be a prisoner, the compound appeared to be deserted.

"The prisoners are probably away on work details," Koloth said, "and will no doubt return before nightfall." He indicated the large opening in the base of the mountain that formed the rear wall of the prison. "According to

K'zeq, that is the main entrance to the network of mining tunnels."

As he peered through his viewfinder, perspiration stung Kirk's eyes, again, and he lowered the device in order to wipe his face. Even without him exerting any real effort, the heat and humidity were sapping his energy. Along with Sulu, he was drinking water by the liter to keep his body hydrated, and both humans were taking vitamin supplements to battle the effects of the stifling heat. It was only a temporary solution, however. The only truly effective remedy for the planet's harsh environment would be to remain on the surface long enough for their bodies to acclimate.

And that was not high on Kirk's list of priorities.

Noticing Kirk's discomfort, Koloth chuckled. "This heat tests even a warrior's mettle, Kirk. You should feel no shame in withering under its influence."

Kirk sensed the sarcasm in the Klingon's tone and smiled back good-naturedly. "I'm just glad I opted to ditch the Klingon disguise. I can't imagine what it would be like with all that makeup on." He'd gotten a taste of that discomfort earlier in the day, when he realized that the artificial skin pigmentation he and Sulu wore retained their body heat. That was enough to convince both men to remove their disguises.

"You should have kept the beard," Koloth noted as he returned his attention to his own viewfinder. "To Klingons, a beard represents courage, which I know you have in no small quantity." He laughed again as he added, "Besides, somehow it made you look more intelligent." Kirk shared the laugh before returning to his own study of the prison compound.

Getting to Pao'la had been easier than he had expected. Other than the prison that was the sole concentration of higher life forms in this entire hemisphere, there was only one other appreciable population center, a spaceport city on the other side of the planet. The idea of beaming anyone up from the prison itself had been thwarted once the cloaked *Gal'tagh* had settled into orbit and conducted a sensor sweep.

Just as K'zeq had indicated to them on Don'zali IV, an energy shield surrounded the prison and inhibited the use of transporters. It also prevented the detection of life forms within its perimeter by passive sensor scans. Koloth had decided that attempting a more invasive sweep would risk attracting attention, possibly from the prison itself but most definitely from the spaceport authorities who maintained tracking stations both in orbit and on the surface. Otherwise, defeating the civilian-grade planetary sensors had been an easy task for both the *Gal'tagh* and the shuttle that Kirk, Sulu, and Koloth had used to make planetfall.

Operating the shuttle under the shroud of its own cloaking device, Sulu and Koloth had piloted the smaller vessel to the surface and found a suitable landing site far enough from the prison to avoid having anyone hear them land. That had been the easy part. The more difficult task had been the long hike on foot four kilometers from the shuttle to a place where they could observe the prison without being spotted themselves.

That had been eight hours ago. After spending so long lying on the unforgiving ground, Kirk was beginning to grow impatient.

"Look," Koloth said, pointing with one hand in the direction of the prison. "Someone's coming out of the mountain."

Through his viewfinder, Kirk could see the first figures emerging from the mouth of the tunnel drilled into the base of the unnamed mountain. In short order, two columns of prisoners, all dressed alike in drab gray utility uniforms, moved slowly but steadily into the courtyard. He also saw dozens of Klingons marching alongside the group, some carrying what looked to be batons of some sort that Kirk guessed were used to discipline the prisoners.

The prisoners represented a myriad number of races, mostly from planets not aligned with the Federation. Regardless of species, and apparently gender, no prisoner sported any hair on their head or face. With the dirt and grime covering their bodies and clothing, few of the prisoners were readily distinguishable from each other. Though the vast majority of prisoners appeared to be from humanoid races, there was no way to be more precise without the sensors aboard the shuttle.

Still, he couldn't help the sense of relief that washed over him as he watched the columns of bedraggled workers exit the tunnel. Somewhere down there, he was sure of it, members of the *Gagarin* crew were waiting to be rescued.

The reports K'zeq had kept said that eight members of the ill-fated ship's complement had been interred at the prison, but that at least two had died within the first year. One had fallen victim to disease, while the *Gagarin*'s captain, the only member of the crew to be specifically named in any of the reports, had been executed. That left six potential survivors, which the shuttle could carry easily. How many of them were still alive, if any? Kirk was convinced that at least some of them had to have survived. Anything else would mean that this mission was a failure, and Kirk would not accept that.

"They look haggard," he said as he peered at the lines of shuffling prisoners through his viewfinder. "Looks like they get worked pretty hard."

Koloth was studying the slow-moving columns as well, silent for a few moments. Then, "They look better than I expected. This group eats better than at most prisons I've seen."

"They can't produce dilithium from the mines if they're dropping dead from malnutrition and disease," Kirk replied.

Koloth didn't comment, instead focusing his attention on the layout of the courtyard. "In order to get at the prisoners, we have to defeat the shield. I doubt we can disable it completely, since it seems the power source is protected inside the prison itself. We have to find a way to penetrate it at a specific point."

Kirk studied the stone wall and the buildings. "Whatever we do, it will have to be fast." They couldn't give the guards any chance to kill the prisoners, get them under cover, or repair whatever damage inflicted on the shield. Kirk was sure there had to be a backup system to take care of any failure in the energy grid. "Our only chance will be to hit them hard and keep them off balance."

"That means a diversionary action," Koloth replied.

Shifting his position, Kirk watched as the prisoners were marched toward a large, squat building on the left side of the compound. He guessed it was a facility that allowed the inmates to clean the day's grime from their bodies, receive their evening meal, or both. As he followed the proceedings, his eyes fell on one of the Klingon guards, who resembled Kirk and Sulu in their disguises more than he did Koloth. In fact, Kirk mused, between here and Don'zali IV he had seen more Klingons of this type in a few days' time than he had in the last fifteen years.

"Koloth," he said, "the Klingons down there, and the

ones we ran into on Don'zali, are they another race that joined the Empire at some point?"

"If it satisfies you to think so, then so be it," Koloth replied sharply. Nothing else followed the simple statement.

Kirk regarded his companion for several seconds, comparing the visage before him with the young Koloth he had first encountered all those years ago.

"That's not an answer," he said. "You have to admit, it's an intriguing mystery. There are a lot of theories floating around out . . ."

"You will not receive any other answer from me," Koloth snapped. "It is not something discussed with those who are not of the Empire." He glared at Kirk as he spoke, and for a brief moment the *Enterprise* captain thought the Klingon might lash out at him.

Instead, Koloth returned his attention to the prison below them, studying the encampment with his own eyes rather than with the viewfinder. Just as the silence between the two men was beginning to grow awkward, he spoke again.

"I apologize, Kirk."

Kirk blinked in surprise. Looking at the expression on the Klingon's face, he could tell the apology was reluctant, as if Koloth was forcing himself to remain civil.

"I would not normally go to the effort to say that," he added, "especially to a human. But you have proven yourself worthy of my respect. I do understand the curiosity, but it is not something most Klingons are willing to discuss. Perhaps one day you will be permitted to understand."

Koloth began packing away his equipment in preparation for the hike through the jungle to where they had established their temporary camp. Kirk did the same, but looked up from his rucksack after a few moments.

"What would Kahless think of your answer?"

The Klingon skewered Kirk with another anger-filled stare. As quickly as it had appeared though, it faded and was replaced with an amused expression.

"I respect you, Kirk, but only to a point. However, to answer your question, I've often asked myself what Kahless would say about many of the things I have said and done over the course of my life." As he continued to secure his equipment, he added, "It may interest you to know that I did not always embrace the teachings of Kahless as I do now. There was a time when such beliefs were largely unpopular. You might say that the Empire went through a time of social and political upheaval. Everything held in high regard until that time was questioned if not dismissed as being old, obsolete. That was the age I was born into."

The two finished packing and started off through the jungle, moving side by side. The walk was not difficult as the undergrowth on the side of the hill wasn't as thick as areas they had traversed to get here from the shuttle.

"So what happened?" Kirk asked.

"My father," Koloth said. "I have never known a finer warrior. He feared nothing." Looking to Kirk out of the corner of his eye, he smiled and added, "Except my mother, of course."

Kirk laughed at the joke. "What about your father?"

"He taught me about Kahless, about honor and courage, how not to bow to the popular thought of others who were more focused on selfish destructive behavior that tore at the fabric of everything the Empire had been built on. Until the day he died, my father never renounced his beliefs."

"What about you?" Kirk asked. "You said you didn't always follow Kahless' teachings."

Nodding, Koloth continued, "As I grew out of childhood, I of course adopted that air of omniscience that graces all children as they enter adolescence and young adulthood. I had no need for the teachings of an old man. Surely you can relate to this."

"Definitely," Kirk replied, smiling now. "I was more than a little headstrong in my youth." He recalled the many rough periods that had colored his relationship with his father during his teenage years. It had taken him several years before he understood just how wise his father had truly been.

Koloth reached out to move aside a drooping tree branch blocking his path. "Exactly, and so it was with me as well. When I grew old enough, I discovered that I was dissatisfied with the society around me. I sought challenge, adventure, glory, and the only place to find that was in the military. When I joined, I met other Klingons who felt as I did, and learned that many of them burned with a fire fueled by the same sense of honor and morality that I had witnessed in my father. I began to realize how he had influenced me in so many ways. It was the one gift that I have learned to treasure, and since that awakening I have spent my life living up to his example and to that of Kahless and his timeless concepts of honor above all."

"Sounds familiar," Kirk said. It had taken his own entrance into Starfleet Academy before he had realized just how much effort his parents had put into raising him. While his father had taught him to go into life with his eyes open, his mother had been determined to make sure that approach was tempered with an equally open mind.

The ground had begun to level off, and Kirk thought he

spied the telltale glow of a fire ahead of them where their camp should be. Surrounded by the trees and underbrush of the Pao'lan jungle, the likelihood of their fire being seen from the prison was almost nil.

"That's not to say there weren't obstacles, of course," Koloth said. "The Empire stands on the foundation created by the principles Kahless teaches us, and without those same principles to support it, the Empire will eventually crumble. Yet even today, many Klingons refuse to embrace all that Kahless has given us. Worse, there are those who merely pretend to honor him, living in deceit in order to curry favor with those in power. In the case of certain members on the High Council, they lie in order to maintain the approval of the people, more and more of whom adopt the ways of Kahless with each passing year." He snorted derisively. "The Empire is undergoing a transformation that may in fact take years if not decades to realize, but it still disgusts me to think that Klingons are capable of such abhorrent behavior."

The fire at the center of the small camp burned brightly as Kirk and Koloth broke into the tiny clearing. It wasn't much to look at, merely three small shelters situated around the earthen pit that Kirk had dug out with his phaser. A trio of folding stools completed the setup.

Kirk looked around but could find no sign of Sulu, who had set out earlier to patrol the surrounding area with a tricorder to insure that they were alone out here. The *Enterprise* captain was tempted to contact him via his communicator, but thought better of it. From what Koloth had told him, the risk of anyone monitoring for unscheduled comm traffic was small, but there was no sense in taking any chances.

As Kirk sat down on one of the campstools, he thought about what his companion had told him. The picture of ne Empire that Koloth had painted didn't match the one Kirk had carried in his head for nearly his entire life. According to accounts he'd read, Klingons encountered by Starfleet captains like April, Garth, and others were described as devious and deceitful, an enemy not to be trusted. Of course, some of those observations had conflicted with earlier reports logged by such legendary captains as Archer and Taggart. It was only later, when he himself had faced off with the likes of Kor, Kang, Korrd, and yes, even Koloth, that Kirk had considered Klingons capable of displaying such admirable qualities.

"It's amazing," he said aloud as Koloth emerged from his shelter with a small pot and a ration pack they had brought from their shuttle. "I never thought of Klingons as capable of being so divided on an issue like what you describe."

Pausing in his efforts to prepare the ration pack's contents for cooking, Koloth leveled severe, glaring eyes on Kirk. "Why does that surprise you so? Do humans always agree on everything?"

Before Kirk could respond, Koloth pressed on. "Do you consider the Empire to be no more than a military state, desiring nothing but war and conquest? Our military may hold a higher point of distinction in our society than Starfleet does within the Federation, but it is not all that we are, Kirk. We have a culture as rich and diverse as yours. We have art and music, we laugh and we love, we live, grow old, and die. Those who embrace Kahless' teachings bring an enrichment to the Empire and remind us to honor all that we are and all that we have."

The rebuke stung Kirk like a physical blow. Balancing what he had always believed to be true about Klingons, what he had seen with his own eyes, and the words Koloth had spoken, he realized that his companion was right. He had always viewed the Klingons, these enemies of the Federation, as nothing more than a threat to be confronted. Of course they had to be so much more, and why hadn't he allowed himself to think of them in that way? After all these years spent exploring new planets, contacting new races, and expanding the base of knowledge, was he still so narrow-minded as to reduce his perception of a species to nothing more than a handful of demeaning adjectives?

As the heat and humidity continued to wrap themselves around him throughout the night like a heavy blanket, the questions running through Kirk's mind burned with an even greater intensity.

Chapter Twenty-four

IF PAVEL CHEKOV had to describe Lorta in a single word, that word would be *methodical*.

Just like him, the *Terthos*'s Klingon security chief had been diligent and untiring in her inspection of the conference hall. For Chekov, it was a side of Klingons that he had rarely seen. The formidable warriors he had encountered during his years in Starfleet had never struck him as the type to waste time on details, the finer points that more often than not brought clarity to a situation. Instead, these people had always seemed focused on the battle, winning through brutal force at any cost.

For nearly three hours, they scanned every millimeter of the room with their tricorders, searching for any clue about the explosion that had ravaged the chamber.

And they had come up with nothing.

"The room is secure," Chekov said as he deactivated his tricorder and let it hang from his shoulder by its carrying strap. "I can't find any sign of a hidden compartment or entrance that someone might have used to place the bomb."

Lorta rose from where she had been kneeling near the front of the room and straightened to her full height, which Chekov noticed for perhaps the twelfth time was several centimeters taller than his own. Her own tricorder was bulkier than his, with a hardened case that Chekov suspected lent itself well to harsh environments. As sturdy as most Starfleet equipment was, it was not unheard of for a tricorder or phaser to succumb to the unforgiving elements of a storm-swept planet or moon. He made a mental note to record his observations in his personal log later. Perhaps it was something the engineers back at Starfleet Research and Development would be interested in hearing about.

She set her tricorder down atop the large, U-shaped conference table. "I too have been unable to find any breach. The room is as secure now as it has been since the beginning of the summit."

Chekov nodded. "And so far we haven't found any record of unauthorized transporter activity in this area from the sensor logs on either the *Enterprise* or the *Terthos*." It had taken almost no time to confirm this information, given that both security chiefs had already ordered all transporter activity to and from the station to be recorded and an alert sounded if anything untoward was registered. Chekov hadn't been so easily convinced, however, and had instructed his security team to scour the *Enterprise*'s sensor logs looking for anything out of the ordinary during the past week.

"If the explosive was not transported into this room," Lorta said, "then it must have been carried in by one of the delegates or their aides, or one of the starbase support staff."

As far as Chekov was concerned, everyone who had entered the room during the morning session was a suspect. In addition to the diplomats and their various assistants, Admiral LeGere had assigned a contingent of Starbase 49 personnel to see to the various needs of the conference attendees to include refreshments, handling of routine communications request, and the like. It made things easier on the delegates, but it compounded Chekov's security concerns tenfold.

Shaking his head, he began to pace the length of the conference table toward the front of the room, noting again how the table's once highly polished surface was now covered with dust and riddled with pits and scars inflicted by debris. A hint of smoke, burned wood and melted plastic still tinged the air of the chamber, offering its own testimony as to what had happened here.

"Everyone coming into the room was scanned before being allowed access. We would have discovered any attempt to smuggle anything like an explosive in here."

Initial scans had pointed to some type of improvised device. He had therefore ordered the entire podium, along with some of the fragments that were the only remnants of the explosive, transported to the *Enterprise*. Scotty was subjecting everything to a barrage of sensor probes that were far more intensive than anything their tricorders could manage.

He hoped the engineer would complete his examinations quickly, though. There had already been pressure from both ambassadors for a report as to the cause of the explosion and, more important, what was being done to prevent a repeat occurrence. Both parties had communicated their discomfort at continuing the peace summit. They had, however, expressed a reluctance to end things now. They agreed that the progress that had been made to this point, as grudging and hard won as it had been, was still significant enough that to conclude the proceedings prematurely would be wasteful.

With that, Captain Spock had gotten Admiral LeGere to arrange for an alternative meeting place elsewhere on Starbase 49. The officer's mess had been converted into a substitute conference hall and the summit had gone forward with negotiations once again. That left Chekov and Lorta free to take as much time as they needed to conduct their investigation. But as he studied the blast-damaged interior of the room around him, Chekov was conscious of the fact that the new conference facilities could also fall victim to attack if he and Lorta did not move quickly enough.

"What is the status of the interrogations?" the Klingon security chief asked.

Chekov winced at her choice of phrase. He had assigned members of his security detachment to take statements from everyone who had been in the conference hall during the morning discussions with the exception of the ambassadors themselves, a duty he had reserved for himself.

"They're not being interrogated, they're being questioned. There is a difference."

Lorta shrugged. "Perhaps for you."

Ignoring the red herring, Chekov retrieved one of his security contingent's datapads from the conference table, Tapping a series of commands on the unit's keypad, he shook his head as he quickly scanned the transcripts of witness interviews taken earlier in the day.

"The accounts of the morning session are nearly the same. Nothing of any real value." Of the statements he had reviewed so far, none had offered any insight as to who or what might have caused the explosion.

"Of course, someone is lying."

Though he frowned at Lorta's blunt statement, he was forced to concede that she was probably right. None of the accounts had given him cause to suspect that anyone questioned so far could be lying, but there simply didn't seem to be any other logical explanation.

His attention was drawn to the sound of a transporter beam and he turned to see a column of energy coalesce and solidify into the form of Montgomery Scott. As the beam released the engineer, Chekov could see that his friend was tired. No doubt he had locked himself inside one of the *Enterprise*'s science labs and worked at a breakneck pace until he had found something worth reporting.

"Scotty," Chekov said, "tell me you've got good news."

Pausing only long enough to glance at the imposing figure of Lorta, twice, Scotty replied in a noticeably downbeat voice. "Well lad, I've completed scans of what's left o' that podium and the shrapnel we dug out of the walls, but I dinna think you'll like it." He cast another look at Lorta. "Neither you, lass."

"What did you find?" Chekov asked.

Holding up the tricorder he'd brought with him, Scotty activated it and handed it to the security chief. "The explosive was placed on the underside of the podium's desktop with a common adhesive strip, no different from the kind ye can find in bulk aboard ship." He pointed to the tricorder's small display screen. "Now, look at this." Lorta stepped closer and peered over Chekov's shoulder at the data displayed on the screen.

"Most o' the fragments that we found embedded in the podium came from what looks to be a standard Klingon datapad. Analysis of the metallic composites, glass, and pieces of other components confirmed it."

"So the explosive itself was hidden inside the datapad,"

Chekov said. Moving to a nearby wall, he ran his hand over one damaged section. His fingers probed the jagged edge of a wound where a piece of shrapnel nearly the size of his fist had been extracted. Even here, nearly the length of the room away from where the podium had been, the force of the explosion had been powerful enough to drive debris several centimeters into the normally resilient material of the wall panel. "We still should have picked it up on our security scans." Returning his attention to Scotty's tricorder, he pointed to one puzzling readout on the unit's display. "What's this?"

The engineer shook his head. "Some kind o' chemical residue. Almost missed it on our scans. When I adjusted the sensors and repeated the sweep, it stood out like a supernova. There was a high concentration o' the stuff near where the bomb was placed, and scattered readings across most o' the shrapnel in the podium and what we found in the walls. I've never seen anything like it."

"*Qo'legh*," Lorta said simply.

Chekov and Scotty looked at her with matching confused expressions. "A highly volatile mixture," she continued, "that can only be created through the combination of three otherwise inert substances. When mixed in the correct manner, it makes for an efficient explosive. It is designed to leave very little in the way of detectable residue."

"That's why you dinna find it with yer tricorders," Scotty said. "I only caught it with the enhanced spectral analysis available on the *Enterprise*. Damn impressive stuff, if ye ask me."

Chekov began to pace, his brow furrowed in concentration. "So the datapad was a fake, probably containing enough real components to get past a routine security scan, but these chemicals were stored in separate compartments inside its casing, which then mixed to form the explosive?"

"That's the ticket, laddie," Scotty replied.

Lorta added, "The chemical reaction is instant, meaning that the explosion was the result of either a timed delay or a communications signal once the device had been placed."

"We would have detected any unauthorized comm signals," Chekov said. "So that leaves the delayed detonation, which makes the most sense now. The intended target may have been the speaker scheduled for that time according to the session's original agenda." Both he and Lorta already knew that according to the session's agenda for that morning, a diplomatic aide to Ambassador Kaljagh had been scheduled to speak.

In his mind's eye, Chekov saw the datapad sitting innocuously underneath the surface of the podium, an internal chronometer counting down the seconds until detonation and unaware of the chaos and suffering it would eventually unleash. That anyone could set such a callous action into motion with total disregard for anyone who might be caught in the blast was both sobering and infuriating to him.

"We may be dealing with a Klingon, but not a trained assassin," Lorta suddenly said.

"What makes ye think that?" Scotty asked.

"Because no one was killed. A Klingon assassin would not waste such an opportunity."

It took an extra second for that to sink in for Chekov. "But why a Klingon at all? Why not a human, or Tellarite, or Andorian?" After all, many races were well represented aboard Starbase 49.

"I base my theory only on the weapon used." Lorta indicated the conference hall and the unchecked damage defacing it with a wave of her arm. *"Qo'legh* is a favored tool of Klingon spies, but the manner in which it was wasted here suggests someone not trained in the art of covert assassination."

"What if whoever planted the bomb wasn't trying to kill anyone?" Scotty asked. "What if, instead, they simply wanted to disrupt the peace talks?"

Lorta nodded. "It is a more plausible explanation, though still one that we have no proof to support."

"If they are out to disrupt the summit," Chekov said, "then they'll have to try again."

"And if we are not dealing with a professional covert operative, then they may make an error that we can exploit. We must be watchful for such opportunities."

Scotty looked around the conference room that still bore the scars of the previous and thankfully unsuccessful attempt. "I hope that happens before someone *does* get killed."

Chapter Twenty-five

UHURA DIDN'T REMEMBER Klingon ships smelling this bad.

Of course, this was the first time she had been aboard such a vessel when there were Klingons around. The food they ate, the substances they inhaled into their lungs, not to mention their own personal hygiene, all conspired to produce a conglomeration of odors that threatened to overpower her.

Only a little while longer, she reminded herself as she sat at the communications station on the *Terthos*'s bridge. She figured it would take another thirty minutes to complete the diagnostic check of the ship's communications systems.

Coming aboard at Murgh's request, Uhura had assisted him in tracking down the malfunction troubling the Klingon vessel's communications systems. One of the ship's engineers had installed an emergency lighting source near one of the intraship relay junctions, causing no small amount of interference to the intercom system in that part of the ship. Working together, Uhura and Murgh decided that the job required a new suite of diagnostic programs to track down and isolate such glitches.

"How's it running now?" asked Lieutenant Brian Connors, his face displayed on one of the communication console's monitors. Uhura had wasted no time calling the computer specialist when it became apparent that she would have a very difficult time understanding the peculiarities of the programming language used to interface with most Klingon military computers. Connors, an *Enterprise* engineer with an affinity for computer languages from a wide range of races, had made short work of the problem.

Studying the results of the diagnostic program on another monitor, Uhura nodded with no small amount of admiration for the young computer expert. "So far, so good. You have a magician's touch, Lieutenant."

"Excellent," Murgh added as Uhura severed the connection. "The system appears to be operating much more efficiently than before."

Uhura leaned back into her chair, raising her arms over her head and stretching her back. Klingon furniture wasn't designed with comfort in mind, and after the past few hours her back muscles were beginning to protest.

"I've also got Connors working on a few other routines that should improve the interface to your computer's Universal Translator as well. It should cut down the time it takes for you to get a translation from languages already on file, and maybe even improve first-contact response time, too."

From the center of the bridge, Uhura heard mocking laughter. Turning in her chair, she recognized Lieutenant Ag'hel, the *Terthos*'s first officer, sitting in the command chair and looking directly at her. The Klingon officer made no effort to hide the condescending smile on her face or the matching tone of her voice.

"Yet another example of Federation technical prowess. It's a pity that such talent is wasted on useless pursuits like teaching computers to talk."

Uhura regarded the first officer with an amused expression. "I don't know about that. Without ship's communications, you can't transmit or receive orders during battle. And an effective translation processor can aid in the breaking of enemy encryption codes. There are more ways to defeat your opponent than simply overpowering them, Lieutenant."

The smile on Ag'hel's face warmed with a new sincerity. "Perhaps there is hope for your species after all, human." She turned in her chair to give the bridge a quick visual inspection, satisfying herself that all was as it should be.

Attempting to turn the conversation to something more interesting, Uhura said, "There aren't very many women in leadership positions aboard Klingon ships, are there?"

"Very few, and none in command," Ag'hel replied, then added with a fierce note of pride in her voice, "I intend to be the first."

Uhura nodded admiringly. The lieutenant had spirit, that much was certain. But it would require more than that to advance to any respectable position of leadership within the Empire. No women held any political power so far as Starfleet Intelligence had been able to determine. As for their military, female Klingons served in all manner of capacities, though as Ag'hel had said, none commanded any vessels of their own. However, several served as first officers, so it could only be a matter of time. How the increasing number of women in power would affect the Klingon Empire, a patriarchal society in the extreme, remained to be seen.

"I hope you succeed, Lieutenant," Uhura said. "Good luck."

"Luck will not be necessary," Ag'hel said, turning away as she rotated the command chair again, surveying the control stations of the ship that had been entrusted to her care.

The next several moments passed in silence as Uhura reviewed the final diagnostic reports from the communications console with Murgh. From the looks of things, the system now appeared to be operating perfectly.

"You are as proficient as your reputation indicates, Commander," Murgh said, nodding in satisfaction at the reports on the computer displays.

As Uhura began to allow herself to be pleased with her efforts, a shadow fell across the console. She turned to see Lieutenant Ag'hel standing no more than a meter away.

"Tell me something, Commander," the *Terthos* first officer said. "Women appear to occupy many seats of power within Starfleet. They command your starships and starbases, making decisions that affect hundreds or even thousands of lives. Do you aspire to such a position?"

I guess I asked for that, Uhura thought before replying. "I've thought about it, certainly. But I'm doing something that I have a gift for and that I love to do."

Ag'hel's expression grew doubtful. "And what about your duty to Starfleet? Does that not have value?"

"Of course," Uhura said. "But I am able to serve Starfleet while doing something I enjoy. Don't you enjoy serving the Empire?"

"Personal enjoyment is not a requirement of loyal service, Commander," Ag'hel replied sharply, though her expression quickly softened. "However, I take great pride in my accomplishments."

Uhura smiled at that. "Maybe we're not as different as we might think, Lieutenant."

She would never know whether or not Ag'hel agreed. The Klingon's response was interrupted as the deck shuddered. A red-alert klaxon began wailing on the bridge, and Uhura saw the Klingons manning various stations around the dimly lit command center turning to their tasks with a renewed sense of frantic purpose.

"Report!" Ag'hel shouted above the din.

A Klingon at the sensor station turned from his console. "We have been attacked, Lieutenant. The starboard nacelle has sustained heavy structural damage."

"Who is attacking us?"

The Klingon shook his head. "I can find no sign of an attacking vessel. The only ship in range is the *Enterprise*."

Ag'hel's head snapped around and her eyes bore into Uhura with an intensity the commander thought she could feel lancing through her heart. Then her own attention was distracted by a shrill beep blaring from the communications console. She turned to read the display monitor, already knowing what she would see.

"The *Enterprise* is hailing us," she said.

If Ag'hel heard the report, she gave no indication of it as she moved toward the command chair.

"Charge weapons," the *Terthos* first officer ordered. "Transfer emergency power to the shields and prepare for tactical maneuvering." Glancing once over her shoulder toward Uhura, she added, "We will demonstrate what happens to cowards who attack from the shadows."

"The *Enterprise* couldn't have attacked," Uhura yelled

over the sound of the red-alert siren. "They would never fire first on an unsuspecting target."

Ag'hel snapped, "The only vessel out there is yours. There is no other explanation."

Flabbergasted, Uhura rose from her chair. "Have you forgotten that your own security chief is investigating a terrorist bombing on the starbase? Whoever was responsible for that might be behind this attack."

When Ag'hel ignored her while immersed in battle preparations, Uhura stepped forward, intending to continue the discussion until she made the Klingon listen to her. She stopped, though, when a large figure moved to block her path.

Murgh.

"Commander," he said, "despite our working together, my loyalty is to this ship. Do not force me to restrain you."

Realizing Murgh was deadly serious, Uhura looked to the forward viewscreen where the *Enterprise* was coming into view. A tactical schematic overlaid itself over the image of her ship, displaying distance and targeting information.

Powerless to do anything but watch the events unfolding around her, Uhura's jaw clenched in mounting frustration.

Is this peace?

Chapter Twenty-six

"RANGE TO TARGET?" Ag'hel asked.

"Six hundred *qell'qams*," replied the Klingon at the sensor station.

On the viewscreen, the *Enterprise* was growing larger as the Klingon ship matched orbits around Starbase 49 and closed the distance. Her ship had faced Klingons before, but for Uhura, watching the confrontation unfold from the bridge of a Klingon vessel was an almost surreal experience.

Behind her, an insistent beeping continued from the communications console. It was the *Enterprise,* she knew, trying to make contact and assure the *Terthos* that they were not responsible for the attack. They might even have information about those who really were responsible.

And speaking of the perpetrators, wherever they were, what if they were preparing for another assault, even now as the *Terthos* crew was distracted with their impending strike on the *Enterprise?*

Uhura turned at the sound of bulky metal doors parting at the rear of the bridge and saw two Klingons enter. Followed by Ambassador Kaljagh, Captain K'tran was an imposing Klingon, having to duck his head in order to cross the threshold of the doorway as he entered the bridge. The leather of his uniform stretched tight across his broad chest, bare and muscled arms rippling as he moved with a grace that belied his size. His hair, long and dark, flowed freely about his head and shoulders and made him seem even taller. Uhura watched as the Klingon captain's eyes took in the scene around him, seeing who manned what station and, most important, what was displayed on the main viewer.

"Silence that alarm," he ordered as he moved to the center of the bridge and his command chair, which Ag'hel vacated. The alert klaxon faded as K'tran settled into his chair and regarded the *Enterprise* on the screen.

"Status."

"My lord," Ag'hel replied, "the *Enterprise* attacked us without warning, inflicting damage to our starboard nacelle. We are moving to retaliate."

Kaljagh stepped forward from where he had been standing near the doors at the rear of the bridge. "They would jeopardize the conference with an act of such blatant hostility after a week of negotiations?"

"There is no other explanation," Ag'hel replied. "There is no other vessel in the area. Only the *Enterprise* could have fired on us."

Uhura had finally had enough. "Captain K'tran, there is no evidence that the *Enterprise* attacked your vessel, and they wouldn't fire without provocation in any case."

Cocking his head at the sound of Uhura's voice, K'tran turned his chair until he faced her. "You are their communications officer."

It was not a question, but instead a statement spoken by someone who was accustomed to knowing everything that occurred on his ship. Judging from that, she could tell the Klingon captain was none too happy to have his vessel gearing up for battle without his having ordered it.

Nodding, Uhura replied, "That's right, Captain. I was assisting Lieutenant Murgh to . . ."

"I read the status reports supplied by my officers, Commander," K'tran said. "Lieutenant Murgh speaks highly of your expertise and selflessness in seeing to the repair of our ship's communications systems."

Kaljagh said, "Would the *Enterprise* launch an attack with one of their own officers aboard our ship?"

"They might if she was spying for them," Ag'hel replied, leveling an accusatory glare at Uhura.

Before Uhura could respond to the charges, K'tran said, "Are you saying, Lieutenant, that you allowed a Federation spy, disguised inconspicuously in a Starfleet uniform of all things, access to the internal systems of my vessel?" Taking a measure of satisfaction from the offended expression on his first officer's face, he added, "Of course you did not, just as Commander Uhura is not a spy from the Federation ship."

Even as Uhura breathed a sigh of relief, K'tran cast a glance toward Murgh, now seated at his console. "Lieutenant, I trust that incessant shriek coming from your station indicates that the communications system is now working properly?"

Murgh rose from his chair in response to the direct address from his captain. "Yes, my lord. We are receiving an incoming hail from the *Enterprise*."

With a look that told Uhura the Klingon captain knew more than he was letting on, K'tran turned to Ag'hel. "Lieutenant, perhaps you should investigate the hail."

The order was given without force or harshness, but Uhura could tell it was delivered in such a manner that K'tran didn't expect any challenge. Ag'hel stiffened at the command, nevertheless, still fuming over the captain's previous allegation. She said nothing, but her eyes communicated her disapproval of K'tran's decision. If the captain noticed her intense expression, or even cared about it, he gave no indication one way or another.

Directing her attention to Murgh, Ag'hel snapped, "Open a channel to the *Enterprise*."

Seconds later, the image on the main viewscreen changed to that of the *Enterprise* bridge. Uhura saw Spock standing in front of the helm and navigator's stations, looking regal in his Starfleet uniform and with his hands clasped behind his back. He gazed out from the screen, his expression impassive as always.

"*Imperial Cruiser* Terthos, *this is Captain Spock, temporarily in command of the* Enterprise. *Our sensors have registered an explosion aboard your vessel. Do you require assistance?*"

With equal calm, K'tran responded, "There is reason to believe that your vessel fired on us, Captain. Perhaps you would care to enlighten us further?"

On the viewscreen, Spock's first reaction was to arch his right eyebrow. Then he said, "*I have been on the bridge since before the incident occurred, sir, and I can assure you that no such action was ordered by anyone aboard this vessel.*" Looking to his left before continuing, he added, "*There is someone else here who can attest to the validity of our claim.*"

A Klingon stepped into the screen's frame. He was dressed not in the uniform of an officer in the Klingon military, but rather in what Uhura recognized as the ornate robes and leather that signified a member of the diplomatic cadre.

"Toladal," Kaljagh said, making no effort to hide the confusion on his face. "What are you doing on the *Enterprise?*"

On the screen, Toladal replied, *"Captain Spock extended an invitation to share his evening meal with me. Additionally, Lieutenant Lorta is working here with the* Enterprise *security officer to investigate the incident in the conference hall. As you directed me to keep informed regarding the progress of the investigation, I saw several advantages to accepting the captain's offer."*

"Perhaps in the future you will consider informing me of your actions before undertaking them," Kaljagh said with more than a hint of irritation in his voice.

Toladal bowed his head formally. *"As you wish, Ambassador."*

With that, Spock took center stage on the viewscreen once more. *"Captain K'tran, the* Enterprise *stands ready to render any support you may require."*

Rising from his chair, K'tran shook his head as he replied. "I will check with my engineer to determine what is necessary, Captain. I also suspect that this latest attack may be related to the earlier incident on board your starbase. The services of Lieutenant Lorta and your security chief may be needed over here as well."

"They are already aware of the situation, Captain, and they will transport to your ship directly. Spock out."

As the viewscreen shifted to display the *Enterprise* once more, K'tran's polite demeanor vanished. "Deactivate weapons! Return us to our original parking orbit!" Spinning on his heel to face Ag'hel, his expression had screwed up into one of barely controlled anger.

"Fool! Were you *trying* to start a war with the Federation in their *own* space?"

Uhura was stunned by the near-instantaneous transformation of the Klingon captain, but it only took seconds for her to understand it. For the benefit of outsiders, K'tran had assumed all responsibility for the *Terthos*'s actions, not allowing anyone else to be perceived as being in control of the situation aboard his own vessel. That would not stop him, however, from dressing down a subordinate who had embarrassed him once other eyes were no longer watching.

Ag'hel, to her credit, snapped to rigid attention before attempting any explanation. "My lord, based on the information available to me, the *Enterprise* was the only possible source of the attack. I was not aware that the ambassador's aide had transported over to meet with their captain."

"I find that odd," K'tran snapped, "considering his departure is recorded in the deck officer's log, which I scanned prior to leaving the bridge and which you should have reviewed prior to assuming your watch."

Before Ag'hel could reply, Kaljagh stepped forward. "Captain, what is important here is the ramifications of this latest attack. I intend to contact the Federation ambassador and discuss suspending or canceling the remainder of the scheduled conferences."

"No," Uhura said, almost instinctively. Too late, she realized that she had almost certainly spoken out of turn and was in all likelihood damaging her status as an invited guest here. The look on K'tran's face seemed to support that notion, but he said nothing.

Instead, he allowed Kaljagh to address the issue. "You have an opinion on this matter, Commander?"

Feeling the eyes of everyone on the bridge boring into

her, Uhura swallowed the tricorder-sized lump that had formed in her throat. "Yes, Mr. Ambassador. Obviously the saboteurs are out to disrupt the meetings here. If you cancel them now after the progress you've made, then you've played right into their hands and they win." Casting a reassuring glance at Murgh, she added, "That would be admitting defeat, and I find it difficult to believe that Klingons even acknowledge knowing the meaning of the word, especially when their opponent doesn't even have the courage to show themselves."

Nodding in satisfaction, K'tran's features softened into a smile that might have been pleasant if not for his jagged, uneven teeth. "Spoken like a true Klingon." Looking to Kaljagh, he added, "I agree with the human. If you allow a coward to chase you away, you dishonor the Empire."

Kaljagh regarded the captain skeptically. "I would think that as a warrior, you would welcome the fight with the Federation."

"As a warrior, I serve the Empire. If it is the Council's wish to seek peace with our enemies, then so be it. I will find battle elsewhere."

Uhura barely managed to contain her sigh of relief. Perhaps there was reason to hope for eventual peace after all.

On the bridge of the *Enterprise*, Spock was entertaining a similar discussion.

Ambassador Joquel, who had arrived on the bridge only moments before communication with the *Terthos* had ended, was adamant. "We cannot allow any further disruptions to these talks! One more of these . . . incidents, and the whole process will crumble. What a disaster!"

Spock agreed with the essence of the statement if not

its distastefully emotional expression. Lasting peace was still an issue that would take many years of trust and co-operative effort to accomplish, but the strides made during this latest round of negotiations were promising. He was convinced that good work had been accomplished here.

The sound of the turbolift doors opening caught his attention and he turned to see Chekov and Lieutenant Lorta step onto the bridge. Spock could tell from the expression on Chekov's face that the security chief had something substantial to report. Chekov, however, schooled his features as soon as he saw Ambassador Joquel and Toladal.

Hoping to deflect their attention from the new arrivals, Spock turned back to the ambassador and Toladal. "Ambassador Joquel is correct," he said. "To stop now would be to acknowledge that peace between the Federation and the Empire is not worth striving for."

Toladal nodded. "I am of the same mind, Captain. I merely speak of the opponents to this initiative, who will no doubt claim these attacks as further proof that peace between our peoples is not possible."

"So long as Ambassador Kaljagh feels the same way," Joquel said in a more measured, but less spirited tone, "then we can continue in spite of all this." Turning to face Chekov and Lorta, she said, "Commander Chekov, I hope that your arrival means you've made some progress."

With an expression that said he was uncomfortable with what he had to say, Chekov replied, "Forgive me, Ambassador, but I am not permitted to comment on an ongoing investigation. I hope to have some answers for you soon."

Not satisfied with the answer, Joquel nevertheless nodded amiably. "I may not like to hear that, Commander, but I do understand your position." Looking to Toladal, she said, "Perhaps we can contact Ambassador Kaljagh and see about salvaging the remainder of the conference."

As the ambassador and the Klingon aide disappeared into the port side turbolift, Spock turned to Chekov and Lorta. "I presume you have new information that you did not wish the ambassador to hear?"

Chekov nodded. "We examined the sensor logs, working backward from the most current readings and looking for anything out of the ordinary." Moving to Spock's science station, the security chief enabled one of the overhead display monitors. An image of the *Terthos* appeared, and Chekov entered another command string that caused the image to zoom forward, magnifying the surface of the Klingon ship's hull until only a portion of the starboard nacelle was visible.

"This is the *Terthos* just prior to 1800 hours," Chekov said. In the corner of the monitor Spock saw that the time index read "17:59:57," with the image frozen at that point. "Now, watch."

Chekov keyed the command to replay the sensor log extract, and they watched as several seconds passed without incident. Then, as the time index moved to read "18:00:24," the surface plating of the nacelle was illuminated by a brief burst of orange light.

"A transporter beam," Spock said.

"More specifically, a Klingon transporter," Lorta corrected as the beam faded and a new object was revealed, attached to the exterior of the nacelle's hull. In contrast to the muted gray-green coloring that characterized K'tinga-class battle cruisers, the narrow, tube-shaped object was dark black in color, with no external markings or identifying symbols that Spock could see.

"The explosive that caused the damage to the nacelle," Spock said.

Lorta nodded, "It is a Klingon torpedo, and it could only have come from the *Terthos*'s own weapons store. I will confirm that with my own visual inspection."

The revelation caused Spock's eyebrow to arch. "Indeed? Most curious. If that is the case, then we can be reasonably certain that our saboteur is either a member of the *Terthos*'s crew or one of the diplomatic team."

Chekov said, "The transporter signal that put it there was piggybacked onto another, and based on the sensor logs, the placement of the bomb was timed to coincide with the transport of Toladal to the *Enterprise*. Obviously it wasn't detected by the *Terthos* crew."

"It was also a beam of very low power," Lorta added, "localized and subdued so as not to trigger sensor alarms on the *Enterprise,* as well."

Chekov said, "We haven't been able to locate the source of the transporter beam, but given the power level, it could only have come from the *Terthos* herself."

Spock studied the image of the *Terthos*'s hull and the ominous dark object affixed to it. On the screen, the time index continued to advance, with seconds passing into minutes and on toward what Spock knew would ultimately happen at "18:14:47."

"Could the detonation have been triggered by a communications source aboard the *Enterprise?*" he asked.

Frowning, Chekov shook his head. "Nothing like that registered on the sensors, sir. Even when we gave the logs a closer look in order to find that." He pointed to the screen.

"You are suggesting that Toladal may be responsible," Lorta said.

Spock's eyebrow rose in response. "I am suggesting no such thing, Lieutenant."

"You do not believe his arrival aboard your ship and

the placement of the bomb is coincidence?" Lorta made no attempt to hide the incredulity in her voice. "The evidence points to Toladal's involvement. Surely your Vulcan logic tells you that?"

Saying nothing immediately, Spock slowly walked around the upper bridge deck, making his way to an opening in the railing surrounding the command area to descend toward the captain's chair. As he settled himself into it, he briefly wondered where its rightful owner might be. Had Captain Kirk succeeded in finding any survivors from the *Gagarin?* Would he be able to affect their rescue and return them home?

Had the entire affair been a ruse, a trap designed to incite an interstellar incident with the Federation appearing as the instigators? Logic told him that was unlikely, based on his analysis of the available information and his assessment of Koloth's character.

Logic also told him something else.

"What I see," he said, "is that you have postulated a theory that is somewhat consistent with the few facts available to us. However, what you have failed to take into consideration is that Toladal was with me at the time of the explosion on the *Terthos,* just as he was with me during the incident on the starbase." Spock locked eyes with the Klingon security chief as he added, "Therefore, I find your theory faulty at the present time. Further investigation will, of course, provide additional information that will allow you to corroborate or discount your hypothesis, or perhaps even formulate a new one."

After many years spent working and living in close proximity to beings who were much less in control of their emotions than Vulcans, he had learned how to gauge what he said in order to reduce the chances of his remarks being taken as insulting or hurtful. However, he knew that the Klingon would chafe at his comments even before he saw her body stiffen in controlled anger. To her credit, though, she said nothing.

Instead it was Chekov who said, "We'll keep at it, sir."

Nodding, Spock said, "That is wise, Mr. Chekov. I'm afraid that time has become an issue in this matter. We must find whoever is behind these attacks before they can launch another one and succeed in injuring or killing someone, to say nothing of the political ramifications if this peace conference fails. The task of preventing interstellar war may well be resting on our shoulders."

Chapter Twenty-seven

STALKING THE CORRIDORS of the *Terthos,* Ag'hel received an odd sense of satisfaction from the way her booted heels echoed off the cold metal deck plating. Those members of the crew she passed must have understood the force behind her footsteps, for they made extra efforts to clear a path for her, saluting her as she walked past. That many of the gestures of respect probably weren't genuine didn't matter to her in the slightest.

During the short duration of her assignment aboard the *Terthos,* she had forged a reputation as a first officer not to be trifled with. That status had been strengthened on more than one occasion with the blood of a foolhardy crew member seeking to challenge her authority. Most of the crew had accepted the outcomes of those duels and obeyed her as honor demanded, but she remained wary for those individuals who would still seek to fight her for her position. No one offered her such a challenge today.

Ag'hel found herself disappointed at that. Her mood at

the moment would be perfectly suited to just such an exercise.

Reaching an intersection in the passageway, she turned a corner and proceeded into the section of the *Terthos*'s living quarters reserved for the use of Ambassador Kaljagh and his party. Not breaking stride, she marched past the pair of guards stationed in the corridor without giving them a second glance.

Ordinarily the dark maroon doors at the end of the dimly lit hallway would not have opened without the authorization of the person occupying the room beyond. Ag'hel, however, had seen to it several days earlier that she was granted automatic access to the living quarters. This of course caused no small amount of furor from the room's inhabitant.

It was another thing that didn't matter to her.

The doors parted at her approach and Ag'hel stormed into the room to find Kaljagh slumped into the only chair his sitting room offered. As she brought herself to a stop just inside the doors, she took a moment to appraise the interior of the ambassador's quarters. The chamber was not nearly as lavish in its appointments as likely characterized Kaljagh's home on Qo'noS or even other, larger ships that had transported him in the past. She'd fought in bars that were better decorated. However, Kaljagh's comfort was not her concern. He was a tool for her to use, nothing more.

Startled by her abrupt entrance, Kaljagh nearly fell out of the chair in his haste to regain his feet.

"Is it standard practice on this ship to barge into the quarters of diplomatic envoys?" he asked.

Ag'hel sneered at the ambassador. "I'm not interested in formalities. We are running out of time and so far our mission is a total failure."

"You can thank Captain K'tran for that," Kaljagh countered as he returned to the chair and reached across a nearby table to retrieve a large, ornately decorated wine goblet from a service tray. Ag'hel figured the ambassador had brought along his own personal assortment of dining implements on this voyage, as nothing so elaborate would ever be found in the *Terthos*'s mess hall.

"Perhaps if your masters had seen fit to include him in this mission," Kaljagh continued, "we would not have to worry about him interfering with our efforts."

"Spoken like someone accustomed to evading responsibility," Ag'hel spat, disgusted that this loathsome coward could take up valuable space on a combat vessel and share the same air as true warriors of the Empire. Were circumstances different, she might have killed him and been done with it.

"I do not question the decisions of my superiors," she continued, "and it would be wise for you to avoid doing so as well. If you had properly carried out your first assignment, we would not have needed a second attempt."

Frustration clouded Kaljagh's features. "With so much riding on the outcome of this mission, why did you give me the task of planting the bomb in the conference hall?" He shook his head in disgust. "Komor and his schemes. It makes no sense to give me this type of responsibility. I am not a spy or commando. I am a politician, and I have no illusions about being anything else."

"A diplomat would not immediately draw suspicion," she said. It was simple, really. In the end, a diplomat caught conducting a terrorist act could well cause as much damage to the peace summit as an actual attack. Additionally, if it kept her from exposing herself, so much the better. While there had been an element of logic to that approach, it had left much to chance.

Too much, unfortunately.

Casting a look of contempt at the ambassador, Ag'hel began to pace the length of the living quarters. Though the room on its own lacked even the most basic of aesthetic features, Kaljagh had certainly attempted to make it more comfortable. One item in particular that interested her was the hide of a large animal she did not recognize, currently serving as a rug placed alongside Kaljagh's bed. Two meters in length, the pelt was covered in thick white fur, and each of its four appendages were accentuated with a set of razor-sharp claws. The head of the animal sported large dark eyes and rows of long, jagged teeth. Ag'hel doubted that Kaljagh had killed the animal, finding it difficult to believe that the politician had even participated in a hunt since his childhood, if then.

Despite what she might think of him personally, however, Kaljagh had raised a valid point with regard to Captain K'tran. Why had she not been allowed to involve the *Terthos*'s commander? During past missions while she was assigned to other vessels, it had been common for her to alert the captain, especially if her task required her to make use of the ship's weapons or other equipment. Did the Council not trust K'tran? If she had been permitted to confide in him, the captain would doubtless have handled the situation with the *Enterprise* much differently. Ag'hel didn't fault the *Terthos*'s commander's actions, for as far as he knew he had been defending the interests of the Empire and the will of the Council by preserving the peace at the conference.

And then there was Komor's insistence that Kaljagh be involved in the operation. It was not a decision Ag'hel had approved of, and her doubts had been proven correct with the mission suffering failure twice already. Even though using Kaljagh reduced her own risk of discovery, she also found herself having to deal with an extra sanitation effort to insure their trail was covered.

"I cannot believe we haven't been exposed yet," Kaljagh said before draining the contents of his goblet. The foul odor of whatever concoction he was drinking reached her nostrils and she grimaced in distaste. Once more she shook her head as she regarded the ambassador.

Had it not been for her, Kaljagh would surely have been caught before planting the first bomb. As it was, the plan had failed, with the ambassador squandering a time-delayed detonation by not taking into account something as simple as a fluctuating schedule in the conference hall. However, it was also her fault for not teaching him to be alert for such unforeseen eventualities. As he had readily admitted from the start, he had no experience with covert operations and the necessity to think independently while undertaking them.

She shook the thoughts of failure away. "We cannot allow ourselves to dwell on these missteps," Ag'hel replied. "Instead we must refocus our energies to completing our mission."

"If we're to continue this course of insanity," Kaljagh said as he rose from his chair, "then I want more involvement."

"As you noted before," Ag'hel replied, "you are not qualified for this type of work. It will only get more hazardous now, and we will have to take extra steps to insure suspicion is drawn away from us."

The ambassador fixed Ag'hel with a steely gaze. "I am not so naive as to think that you or the Council cares one way or another if I am discovered. Therefore, I want steps taken to protect myself. This may be just another assignment for you, Lieutenant, but my stake is more personal.

Komor forced me into this situation and I intend to see it to the end, whether we succeed or fail."

Ag'hel didn't know Komor's reasons for tasking Kaljagh, and really didn't care so long as her own exposure wasn't threatened. As a deep-cover operative reporting directly to the High Council, she had been given assignments on many occasions where she had not known the primary or ultimate objective. For her current mission, she could only deduce that the Council had reason to distrust the Federation's motives for participating in the peace conference. She had to trust that Chancellor Kesh was acting in the best interests of the Empire.

Now, though, she knew that to simply incite a confrontation between the *Terthos* and the *Enterprise* would not be sufficient. No, her next action would have to be catastrophic enough that it caused an immediate end to the summit and cast a suffocating shroud of doubt over the entire peace process.

In short, she would have to start a war.

Chapter Twenty-eight

STEPHEN GARROVICK wanted nothing but to sleep for about a hundred years.

On top of the already exhausting workday, the prisoners had to deal with increased transit time from the compound to the area of the mine being worked. A new section of the vast underground cavern had been discovered to contain rich dilithium deposits, and Korax was anxious to exploit the find. In order to keep his already impressive level of productivity from faltering, the prisoners were now awakened earlier each day for transport into the mine and returned later in the evening following the completed work shift. Even using the automated railcar system that had been built for just such purposes, it still required nearly two hours to move the prisoners to and from the compound.

Garrovick figured he was lucky if he was getting four decent hours of sleep each night, and that was without being awakened by any of Sydney's nightmares, which were occurring with greater frequency. He wasn't sure what might be causing the dreams, but he could guess. Khulr had been leaving her alone the past few days, perhaps on Korax's orders. The Klingon wouldn't allow her any kind of lasting peace, though, of that he was certain. Garrovick figured she was both anticipating and dreading her next encounter with the malicious head guard.

"You look like I feel," Sydney offered as they shuffled alongside one another. Garrovick could see that the longer workdays and lack of sleep were beginning to take their toll on the former security chief. At least they were being fed decently, otherwise the problem would have been magnified.

As they emerged from the tunnel and into the prison courtyard, the first thing Garrovick noticed was that the sun had gone from the sky. Illumination was being provided by large lamps affixed to the top of the prison wall and spaced forty or so meters apart around the perimeter of the compound. Beyond the wall Garrovick could see the shadows of the tree line. The tops of the trees were moving in a gentle breeze that neither he nor anyone else inside the wall could feel because of the forcefield surrounding the prison. Though he couldn't see it, Garrovick could still hear the faint hum that confirmed the energy shield was in operation. More so than even the wall itself, the field's omnipresent droning hammered home the prisoners' sense of isolation and helplessness.

"I wonder what sumptuous feast our hosts have prepared for us this evening," Sydney asked, wiping her forearm across her brow and bringing it away covered with sweat and grime. The joke came out hollow and sarcastic, lacking her usual tone of levity. As it had everyone else, Kawaguchi's death had hit her hard, harshly reminding them that their lives here were fragile and vulnerable every day, and not just from their captors.

"I'm not all that hungry, anyway," he said. "I just want to sleep."

Sydney scowled at him. "You're the one who's always telling me to eat and keep my strength up. Leadership is by example, Stephen. The others need to see you coping with this."

She was right, he knew. He'd preached countless times to the remaining *Gagarin* crew about the need to take advantage of meals and water at every opportunity. He reminded himself that he couldn't let any sadness he felt over the loss of Kawaguchi drive him to do something foolhardy, like depriving his body of needed nourishment. Not here, and definitely not now.

"mev!"

Like a squad of first-year Academy cadets, the columns of bone-weary prisoners halted their march at the barked command to stop. Just as it happened every night, they would soon be directed into the drab warehouse building where fellow prisoners prepared and served the meals for the entire inmate population. There they would be fed before being allowed the opportunity to take care of various personal-hygiene needs before being secured in their cells for the night. Within the tiny chambers, they would seek refuge and a few precious hours' rest until they were awakened in the morning to start the entire mind-numbing routine all over again.

But then, the routine was blown completely to hell.

Deafening thunder and blinding light erupted outside the prison wall near the base of the mountain. Flames and sparks shot into the air, illuminating the jungle that lay a few dozen meters from the outside of the prison wall.

"What the hell was that?" Sydney shouted as chaos engulfed the scores of bedraggled prisoners. Alarms blared and guards shouted and motioned for the prisoners to move away from the cavern as another explosion shook the compound, this time on the opposite side of the prison.

The interior of the compound was deteriorating into total bedlam. Guards were ordering prisoners to evacuate the open area of the courtyard, but they were having little effect. The clamorous alarms only contributed to the confusion, drowning out the shouted orders of the guards and the cries of panic from the inmates.

Garrovick caught motion out of the corner of his eye and snapped his head around to see the telltale signature of a small vessel's plasma trail streaking just above the tree line. Judging from the emissions, he didn't think it could be anything bigger than a small personnel transport.

We're under attack?

Even as the ludicrous notion began to take hold in his mind, another explosion rocked the ground beneath Garrovick. All around the prison wall, the energy field flared and flickered, as if the protective shroud were under its own assault.

"Somebody's breaking through the shield!" Sydney called out, grabbing his arm and directing his attention to where a gap in the forcefield had formed outside the massive doors providing the only entrance into the prison. Garrovick knew that the shield surrounding the compound was created by a series of power generators installed within massive metal columns that formed a ring around the prison facility. The attacking shuttle had succeeded in disabling one of the generators, a feat that would have been impossible from the interior of the prison. After all, the energy shield was designed to keep people inside the compound.

Yet another thunderous roar washed over the courtyard, and Garrovick saw the metal doors disintegrate in a hellstorm of disruptor energy.

"Stephen!"

Sydney pulled Garrovick at a run toward the relative safety of a nearby cell-block building. All around them, prisoners sprinted for cover, racing for the cell blocks or the warehouses or anything that might provide concealment.

As he ran, the sound of racing engines caught Garrovick's attention. He looked over his shoulder toward what remained of the giant doors in time to see a small ship streaking through the entrance and into the courtyard. The vessel's design was easy enough to recognize.

"I don't believe this!" he said as he and Sydney ran underneath the sheltered walkway of a cell block's first level. "We're being attacked by Klingons!"

The small shuttle moved incredibly fast despite the cramped confines of the prison courtyard and the umbrella of the still mostly functional forcefield. Garrovick had to admire the skill and utter audacity of the vessel's pilot.

As abruptly as it had appeared, the ship began attacking the interior of the compound, weapons blazing as disruptor energy lanced out to strike guard towers and the prison's main headquarters building. The effect was staggering, with the Klingon guards ceasing their attempts to maintain control and instead running for cover.

Garrovick was surprised when a familiar tingling sensation, one he hadn't felt in years, began to envelop his body. A hum of energy started to assert itself over the sounds of pandemonium around him, growing in pitch until he could almost hear nothing else.

Transporter beam!

* * *

"Clear the pad!"

The command, barked in Federation Standard, came even before Garrovick had finished materializing. A quick look to either side of him showed that in addition to himself and Sydney, Sinak occupied the cramped, three-person transporter platform. Garrovick turned to the source of the clipped order and saw a human manning the transporter console.

And not just any human.

"What the hell . . . ?" Sydney began.

Garrovick blinked, still not believing his eyes. How long had it been since their paths had crossed? Ten years? Fifteen?

"Captain Kirk?" he asked, his voice cracking under the strain of disbelief. "How . . . ?"

Of course, Garrovick knew that if anyone could pull off the impossible, it was Kirk. He'd made a career out of it, after all.

"Fascinating," Sinak added.

"Move!" Kirk commanded again, then he looked at Garrovick. "How many more of your crew are down there?"

As Garrovick and the others vacated the transporter platform, the shuttle pitched to starboard and everyone in the room could hear hull plates groaning in protest.

"Somebody doesn't want us to leave," Sydney said, holding on to a support column as the shuttle lurched under another impact.

At the transporter console, Kirk said, "Sulu can handle that." He looked at Garrovick again. "How many more are down there?"

"Two," Garrovick replied, then supplied the names when Kirk asked. He watched as the captain's fingers moved across the computer console that Garrovick saw had been configured to display information in Federation Standard rather than Klingon.

"I've tied the transporter controls into the ship's computer," Kirk explained as he entered commands into the console. "We've loaded the medical and biological information on the *Gagarin*'s crew into a database, and the sensors are scanning the prison looking for any matches. It takes time, but we can speed things up if the computer knows exactly who to look for."

The ship shuddered again under another assault, followed by the crackling of overhead intercom speakers.

"Captain! They're bringing weapons emplacements online. We can't get them all before one of them causes us serious damage."

Working at the console, Kirk replied, "Almost there, Sulu. Stand by to get us out of here on my command."

Realizing that the attacking ship wasn't targeting anyone on the ground, Korax emerged from the headquarters building and out into the courtyard, a disruptor in his hand. Beside him, Khulr and Moqlah both carried disruptor rifles outfitted with targeting scopes. Still recovering from the injuries he had suffered in the mine, Moqlah was favoring his left side while cradling his weapon in the crook of his right arm.

"Get the shield repaired!" Korax shouted into the communicator he carried in his other hand. "Quickly, before they can escape!"

Who would want to attack them here, this all but forgotten hellhole on the fringes of the Empire? The dilithium might make a tempting target, but the vessel was too small to make off with any appreciable amount of the mineral. Whatever they could carry wouldn't be enough to justify the risk of such brash action.

"Commander, look!"

Khulr was pointing into the courtyard, where a transporter beam had wrapped itself around one of the prisoners. Even though the figure was covered in dust and grime from the mines, Korax recognized the orange-hued skin of an Efrosian. There was only one Efrosian currently being held in the prison.

And just like that, the answer was there.

"They've come for the Starfleet prisoners!" he growled, turning his attention to the shuttle still hovering above the floor of the compound, bobbing and weaving even as it continued to fire on targets of opportunity. The nose of the ship turned toward the building that housed Korax's personal shuttle as well as the prison's small fleet of ground transport vehicles. Disruptors flared again and twin beams of energy penetrated the wall of the hangar, chewing into its thermoconcrete surface with ease.

The ground rocked under another explosion and fire erupted from the hangar's windows and doors. Shards of glass and chunks of metal and thermoconcrete sailed in all directions. From where he stood, Korax knew that the explosion had consumed his shuttle.

In the courtyard, the shuttle continued to attack even as weapons batteries were being brought to bear. Whoever was manning the weapons on the ship was an exceptional marksman, Korax admitted. They were removing, with surgical precision, anything on the ground or on the prison wall that might pose a threat.

But Korax's guards were beginning to lock on to the ship with disruptor cannons. The pilot of the vessel couldn't be that good, he decided. It was only a matter of time.

The nose of the craft swung in their direction, disruptors still firing. Barely forty meters away and flying only ten or so meters off the ground, Korax was able to see through the clear plexisteel windshield. A Klingon and what looked to be a human sat in the cockpit. He managed only a momentary glimpse of the magnified image from the scope's viewfinder before the shuttle banked away.

But it was enough.

"Give me your weapon," Korax snapped, grabbing the disruptor rifle from Moqlah's hands and pulling the weapon into his own shoulder. Peering through the targeting scope, he sighted in on the ship's cockpit.

"No!"

It couldn't be!

Korax recoiled back from the scope in shock. The Klingon at the ship's controls looked to be none other than Koloth! Could his former commander really be here now? More than anyone or anything else, Koloth was the reason Korax had been all but banished to this useless backwater planet.

And now he was here, abducting Starfleet prisoners? Was he working for the Federation? Had he forsaken the Empire he had long professed loyalty to, or had he simply gone mad?

Reaching for his communicator, Korax shouted into the unit, "Lock all weapons on to that ship! Target its engines only! I want it captured, not destroyed!"

Moqlah saw a transporter beam claim another prisoner, and wondered how many people had been taken in this manner. Further, he thought he recognized the figure as that of a human.

Could it be?

With Korax and Khulr both looking away from him, he

let a small smile escape his lips. Had someone from the Federation mounted a rescue operation to retrieve their comrades after all this time? With the courtyard embroiled in chaos from the attack, there was no way to be certain which prisoners were being taken, but as Korax had already pointed out, the Efrosian member of the *Gagarin* contingent had just been swept away in a transporter beam.

It made sense, really.

At long last, it seemed that justice was being paid to Garrovick and his people. Perhaps their rescue would bring the entire despicable story of their ship's capture and the treatment suffered by its crew to light. The Council would not be able to deny what had happened, and it would be the first step toward restoring both honor and his faith in the Klingon Empire.

"Sulu!" Kirk's voice blared through the intercom in the shuttle's tiny cockpit. *"I've got all of them. Get us out of here!"*

"Aye, aye to that," Sulu said, more to himself than anyone else. His hands manipulated the controls of the ship as if the *Enterprise* helmsman had been piloting Klingon vessels all of his life.

From his own seat, Koloth marveled at the human's flying. As with the *bat'leth,* Sulu had displayed an uncanny ability to acquire new skills in impressively short periods of time. His natural talent for flying allowed him to pilot the shuttle while Koloth himself concentrated on manning the ship's weapons.

"Sensors still show the breach in the forcefield," he reported. "But it won't last long." Penetrating the electronic barrier had been easy enough, with the Klingon disabling the power generator for the section of the energy shield covering the entrance to the compound. He knew, though, that emergency systems would soon kick in. In fact, he was surprised that it hadn't already happened. Koloth guessed that such systems were manually operated rather than controlled by computer. After all, how often could such emergency measures be needed out here in the middle of nowhere?

The shuttle lurched again, and this time an alarm sounded in the cockpit.

"Impulse generator is offline," Koloth called out as he glanced at the status displays. Though Kirk had been lowering and raising the shields in coordination with his use of the transporter, the protective fields had borne the brunt of intense punishment from several of the weapons emplacements while activated, and their energy levels had been dropping throughout the rescue operation. They had now weakened to the point that the ship itself was taking damage.

Koloth didn't have to add that without the impulse generator, the shuttle did not have sufficient power to escape the pull of the planet's gravity. They would not be able to achieve orbit, much less a rendezvous with the *Gal'tagh*.

Glancing over, he saw that Sulu appeared concerned only with getting the shuttle out of the firefight while it was still in one piece. Tapping the helm's controls again, the ship banked under his touch and headed for the gap in the energy shield.

Another strike rocked the ship, accompanied by a slew of alarms as warning indicators all across the console lit up and demanded their attention.

"I've lost attitude stabilizers," Sulu called out over the alarms. "Helm is going unresponsive!"

Koloth stabbed at controls on his own console, attempting to reroute power from nonessential systems. It was hopeless, though. The last attack had damaged the ship beyond even Sulu's powers of compensation.

"I'm not going to be able to get much altitude," Sulu said as he fought the increasingly sluggish controls. He had managed to clear the prison wall and emerge from the confines of the energy shield, but now it was a struggle to keep the shuttle from slamming into the towering trees of the surrounding jungle as the ship clawed for altitude.

"Koloth, we're going to have to set down before we crash."

"Kirk!" Koloth called into the intercom. "Prepare for emergency landing!"

Even as he reached for the sensor controls to search for possible landing sites, Koloth felt the ship shudder around him, and then the bottom seemed to fall out from beneath his chair.

Outside the shuttle's canopy, the trees loomed closer.

Chapter Twenty-nine

"RED ALERT."

The voice of the *Enterprise* computer was nearly drowned out by alarm klaxons as the bridge illumination turned a deep crimson.

Spock swiveled in the captain's chair to face the science station where Chekov and Lorta had been working steadily for several hours. They had taken advantage of what had until now been a characteristically uneventful duty shift during ship's night.

"Mr. Chekov?" he prompted.

As the computer automatically silenced the alert sirens, Chekov said, "Transporter beam detected. Sensors are attempting to track it."

The two security officers had set sensors to scan for the Klingon transporter signature that had been used during the previous attack. The ship's computer would then locate the target of the beam and lock on to whatever materialized with the *Enterprise*'s own transporters so that it could be beamed away safely.

More important, the ship's computer and sensors would also have all the information they needed to track the transporter beam to its origin point.

Spock's eyes flickered to an overhead monitor showing a technical schematic of both the *Enterprise* and the *Terthos*. Pulsing blue crosshairs tracked across the representations of both ships and within seconds a point on the *Terthos*'s hull was illuminated and magnified on the display.

"There, on the secondary hull," Lorta said as she pointed to the monitor.

Chekov added, "It's near their engineering section." His head snapped up in alarm. "It's another Klingon torpedo, sir."

"Open a channel to the *Terthos*," Spock ordered as he returned to the command well and moved to stand in front of the helm console. Within seconds, the picture of space displayed on the bridge's main viewer was replaced with the image of Captain K'tran.

"Captain," Spock said, "another explosive has been transported onto the outer hull of your ship near your engineering section. I suggest immediate evacuation." Looking back at Chekov he asked, "Do you have a transporter lock on the torpedo, Mr. Chekov?"

Slamming his hands down on the console, Chekov swore in his native Russian language before replying. "Negative. The torpedo has been fitted with a transport inhibitor."

On the viewscreen, Montgomery Scott moved into view. The engineer had been assisting the *Terthos* crew with repairs following the last attack, a wise use of the experience he had gained working with Klingon technology over the years.

"*Tractor beam,*" Scott offered. "*Ye should be able to yank that beastie off easy enough.*"

"Agreed," Spock said, already turning to issue the

proper order. The lieutenant manning the helm entered the instructions to her console, but shook her head after a few seconds.

"No effect, sir," she reported. "Whatever's interfering with the transporter must be disrupting the tractor beam as well."

On the viewer, K'tran said, *"Captain Spock, can you use your weapons to destroy the torpedo?"*

Lorta turned from the science station. "That might detonate it, Captain. Considering where it's placed, it could do serious damage to the engineering area. If the antimatter containment field is disrupted, the entire ship could be destroyed."

She was interrupted by a beeping tone from the console.

"Sensors have traced the transporter signal," Chekov said. "It came from the *Terthos* herself."

"Is there any indication as to when the torpedo might detonate?" Spock asked.

Chekov consulted the sensor displays before replying. "No evidence of any timing mechanism. The weapon does contain a transceiver assembly, though. It could be waiting for a remote detonation signal."

"Perhaps we can jam its ability to receive such a signal?" Lorta suggested.

"Possible," Spock said. "Provided the transceiver isn't shielded like the rest of the weapon."

From the viewscreen, Scotty said. *"We canna take the chance, Mr. Spock. We hafta get that thing off the hull."*

Coming from anyone else, Spock would have considered the statement to be born of rampant emotionalism. However, he had never known the engineer to make any suggestion lightly.

"You have a proposal, Mr. Scott?"

* * *

No sooner had the torpedo dematerialized from the cargo transporter pad than Ag'hel set about covering her tracks. As before, she would have to take carefully plotted steps to remove all traces of her activities from the security logs maintained in the *Terthos*'s main computer.

She pulled her communicator from a compartment on her wide leather belt and activated it. All she had to do was adjust the device to the proper frequency and open the channel. There was a risk that her call would be traced, but it was only a slight one. Ag'hel had instructed the ship's computer to forgo logging her outgoing signal, again using her override code. When her business here was finished there would be no record of her communication, transmitting an apparently random hailing signal. Kaljagh would know immediately that the torpedo had been planted and that he could detonate it at his command.

Ag'hel had adjusted the torpedo's yield so that the danger to the *Terthos*'s antimatter system was minimized, thereby preventing the complete destruction of the ship. But the damage caused by the torpedo would still be devastating, given the weapon's placement near an area of the ship where the crew was highly concentrated. Casualties would be massive, and the ship would be crippled.

The successful execution of this strike was critical, she knew. If the results were as lackluster as those generated by the first two attacks, she wasn't certain they would get another opportunity before the conference ended or the Council members directing them opted to sever ties with their operatives.

Completely.

"Do not move."

Ag'hel whirled around at the sound of the voice to see Captain K'tran's massive frame filling the doorway. Lieutenant Lorta and the human security officer from the *Enterprise* flanked him. All three were armed.

"It is over, Ag'hel," Lorta said. "We know that you are behind the sabotage."

Ag'hel would never surrender so easily. "What are you talking about?" Mentally, though, she was retracing her steps. Had she left a clue for the two security officers to discover? She had faked the inventory reports detailing the number and status of the ship's torpedoes. The reports had implicated the munitions officer and K'tran had ordered him thrown in the brig to await trial and execution. She had performed similar acts on the transporter and communications logs to cover her tracks. How could any trail, if indeed one had been left, lead back to her?

The hand holding her communicator was still partially concealed by her body. Moving her thumb almost imperceptibly across the familiar face of the device's faceplate, she managed to press a control without being noticed.

"You can thank Lieutenant Connors on the *Enterprise*," Chekov said. "It was his idea to plant an additional identifier stamp on all computer entries. The requests you made to update the armory and transporter logs were encoded with a unique designator identifying the access terminal that you used, which happened to be the one in your quarters." The small security oversight program had been the *Enterprise* computer specialist's last task for the *Terthos*'s main computer.

Lorta added, "It also recorded the request you made from that transporter console just a few minutes ago to delete all evidence of the communication you were about to make."

Ag'hel was impressed, having failed to anticipate such a ploy. It could be argued that the faux pas was understandable, since most Klingons serving aboard fleet vessels possessed little if any comprehensive software programming expertise. Such work was generally left to support personnel when a vessel reported to a maintenance facility. She had not foreseen the possibility that a Starfleet computer engineer would be proficient in a Klingon programming language. She made a mental note to include this in her report, assuming she survived long enough to make one.

"Clever," she said, holding up the communicator that still rested in her hand. "But not clever enough."

Before anyone could react, Ag'hel's thumb pressed the transmit button.

Chapter Thirty

"ALLOW ME TO SAY that the accomplishments of the past several days are among the most satisfying of my career. Having lived in an age where war with the Klingon Empire was always a distinct possibility, it is gratifying to see that peaceful relations are achievable. It is my hope that our peoples will continue to build upon the work we have begun here today."

Applause erupted in the conference hall at Ambassador Catherine Joquel's remarks. The Federation diplomat's speech marked the end of the peace summit. Opinions in the room were mixed as to whether or not any lasting good would come from the efforts expended during the past week, but that did nothing to dampen the positive feelings of success permeating the atmosphere of the conference.

Standing just behind and to the right of Joquel, Ambassador Kaljagh felt the communicator concealed in his robes vibrate. He had set the unit to tactical mode to silence the normally audible tone emitted when it received an incoming transmission. As he pretended to listen to Ambassador Joquel's speech, Kaljagh felt the communicator's vibration cease, then start up again. The pattern was repeated three more times, finishing out a sequence that the Klingon had been dreading.

Something has gone wrong. Detonate the torpedo.

His first instinct was to fumble for the communicator and send the signal that would trigger the explosive, but he realized that was foolish. Now more than ever, he could not afford to bring attention to himself.

With forced casualness Kaljagh moved his hand into the pocket of his robe until he found the communicator. Keeping his eyes on the audience as Joquel continued to speak, his fingers searched for the control to activate the preprogrammed sequence that would be transmitted to the receiver assembly inside the torpedo's casing.

Within seconds, it would be over.

"In closing," Joquel continued, "I would like to say that I . . ."

The ambassador's words died in her throat and everyone's attention was drawn to the center of the room as four columns of transporter energy appeared. They solidified into the forms of Spock, K'tran, Chekov, and Lorta. All four officers were armed and no sooner had they finished materializing than they turned and aimed their phasers at Kaljagh.

"Please do not move, Ambassador," Spock said. "You are under arrest."

"What the hell is going on?" Joquel demanded, making no effort to hide her displeasure. She was not alone, as the audience members began to voice their surprise and disapproval of the interruption. The confusion of the situation was compounded when the main entrance to the conference hall opened and armed officers, both Starfleet and Klingon, began to file in.

Spock didn't respond to Joquel as he turned to insure that his order to have the room evacuated was being carried out. Only Toladal, rising from his seat at the front of the room, refused to leave. Chekov looked to Spock for guidance, who nodded for the ambassador's aide to remain. Only then did he return his attention to Joquel.

"I apologize for the intrusion, Ambassador. I must report that we have found our saboteur."

"Ambassador Kaljagh?" Joquel asked, her voice heavy with incredulity.

"That's outrageous!" Toladal replied with equal disbelief. "Captain Spock, you can't be serious."

"We have proof," K'tran said as he stepped forward. "My own first officer has been revealed to be a spy, working for someone on the High Council. We have already discovered her tampering with computer records aboard the *Terthos* to mask her activities, including two separate terrorist attacks on my ship." He held up a communicator for everyone to see. "She used this to contact the ambassador just a few minutes ago; however, we were able to jam her communications signal. Once we arrested Ag'hel, we initiated contact ourselves, and our sensors determined that Ambassador Kaljagh received the transmission."

Spock said, "The ambassador has the means to detonate a torpedo that was attached to the hull of the *Terthos*."

All eyes in the conference hall turned to Kaljagh, whose expression remained neutral, just as it had since Spock and the others had arrived.

"Ambassador," Toladal said, his voice pleading, "please denounce these lies!"

Instead of replying, Kaljagh suddenly exploded into motion. His left arm jerked free of his robes and light glinted off the polished finish of a *d'k tahg* knife. His right arm also moved as he stepped behind Joquel, the forearm coming to rest across the ambassador's throat. As Kaljagh placed the edge of the knife's large blade just under her left ear, Spock and the others could see a communicator in his right hand.

"You will lower your weapons, or I will kill her and detonate the explosive."

No one moved in the room. All weapons remained trained on the raised dais, though Spock was sure that none of them had a clear shot. Studying the Klingon's face, Spock thought he detected uncertainty.

"Hold your fire," he ordered.

"Stun them both," K'tran countered. "Then take the communicator from him."

Spock shook his head. "We do not need to take the communicator, Captain, as it has been rendered incapable of transmitting the detonation signal to the torpedo. However, Ambassador Joquel could still be injured by the knife even if we stun them both."

"You are lying!" Kaljagh said, holding up the communicator for emphasis. "You couldn't possibly have discovered our activities in time to defend against it."

Despite the knife threatening her, Joquel's demeanor remained controlled. "It doesn't make sense, Kaljagh. You've worked as hard as I have to make this summit succeed."

"After all the good that has come from our work here," Toladal said, "why would you attempt to destroy it? What could possibly be worth sacrificing the lives of Klingon warriors?"

"It was not my plan to kill," Kaljagh replied. "I am not an assassin."

"That much is obvious," Lorta said derisively. "A true Klingon field operative would have succeeded where you consistently failed."

Kaljagh nodded. "With that I will not argue. I had no choice in the attacks that were made, or in the selection of targets."

"Are you a puppet?" K'tran asked. "Who controls you?"

Kaljagh was silent for several seconds, his eyes cast downward toward the floor. Spock got the distinct impression that the Klingon was weighing the consequences of his answer. Finally, Kaljagh looked up at them once more and uttered a single word.

"Komor."

Spock recalled that Komor was a member of the Klingon High Council of some tenure and standing, having held the seat for many years.

"Impossible!" K'tran snapped. "Komor would never betray the Empire by engaging in such cowardly tactics." Kaljagh's expression grew angry as he replied. "I have the proof recorded in my personal computer files. Have your security officer test their authenticity. Komor controls me, as you describe it, because he threatened to kill my family." He looked into the faces of those who now stood in silence before him, judging his every word. "My wife and three children, one of them a newly born son. Komor threatened to kill them all unless I obeyed their commands."

"He will not succeed, Ambassador," Spock said. "We have captured Lieutenant Ag'hel. We have her private computer files as well as yours. We have all the proof we require to expose this conspiracy. If you injure Ambassador Joquel, you will undermine everything you have accomplished here."

"What about my family?" Kaljagh demanded. "How can you guarantee their safety?"

It was Toladal who provided the possible answer. "There is someone on the Council who may be an ally."

Of course, Spock thought. Gorkon, who had sent Koloth the information about the *Gagarin* and who had supported the rescue operation. Toladal had spoken highly of him during the past week, and Spock had learned enough about the ambassador's aide to deduce that the Council member was a being of integrity and sound character.

"We can contact Gorkon directly," Toladal continued. "He will see to it that your family is removed from danger."

The knife wavered for the briefest of intervals, and Spock glanced to his left to see whether or not K'tran might take advantage of the small lapse and try to fire on the ambassador. Thankfully, he didn't, and seconds later Spock's patience was rewarded as Kaljagh lowered the knife. He released his hold on Joquel, and everyone watched as he moved slowly to the head table and dropped down into his seat. His shoulders sagged visibly as he laid his knife and communicator down atop the table.

"I only wanted to protect my family," he whispered to no one. "What have I done? How many have died because of my actions? How many more will die before this madness ends?"

Then he turned to Spock. "Captain, Komor and other Council members are very worried that Koloth and your Captain Kirk will succeed in their mission to retrieve any Federation prisoners being held in Klingon territory. If that happens, it will cause an uproar across the Klingon Empire and could result in an upheaval of the Council. They will do whatever it takes to prevent that."

"What is he talking about?" Joquel said, directing her gaze to Spock. "What is Captain Kirk involved in?"

Spock spent the next several moments relaying the information regarding the loss of the *Gagarin* and the subsequent discovery that some of her crew had become prisoners of the Empire. The look of confusion on Joquel's face turned to shock as Spock described the mission that Captain Kirk had undertaken with Koloth's help to find and rescue at least some survivors of the ill-fated ship.

"They cannot allow that information to become public knowledge if they want to remain in power," Kaljagh said. "There are too many Klingons who would denounce Kesh and Komor and their partners and fight for their removal from office."

Spock replied, "He must have believed that if an interstellar incident were to erupt during what should have been a peaceful meeting between officials of the Federation and the Empire . . ."

"It would give Kesh and Komor time to clean up their affairs," K'tran completed the thought. "In addition, if they are able to capture Kirk in our space, they will accuse the Federation of using the peace conference as a cover to launch a covert espionage mission. They will even proclaim Koloth a traitor to the Empire to strengthen the deception." The *Terthos*'s captain's upper lip curled in a snarl of disgust. "Cowards."

"I don't understand, Ambassador," Toladal said. "Why involve you at all? If Lieutenant Ag'hel was a spy working for Komor, why did he need you to plant the bombs?"

Kaljagh sighed heavily, as if relieved that he could finally confess his multitude of sins. "Eight of your years ago, I was a court magistrate, one of several who presided over the trial for the crew of the Starfleet ship. It was a trial in name only as members of the High Council, specifically Chancellor Kesh and Komor, had already decided their ultimate fate. There was never any intention of returning the prisoners.

"As I moved into politics, I tried to put the entire distasteful episode behind me. I worked in the diplomatic corps. We furthered relations with the Federation to the point that revealing the Council's actions of years ago would do more harm than good. Kesh and Komor know that the tides are turning and that peace with the Federation is inevitable. The only way they can hope to remain in power is to accept the evolving reality and position themselves to benefit in spite of the changes that will surely affect our society."

"And that means removing any evidence that Federation prisoners have been held in Klingon space," Chekov said.

"Exactly. The fact that I was attending the peace summit was an added bonus to them. I am one of very few Klingons who are even aware that Starfleet officers are being held illegally."

Kaljagh turned his attention to Spock. "Captain, you should know that Komor has dispatched a warship to follow after Koloth and your captain with orders to destroy the prison facility on Pao'la. No proof of the prisoners' existence will remain."

"Good lord!" Joquel's expression was one of stark horror. "They would order so many deaths merely to keep their secret?"

"They will stop at nothing, Ambassador," Kaljagh replied. "Even if Koloth and Captain Kirk succeed in rescuing any of your people, they will never be allowed to leave Klingon space alive."

Joquel's face was now a mask of pure fury. "We have to do something. We can't just stand by while corrupt politicians commit these heinous crimes."

The conversation was interrupted by the beeping of Spock's communicator.

"Spock here," he said into the unit as he flipped its antenna grid open.

"Captain," said Lieutenant Clev, the Andorian communications officer assigned to gamma shift, *"sensors have detected a change in the torpedo's readings. It's activated itself."*

Spock's eyes moved to focus on Kaljagh's communicator, untouched since the ambassador had abandoned it.

"It armed itself?" K'tran's voice was laden with disbelief.

Chekov replied, "That, or the torpedo was programmed with a fail-safe option, designed to trigger a detonation after a given length of time."

Dumbstruck, Kaljagh jumped from his chair. "I did no such thing! I was supposed to send the signal myself."

"Ag'hel," Lorta said. "It must have been her."

Spock returned his attention to his communicator. "Mr. Clev, how much time until the weapon detonates?"

"Unknown, sir. We're trying to determine that with sensors now."

"Patch me through to Mr. Scott."

Chapter Thirty-one

ONE OF THESE DAYS, I'll find an easier way to make a living.

As fast as the bulky magnetic gravity boots would allow, Scotty walked across the surface of the *Terthos*'s hull, the helmet of his Starfleet-issue environmental suit echoing the sound of his own breathing. Beside him K'vyr, the engineer of the *Terthos*, maneuvered in similar fashion. The ship's transporter had deposited them twenty meters away from the torpedo, sufficient enough distance from the explosive that they could get a good look at the device before moving closer.

Scotty scanned the explosive with his tricorder. "Aye, she's active all right. Chekov was right, there is a transceiver inside the casing, but I dinna think I can get at it."

"Such an attempt may detonate it," K'vyr replied.

"Aye, she may be designed to go off if we tamper with it. I think our original plan is still the safest." Though Chekov and Lorta had succeeded in finding and blocking the frequency of Ag'hel's and Kaljagh's prearranged communicator signals, Scotty would not be able to relax until the torpedo itself had been disposed of.

All things considered, though, I'd rather be in a pub on Argelius.

"It is also the option that will take the least amount of time," K'vyr said, already retrieving from his belt the cutting torch he had brought with him.

To remove the torpedo from the *Terthos,* Scotty and K'vyr would have to cut out a measured section of hull around the weapon large enough for the *Enterprise* tractor beam to lock onto without being disrupted by the inhibitor inside the torpedo's casing. K'vyr had already seen to it that the entire section inside this area of the hull was evacuated and the compartment sealed and depressurized in order to minimize possible damage to the interior of the ship.

Cutting through the hull of the Klingon ship was slow going. Though the plating wasn't composed of trititanium as on Federation starships, it was still dense material, no doubt chosen for its ability to withstand combat conditions even when unshielded. It was tiring work, made worse by the threat that the torpedo might go off at any moment. Scotty tried not to think about that, concentrating instead on the task at hand as he guided his own torch across the surface of the *Terthos*'s hull. The task proceeded for several minutes without incident, with both engineers working steadily.

Though he couldn't hear the alarm of his tricorder, he had strapped it to his forearm so that he would be able to see the unit's display panel. Because of this, Scotty saw the indicator light as the tricorder's sensors detected what he had programmed them to look for, and hoped they would never find.

He swore a particularly vulgar Scottish oath before

saying to K'vyr, "She's activated herself somehow. No signal was received, so she musta had some kind of programmed delay."

"Is there any way to determine how much time we have?" K'vyr asked, his attention still on the cut he was making in the *Terthos* hull.

"Aye, but it'll take time to adjust the tricorder, and I'd rather spend that time cutting."

So focused was he on the job that he thought he might have a heart attack when Spock's voice blared in his ears.

"Spock to Scott. We have detected the activation of the torpedo. Ship's sensors have determined that five minutes and thirty-six seconds remain before it detonates. Move clear immediately for transport to the Enterprise."

Scotty exchanged looks with K'vyr. Both engineers knew that if the torpedo detonated while still attached to the hull, the damage to the *Terthos* would be considerable, even assuming the ship's antimatter containment system survived the blast.

"We are almost finished," K'vyr said, continuing to work.

That was good enough for Scotty.

"Mr. Spock, evacuate the ship's secondary hull sections. We're going to keep working."

"I find that course of action ill-advised, Mr. Scott."

"Yer tellin' me, but I dinna spend all that time helpin' to repair this ship to see it get blown apart. We've got five minutes, and I intend to use 'em. Have the tractor beam stand by and the transporter room ready to lock onto us. It's gonna be mighty close."

There was several seconds of communications silence as the two engineers continued to guide their cutting torches, and Scotty spent that time willing the metal of the hull to part faster.

"Agreed," Spock finally replied. *"However, I suggest you work quickly. It would be most unfortunate if I were forced to explain your loss to the captain."*

At the science station on the *Enterprise* bridge, Spock called up the sensor readings of the torpedo still attached to the *Terthos*'s hull. A scan of the weapon's interior showed one heavily shielded area. Given more time, he might be able to find a way to penetrate the shielding with sensors. Such a task would undoubtedly take more than the four minutes and fourteen seconds remaining until detonation.

"Sir," Lieutenant Clev called out from the communications station. "Captain K'tran has sent a message from the *Terthos*. He reports that Lieutenant Ag'hel is proving to be uncooperative in providing information to disarm the torpedo."

Spock had expected nothing else. As a seasoned covert operative, Ag'hel would no doubt possess the skills needed to insure she didn't reveal any useful information in the time remaining to them.

He heard the hiss of turbolift doors behind him and turned to see Chekov and Ambassador Joquel step onto the bridge. Spock noted the ambassador's concerned expression, whereas Chekov simply looked tired.

"Lieutenant Lorta and Ambassador Kaljagh are still on the starbase, sir," Chekov said to Spock. "The ambassador has been remanded to station security for the time being until the matter can be investigated fully. Admiral LeGere sends his regards."

Joquel stepped from the turbolift alcove. "I intend to voice my support for Kaljagh. The accomplishments he helped bring about should not be overshadowed by his unfortunate involvement in this affair, considering how he was coerced."

Spock nodded in agreement. Having reviewed the draft versions of the treaty that Joquel and Kaljagh had drawn up, it was obvious that the Klingon ambassador had been committed to the peace process, despite the role he had played in the acts of sabotage. He had no doubt that Joquel could convince any Federation inquiry board of Kaljagh's contributions.

But now, Spock had more pressing concerns.

Joquel seemed to sense this as well. "Captain, have you had any luck deactivating the torpedo?"

"No, Ambassador," Spock replied. "Given the time restraints, our only option is to trust in the expertise of Mr. Scott and the *Terthos*'s engineer."

The turbolift doors opened again, this time admitting McCoy onto the bridge. From Spock's observation, the doctor appeared to be his usual agitated self, a theory confirmed when McCoy actually spoke.

"I just heard that Scotty went outside in a spacesuit to pry that torpedo off that ship's hull. Whose idiotic idea was that?"

"That would be Mr. Scott," Spock replied.

McCoy was anything but pleased at the confirmation. "Did anyone bother to tell him that the damned thing might go off?"

"He is aware of the risks, Doctor. Nevertheless, he presents us with our only viable option for dealing with the current situation." Spock knew that McCoy was only voicing concern for his friend, but emotionalism could not be allowed to cloud the issue. Time was short, and the dilemma they faced was fast approaching critical.

Looking to one of the bridge's chronometers, Spock saw that only two minutes and eight seconds remained until detonation.

* * *

Almost there.

Starting at a point near the head of the torpedo and moving in opposite directions, Scotty and K'vyr had begun cutting out one side of a crude rectangle. They worked to join up again at the opposite end of the weapon, and Scotty could see that only a few meters separated them now.

Scotty checked his tricorder. "One minute, twenty-seven seconds left. How are you coming, lad?"

K'vyr replied without looking up. "It will take us nearly a minute to complete the cutting," he said even as he continued to work.

Damn! Scotty knew that even if he and K'vyr could finish cutting the section of hull plating free, the *Enterprise* still had to get it away from the ship before the torpedo detonated. At this proximity, the explosion could still do tremendous damage to the *Terthos,* whose shields could not be raised until the tractor beam pulled the weapon far enough away.

They weren't going to make it, not by a long shot.

Movement in the corner of his eye caught his attention and he turned his head to see the *Enterprise* moving in their direction. Already less than two hundred kilometers away, he judged, the mighty starship was closing the distance rapidly. Why would Spock move the ship so close?

Of course! He meant to use the *Enterprise*'s shields to protect the *Terthos* in case they were unable to move the torpedo outside the Klingon ship's own shield perimeter.

"Bless ye, Spock. I knew I could count on you."

Spock replied, *"You will need to move clear before we can engage the beam. Forty-five seconds remain until detonation. Stand by to be transported aboard."*

Scotty looked down at the hull and saw that less than

two meters remained to be cut. There was no possibility of them finishing the job in the time left to them.

"That'll have to do, lad. We've got to get clear." Scotty guessed that the *Enterprise* had moved to between fifty and sixty kilometers away. With full power to her shields he was sure the ship would be able to withstand the brunt of the explosion.

To his credit, K'vyr had not let even the approach of the *Enterprise* distract him from his task. With his torch still slicing into the heavy hull plating, he said, "At this range, your ship's tractor beam will have to be calibrated precisely to avoid further damage to the surrounding hull or the interior compartment. Every centimeter we cut out of the way will help them."

Though he could almost hear the seconds ticking away in his head now, Scotty knew the Klingon was right. If the situation were reversed, he'd fight just as hard to save the *Enterprise*.

"Have your ship engage its beam," K'vyr said, still guiding his torch across the hull.

Scotty relayed the order and seconds later he felt the power of the beam as it latched on to the partially severed section of hull plating, its warm gold hue enveloping the area he and K'vyr had cut out. Though the sound didn't travel to him, of course, the engineer imagined he could hear metal protesting as it was pulled away by the power of the starship. Spock was obviously holding back the full strength of the beam out of consideration for the two engineers' fragile bodies as well as the potential harm the beam could cause to the *Terthos* herself.

Nevertheless Scotty still saw the partially severed section of plating move, beginning to wrench itself from the hull. K'vyr continued to cut, slowly freeing the section centimeter by precious centimeter.

It was all taking too long.

"Spock, increase power," Scotty called into his helmet communicator. Reaching out to grab K'vyr's arm, he said to the Klingon, "We're outa time. Let the *Enterprise* take it from here."

The engineers scrambled clear, moving as fast as their bulky suits and magnetized boots would let them. Behind him, Scotty could almost feel the *Enterprise*'s tractor beam increase its pull on the nearly severed hull section. He turned in time to see the hull plate and the torpedo attached to it tear free, enveloped in the beam's unyielding grip.

All that remained now was for the tractor beam to pull the explosive beyond the Klingon ship's defensive perimeter so the *Terthos* could raise her own shields. Did they have enough time for that? Scotty looked down at the tricorder still strapped to his forearm.

Five seconds.

"Enterprise! Beam us . . ."

". . . aboard!"

No sooner had the transporter room solidified around him than Scotty felt the telltale vibration in the deck. It wasn't much, hardly a shudder, but the engineer had felt the *Enterprise* deck move beneath his feet enough times over the years to know when an explosion had occurred outside the ship. The fact that he had felt anything at all through the shields was evidence of just how close the detonation had been.

"Transporter room," Spock's voice called from the intercom. *"Do you have them?"*

Behind the protective window that shielded the transporter console, the Tellarite manning the station replied, "Yes, sir. Captain Scott and Lieutenant K'vyr are safely aboard."

"Did we do it, Spock?" Scotty asked.

"Affirmative. The torpedo detonated outside our shields. The Terthos *was unable to raise her own screens in time, so we extended ours to protect her. No damage has been reported on either ship, Mr. Scott."*

Only then did Scotty permit himself a sigh of relief even as he unfastened the latches on his suit's helmet.

"Well, it looks as though I haven't run out of luck yet."

The engineers helped one another out of their environmental suits, after which Scotty allowed himself the luxury of sitting down on the transporter platform. He was just leaning his back against the bulkhead when the entrance to the room hissed open to admit Spock and Ambassador Joquel.

"Gentlemen," the ambassador said, "your actions today were truly exemplary. In addition to saving the *Terthos,* you added a final positive note to this peace conference. Your ability to work together despite our peoples' ideological differences is worthy of emulation."

"We did all that, did we?" Scotty asked K'vyr.

The Klingon nodded. "It appears so."

Exhaling audibly, Scotty wiped his brow and shook his head. "I am truly gettin' too old for this type o' nonsense."

"It doesn't seem as though age has affected your ability," K'vyr noted. "I think you should continue to perform your duties for as long as you are able."

"Agreed," Spock added. "A most logical observation."

Joquel turned her attention to Spock. "Captain, there is still the matter of Captain Kirk. He's still at risk in Klingon space. Is there anything we can do to help him?"

Spock considered Kirk and Sulu and the new danger awaiting them. If what Kaljagh had told them was true, no longer could they only concern themselves with discovery in Klingon space and condemnation as spies. Now there were forces at work actively searching for them.

"Our own efforts to launch a rescue mission would be hampered at best, Ambassador. Even in the unlikely event that we could secure permission to enter Klingon space, we do not know Captain Kirk's present location. In light of this, I am afraid there is very little we ourselves can do at the moment."

For a brief moment, Spock was thankful that McCoy was not present to hear the hint of suppressed frustration that had almost escaped his lips.

Chapter Thirty-two

IT WASN'T THE FIRST TIME James Kirk had been hunted.

He'd been pursued by a relentless Gorn and had engaged in the ultimate game of "cat and mouse" with an omnipotent adolescent who'd called himself Trelane. He'd been chased through the subterranean tunnels of Janus VI by a creature that consumed solid rock, and had been hounded by an entity at the center of the galaxy who'd had the supreme arrogance to pass itself off as God.

And he'd been hunted by Klingons as well, but never like this. Never before had he found himself plunging headlong through the dense jungle of a remote planet, deep in the heart of enemy territory and with no way to contact anyone who could come to his aid. His beloved *Enterprise* and her crew, who had rescued him from mortal danger more times than he could remember, was days away at high warp. Even Koloth's ship was out of reach, with orders to wait until it received a signal from the shuttle that had brought Kirk, Sulu, and Koloth to this all but forgotten world.

Only now, Kirk hoped the *Gal'tagh* would pick up the signal being emitted from the shuttle's distress beacon.

Fighting the dying controls of the Klingon shuttle all the way to the ground, Sulu and Koloth had managed to land the mortally damaged vessel. With its flight stabilizers all but gone, the ship had been little more than a flying rock. Only Sulu's consummate skill with what little control remained of the ship's thrusters had enabled their fall to the jungle floor to be more guided descent than plummeting crash. Even so, the landing had been a hard one, throwing the occupants of the shuttle around the interior of the vessel.

Everyone had suffered some form of laceration or bruising, but Ra Mhvlovi had faired worst of all. The Efrosian's right leg was broken in two places, for all intents and purposes rendering him an invalid. A lightweight yet durable stretcher now bore his weight, and Sinak and Sulu were manning the stretcher at present. Kirk had ordered everyone to take turns carrying their injured comrade, twenty minutes per interval in order to conserve the group's strength for as long as possible in the overpowering heat of the Pao'lan jungle. Sulu had already administered tri-ox compound to everyone to help them breathe in the thick air, as well as giving vitamin supplements to all of the *Gagarin* survivors. The vitamins couldn't completely compensate for the generally weakened condition of the prisoners, but it might be enough to keep them going until the *Gal'tagh* returned.

Koloth led the ragtag group through the jungle, a disruptor pistol in his right hand. Strapped to his back was the same *bat'leth* Kirk had seen the Klingon use to spar with Sulu back on the ship. If the heat bothered Koloth, he didn't show it. In contrast, sweat ran freely down Kirk's face and saturated the tunic he wore. With the sun just starting to rise, he knew the heat would get worse as the day wore on.

Koloth turned to look over his shoulder at Kirk. "Any sign of them?"

For what seemed like the hundredth time, Kirk checked his tricorder. Once again, the device revealed no indication of pursuit behind them. The fugitive group of prisoners and their would-be rescuers had a healthy head start, however.

Despite the damage it had suffered during the rescue operation, the shuttle had still managed to travel nearly sixty kilometers before Sulu and Koloth had been forced to land. With the damage they had inflicted on the camp's lone personnel shuttle and pool of ground-transport vehicles, it would take the Klingons at the prison a while to mount any kind of pursuit.

"I wouldn't count on that," Garrovick said when the topic was broached. "Korax won't stand being made a fool of on his own turf. He'll come after us even if he has to crawl through the jungle on his hands and knees."

Koloth started at the name of the prison commander. "Korax," he said, nodding his head as he drew the name out. "So this is where the Empire saw fit to banish him."

"You know him?" Kirk asked.

Smiling, Koloth replied, "He was my first officer aboard the *Gr'oth* all those years ago when you and I met on that space station." With a glint of mischief in his eye, he added, "I believe some of your men introduced themselves to Korax in the station's bar."

Kirk groaned as he remembered the incident at station K-7. The bar fight between the Klingons and members of the *Enterprise* crew had not gone over well with the Federation officials on the station. Kirk hadn't been too thrilled about the altercation, either, and doubted he'd ever forget that day. He'd had to dress down a group of his officers as if they were a squad of raw cadets who'd failed a barracks inspection. Making matters worse was the fact that his chief engineer had started the whole thing!

Kirk's reverie was broken as he realized someone had moved up on his right side to walk along beside him. Looking up, he saw that it was Garrovick.

"You have no idea how good it was to see you when we materialized on that transporter pad. I thought I was dreaming."

The *Enterprise* captain turned his head to get a better look at the younger man. The years of captivity had not been kind to him, Kirk noted as he studied Garrovick's sunken cheekbones and eyes. His skin was pale and pasty, no doubt the result of all the time spent working in the underground mines. While he still had most of his teeth, years of improper diet and dental hygiene had taken their toll even against advanced Federation dentistry techniques. The lack of any facial or body hair only accentuated the fragility of his appearance. Kirk was awestruck that Garrovick and the others had survived as long as they had.

Noticing Kirk's glances, Garrovick said, "Don't worry, it looks worse than it is. Aside from a few missing teeth and minor injuries, I've been lucky."

"You've done incredibly well to have survived this long, Stephen," Kirk said.

"I'll be happy to tell you all about it when we get back." A twinkle appeared in Garrovick's eye. "I have several tall stories you might like to hear."

The familiar words rang in Kirk's ears, reminding him of when Garrovick had been a young ensign aboard the Enterprise, fresh out of the Academy and with his entire life ahead of him. He was older now, a good portion of the wisdom he now possessed having come at an incredible price.

"Klingon prisons are no picnic, from what I've been told," Kirk said. "Especially for humans."

Garrovick shrugged. "Korax doesn't usually tolerate abuse toward the prisoners, probably because he doesn't get enough replacements to keep his dilithium quota up. He doesn't have any choice but to keep us reasonably healthy."

"It could also be that he had orders to see that no harm came to you or any of your crew."

Garrovick shook his head as he reached out to brush aside a vine drooping across his path. "If that's so, then the order only came after he took over the camp. It sure didn't come in time to save Captain Gralev."

Kirk nodded tightly in agreement. "I know about what happened to her. It was part of the information Koloth provided. He's the reason we came looking for you."

At the mention of the Klingon's name, Garrovick's expression turned questioning. "Did we sign a treaty with the Klingons or something?"

Shaking his head, Kirk replied, "No, I'm afraid not, though we might finally be close to it." Kirk relayed the events that had begun at Starbase 49.

"So the Klingons denied even having us in custody all this time," Garrovick said. "We didn't want to accept that, but after a while it just sort of seemed inescapable. When you live in a vacuum for years, it's easy to think everybody's forgotten about you. Well, I guess I should be thankful that Mom thought I was dead rather than a prisoner. That would have been harder for her to take, I think." At that thought, he looked at Kirk again.

"Did Koloth have any information on the rest of the crew? They only brought a handful of us here. I'd always assumed that they'd separated us and sent us to different gulags around the Empire. Other than those who were brought here with me, I haven't heard about anyone else from the *Gagarin* since the attack."

Kirk shook his head. "He didn't have anything else. But now that we know some of you survived, we have reason to confront the Empire about the rest of the crew."

"Then that's another reason for us to get the hell out of here."

Turning at the sound of the new voice, Kirk and Garrovick saw Sydney Elliot walking three paces behind them. Kirk marveled at her stealth, not having heard her approach.

"Captain Kirk, I'd like to introduce Ensign Sydney Elliot, formerly a member of the *Gagarin*'s security detachment."

Elliot disregarded the introduction. "Captain, you know they'll kill us all rather than let us escape. They can't afford to have their little secret get out."

"I don't think it's that simple, Ensign," Kirk replied. "If they'd wanted you dead, they would have killed you years ago. As potential pawns in a larger political game, you're far more valuable to the Klingons alive."

An insistent beeping from his tricorder begged for Kirk's attention.

"Koloth," he said as he studied the device's small display, "they're coming." As the Klingon walked back to join him, Kirk held up the tricorder for him to see.

"How soon before they overtake us?" Koloth asked.

"Maybe two hours, unless we keep moving. They're moving pretty fast. I guess we didn't do a good enough job of taking out their transportation." Kirk examined the tricorder's scan results once again. "It looks like only two vehicles following us." Looking at Garrovick he asked, "How many people will one of those things carry?"

"A dozen or so," Garrovick replied.

Koloth glanced around at the jungle surrounding them. "The terrain here will eventually force them to follow us on foot, but they will still move faster than us. We will have to stand and fight."

Frowning, Kirk considered their prospects. He had no doubt that the Klingons would find them. Even though he and Sulu had removed the bracelets with their transponders from the ankles of the prisoners, Korax and his men would have tricorders with them. Using the shuttle's crash site as a starting point, it wouldn't take them long to triangulate on the fugitives' position.

They numbered eight, including the wounded Ra Mhvlovi, while there were at least twenty-four Klingons pursuing them. They would all be armed to the teeth, whereas except for he, Sulu, and Koloth, no one else in the fugitive party would be up for any type of sustained fighting. The phasers he and Sulu had brought and distributed among the prisoners would help, but in the end sheer numbers would work against them.

"There's no way we'll beat them in a stand up fight," Kirk said. "We need to find a place to hole up." He adjusted the tricorder's scan controls and turned in a slow circle until he found what he wanted, then pointed into the jungle.

"That way, there's a small plateau. We can use that as a defensible position."

Koloth balked at the idea. "Hide and wait for our enemies to come to us? What kind of way is that to fight?"

"We have to hold out long enough for the *Gal'tagh* to return," Kirk replied. "We don't stand a chance out here in the open." He didn't want to add that there was no way of knowing if Koloth's ship had even received the weak distress signal sent out by the damaged shuttle.

"It is honorable to die fighting for a cause you believe in," Koloth said, his voice hardening.

Kirk didn't reply immediately, instead taking a few seconds to scan the faces of Sulu and the prisoners who had by now gathered around them. He saw the looks in their faces, combinations of fear, resignation, and resolve. It was as if each of them had come to the conclusion that today would be the last day any of them would spend on this world, one way or another.

Elliot fixed Kirk with a glare of fierce determination. "I'm not going back to that hellhole, Captain. Either I leave this godforsaken planet or I die trying, and I'm taking as many Klingons with me as I can." She tightened her grip on the phaser in her hand.

Kirk saw in her tired eyes the unforgiving existence that had been her lot in life during these past years. He didn't want to imagine the harsh realities that the young security officer and her companions had faced while in captivity. Were he in their position, he knew he would feel the same way.

Turning to look back at Koloth, he said, "My mission is to get these people out of here, Koloth, and that's precisely what I intend to do, any way I can. If that means we hide and ambush them, then so be it."

Regarding Kirk for several seconds, Koloth finally nodded, a small smile forming on his lips. "Coming from any other Earther, I would have considered your words to be those of a coward, Kirk. But I know better than that." He gestured into the jungle with his free hand. "Lead us."

As he led his ragtag group of followers deeper into the jungle, Kirk's thoughts turned to the coming battle. There could be no compromise, no quarter given. There were only two possible outcomes.

Either they would succeed, or they would die.

Chapter Thirty-three

KORAX WANTED BLOOD.

Specifically, he wanted Koloth's blood. He hadn't been sure of the Klingon's identity when he had first spied him through the canopy of the shuttle. After turning that fleeting image over in his mind during the past few hours, however, Korax was now certain he was pursuing his former commander through the Pao'lan jungle. He would have every cursed *petaQ* on that shuttle executed in the courtyard while the prisoners they'd tried to rescue watched, but he wanted Koloth for himself. For whatever reason, fate had delivered into Korax's hands the one most responsible for the ruin his career had become, and he was determined not to waste the opportunity.

"How far?" he growled.

Beside him, Khulr consulted his tricorder. "Less than two *qell'qams,* Commander. Eight life signs. Three Klingon, three human, a Vulcan and an Efrosian. They are stationary, near a small rise." He pointed off into the jungle.

Finding the downed shuttlecraft had been simple, and Korax had not been surprised to find five ankle bracelets lying among the discarded equipment inside the ship. The prison's central computer wouldn't be able to help him track the escapees, but he didn't need the assistance. Without their ship they were forced to move on foot, perhaps while carrying injured members of their party. Sooner or later Korax would overtake them.

If he could just get through this cursed jungle.

He scowled as he looked into the undergrowth, which appeared to be even thicker than that which they had just spent the last two hours slugging through. The trees and thickets had grown so dense that Korax had been forced to order the pursuit continued on foot. It was slow going, but he didn't care. He would claw his way through this hellish jungle for the rest of his days if it meant claiming vengeance on Koloth.

Had things been different, Korax may well have advanced to a position of power and prestige within the Empire. But Koloth, rather than standing by his side and pledging his faith and support, had instead forsaken him, casting him away as he pursued his own goals.

That, and *enlightenment*.

Koloth had embraced the teachings of Kahless, like so many others who had turned away from aspirations of conquest and the power to be had by subjugating those who were weaker. Instead, they searched for honor and glory, living their lives by a rigid code set forth centuries before and which had until only recently been relegated by many to the realm of myth or even children's tales. And for what? Those who followed Kahless' path believed that upon their death, the mighty Klingon warrior who defined their existence would welcome them into the afterlife where they would reap the rewards of their loyalty.

Korax had never believed any of it, but did it explain why Koloth was here? There were those Klingons in the Empire who regarded the taking of captives during battle to be a grievous violation of honor. Was that what had brought Koloth to Pao'la?

Or was it simpler than that? Perhaps Koloth had turned traitor and was now working for the Federation. After all, he had seen a human in the shuttle's cockpit, sitting next to Koloth.

Somehow, despite the hatred for Koloth that he had developed over the years, Korax couldn't make himself believe that his former commander was capable of such treason. Though he might take issue with individuals in positions of power, Korax was certain that Koloth's loyalty to the Empire was absolute. But if the action he'd undertaken was unfavorable in the eyes of those on the High Council, then Korax knew he might have the opportunity to redeem himself. Perhaps he could restore his career while he was still young enough to enjoy it. At the very least he should be able to parlay his transfer from this hellhole.

Of course, to accomplish any of that, he had to catch Koloth first.

His communicator beeped for his attention. Korax grabbed the device from his belt and activated it.

"What is it?"

It was Moqlah, to whom Korax had given the task of restoring order to the prison. *"Commander, we have received an incoming message from the warship* Zan'zi. *They inform us that they will soon enter standard orbit. Her captain demands to speak to you."*

Why would a Klingon ship be here? Was it related to the escape of the prisoners? Koloth would need a vessel to get him off the planet, so was the *Zan'zi* his means of escape? If that was the case, then why contact him?

Korax decided that he had neither the time nor the desire to deal with this new development.

"Moqlah, inform the *Zan'zi*'s captain that you have not been able to locate me, but that you are working to do so. Contact me when the ship makes orbit." He didn't even wait for Moqlah's response before severing the connection and replacing the communicator on his belt.

As he continued to lead the column of Klingons in silence, he considered the ship approaching Pao'la. The more he thought about it, the more he realized that the *Zan'zi* couldn't possibly be part of Koloth's plan to leave the planet with the Starfleet prisoners. However, he could come up with no other reason for the ship's arrival that made any sense. The only ships that visited the planet did so according to a rigid schedule. Prisoner transfers were coordinated in advance, and supply ships visited at regular intervals. There had never been any deviation from the schedule in all the time that Korax had commanded the prison facility here.

Something was wrong here, Korax could feel it. Whatever it was, though, would have to wait until he resolved his current problem. His first priority was recapturing the escaped prisoners and their rescuers, preferably before the *Zan'zi* made orbit.

His eyes scanned the jungle around him as he moved through the undergrowth. Except for a single soldier walking point, the rest of the twenty guards he had brought from the prison were behind him. The woefully small number was all that would fit into the two ground transports that had survived the devastating attack on the compound. Between that and the widespread power outages, including damage to the energy shroud, which was the only thing protecting the entrance to the prison, Korax could spare very few men to hunt down the fugitives.

The undergrowth was beginning to thin somewhat, and he could detect the gradual incline of the ground beneath his boots. They had to be getting close.

"Khulr," he said, instinctively lowering his voice as if aware that those he hunted might overhear him. "Where are they?"

Consulting his tricorder again, Khulr pointed in the direction they were already headed. "They still haven't moved. They must be hiding."

"Do they know we're here?" It didn't seem possible that they could make their approach undetected. Surely Koloth had brought at least a single tricorder with him?

Khulr replied, "They are close together in a ravine at the base of a small hill." Analyzing the readout on the tricorder again, he added, "Given their position, we can surround them easily."

Checking the charge on his disruptor, Korax nodded in satisfaction. "Excellent. Inform the others as to how we'll proceed." He was already beginning to feel the beat of his heart quickening and the rush of blood in his veins as he anticipated the coming confrontation. He thought of Koloth, doubting that his former commander was unaware he was being pursued.

Good. It made the game so much more enjoyable.

I'm coming for you, Koloth. Do you know who it is that hunts you?

"Follow my lead," he said to the group as Khulr finished briefing them. "I want them taken alive. Kill any of them and you will die here by my blade." Pausing until he was confident that his orders were clear, Korax set off toward the ravine, Khulr's tricorder in his free hand. The sound normally made by the unit was muted, so he had to rely strictly on its directional readout.

He was aware of his breathing growing shallow and

rapid. His senses were becoming increasingly alert, and he was able to hear his men as they began to move in their assigned directions. Korax could see the envelopment playing out in his mind's eye. Koloth and the others were quickly becoming the apex of a semicircle, with Klingons approaching them on three sides. The rise of the plateau on the far side of the evolving formation would prevent easy retreat in that direction. In short, there was nowhere for the fugitives to go that wouldn't bring them into contact with one or more of his men.

Stepping around a large thicket, Korax got his first look at the ravine, which was actually little more than a depression. Just as Khulr had said, it was small, less than two meters deep. Partially concealed by a line of dense undergrowth, the position did offer favorable concealment. However, the very vegetation that blocked the gully from view also masked his own approach.

He looked around for his men. Spaced at irregular intervals among the trees were patches of black, the Klingons' uniforms contrasting against the dull browns and pale greens of the jungle. Korax was pleased to note that his soldiers moved with surprising stealth, especially considering the lack of opportunities they had to train for such situations. He waited several more seconds, mentally counting off the time while his men moved into position before starting forward again.

Every nerve tingled as he moved, his disruptor aimed ahead of him. He strained his ears but could hear no signs of movement from the depression. His initial suspicion that this might be a trap begged for his attention, but he ignored it. Koloth was here, somewhere.

The tricorder vibrated in his hand.

Startled by the unexpected sensation, Korax stopped his advance and brought the unit up.

"What is this?" he whispered, barely audible even to his own ears as he watched the tricorder's previously coherent display deteriorate into a chaotic jumble.

This made no sense! The tricorders supplied to the prison were all shielded against any disruptive influence caused by the overabundance of mineral deposits indigenous to this planet. A quick check of the unit's power supply showed that it was fully powered.

So what was causing this havoc?

A jamming field.

"No," he blurted out, but it was the only option that made sense. A jamming field was in operation somewhere nearby, most likely being used to conceal Koloth's true position. And that meant . . .

Lunging forward, Korax leapt over the parapet of the ditch, disruptor raised to fire but already certain there would be no targets waiting for him.

Except a tricorder.

He didn't have to look at it lying at the bottom of the ditch to know that it had been programmed to emit signals approximating the life signs of the fugitives.

Koloth had tricked him!

The oath that escaped Korax's lips was one he had learned as a boy. It was particularly vulgar and had earned him a slap across the mouth when he'd had the incredible lack of good sense to utter it in front of his mother.

But it seemed so appropriate to say now.

And he said it again when the ground exploded near his feet.

Chapter Thirty-four

"FIRE."

As one, the eight runaways unleashed a barrage of firepower at Kirk's command. Their elevated position at the top of the plateau offered them ideal concealment and protection from which to launch their assault.

"That's Korax," Koloth said as he peered down into the gully with his viewfinder. "It's been a long time, but I'd recognize that face anywhere." He shook his head in apparent disgust. "And to think that I once called him friend."

Kirk's ruse had worked. Using a tricorder they had brought with them from the shuttle, he and Sulu had rigged it to transmit false readings that simulated their life signs. It had been Sulu's idea to substitute Klingon patterns for himself and Kirk because, after all, why announce that humans were involved in the rescue attempt if they didn't have to? They still had a chance to get out of here without tipping their hand. All they needed was a little bit of luck.

Rigging the dampening field to conceal their true position had been a different matter, though. Klingon tricorders didn't have the power necessary to create the field in such a way that it wouldn't be detected by other scanning devices, so Sulu had used the Starfleet-issue unit he'd brought along from the *Enterprise*. It had required reprogramming the device almost from scratch, something Sulu had learned from Scotty some years before. Once operational, the dampening field would mask their presence from portable tricorders unless they were programmed to detect such an anomaly. The shroud had allowed them to take up defensive positions on the top of the hill and wait for their pursuers to arrive.

Below them, Kirk watched those Klingons who had stepped out of the cover of the jungle jump back as he and the others opened fire. His own first shot, aimed at Korax, had missed the Klingon by mere centimeters. As he sighted in for another shot, Korax jumped out of the ditch and backpedaled for cover, his disruptor firing in the general direction of the fugitives' position.

"I think they're upset with us," Sulu said as he checked the setting on his phaser again.

Kirk had ordered all weapons placed on stun, determined not to kill anyone unless it became absolutely necessary. They were momentarily protected on this hilltop, but he knew it was only a matter of time before the Klingons adjusted their strategy. The jungle still provided sufficient cover for them to move on the hill, and both of the fugitives' tricorders had been employed to set up their distraction. None remained that they could use to track their opponents' movements.

As quickly and as furiously as the Klingons' return fire had come, it faded away. Kirk listened but could hear no signs of movement below as the jungle became quiet once again.

"You don't suppose they got bored and went home?" Garrovick asked, chuckling at his own attempt at humor.

"Not likely," Koloth replied as he scanned the low ground with his viewfinder. "Korax did not come this far to give up so easily. We must prepare for a direct assault."

The hilltop, perhaps thirty meters in diameter, was covered with low-lying vegetation and small trees. It rose high enough from the jungle floor that Kirk could see the tops of the surrounding trees for kilometers in every direction. The terrain offered limited visibility, which would make it difficult to detect the approaching Klingons.

"It's going to be tough defending this much area with just eight of us," Cheryl Flodin said as she wiped perspiration from her forehead. Kirk did the same, realizing that the oppressive heat was beginning to get to them all. Even with the tri-ox compound Sulu had provided, they would be exhausted by nightfall at this rate.

"We only have to hold long enough for Koloth's ship to arrive," Kirk told her in what he hoped was a reassuring voice. He wouldn't patronize the ensign, or any of her companions for that matter. Everyone here knew the situation and the stakes if they failed. Still, there was no reason to surrender all hope of escape. They weren't captured yet.

He looked to Koloth. "How long?"

"Assuming they did not receive the shuttle's signal, our scheduled rendezvous time is not for several hours."

Kirk nodded soberly. They had activated the shuttle's distress beacon soon after setting down, but it had been questionable as to whether or not the damaged vessel would be able to supply power long enough for the signal to be picked up by anyone.

He watched as, within moments, Sydney Elliot organized the group into a defensive perimeter, defining fields of fire for each member. She moved quickly, as if sensing the approach of their enemy through the jungle. As she passed by Kirk's position on the way to her own, she knelt next to him.

"Looks like we're all set, Captain."

Kirk nodded appreciatively. "Nice work, Ensign. Good to see that being out of action all this time hasn't dulled your skills."

"Some things you never forget, sir." Elliot smiled as she said it, but Kirk could see the tension in the young woman's eyes. She was preparing for battle, yes, but there was more to it. He remembered what she had said earlier about refusing to be recaptured, but he suspected that the source of the fire burning within her ran deeper still.

Before he could ask her about it, however, Elliot was gone, moving off to her own position.

Kirk scanned the jungle with his viewfinder. Nothing stood out from the lush vegetation, no telltale sign revealing the presence of Klingons offered itself. The Klingons were doubtless employing their own tricorders now, trying to penetrate the dampening field Sulu had created. The *Enterprise* helmsman had increased the power output to cover the increased distance between the group's members, but it meant that the field's overall integrity had been compromised. There was now a very real possibility that their positions could be pinpointed.

"Here they come!"

It was Flodin, shouting as she let loose a barrage of phaser fire. One, two, three shots, but no return fire. Kirk listened but heard no other signs of movement from the jungle.

The Klingons were obviously probing, trying to determine the fugitives' positions. The only thing the group could do was hold fast and make sure none of the Klingons broke into their perimeter during a diversionary action.

Light exploded near Kirk's head as a disruptor bolt tore into a thicket less than a meter to his right. He rolled away from the blast just as another shot followed, scorching the mound of earth he'd been hiding behind only an instant earlier. Kirk brought his phaser up and fired in the direction the shots had come from, not really expecting to hit anything. His eyes scanned the jungle but he could see no sign of any Klingons.

Somewhere behind him and to his left he heard another phaser fire. Envisioning the mental map he had made of the group's positions, he guessed it was Lieutenant Sinak dealing with an interloper. More phaser fire followed from further behind him. That would be Garrovick.

"Conserve your phaser charges," he called out to the rest of the group. "They're trying to bait us. Wait until you have a clear target before firing." He wasn't concerned about giving his own position away. Whoever had fired at him moments before knew where he was.

The probing actions were coming faster now, the Klingons beginning to push forward and testing their quarry's resolve. The strategy they were employing gave Kirk one valuable piece of information, however. Korax wanted the prisoners taken alive if at all possible.

Perhaps that was something Kirk could use.

Then he heard phaser and disruptor discharges erupt in a flurry behind him and he knew that the battle had finally begun.

Chapter Thirty-five

STEPHEN GARROVICK had barely settled into his assigned position when weapons fire broke out all around him. Down below, he could see movement in the jungle as the Klingons began to push forward, using the dense undergrowth for concealment. Flodin and Sinak engaged targets within their respective fields of fire to his left and right, responding to the plan Elliot had mapped out.

"Keep them pinned!" he heard Elliot call out above the din of the rapidly escalating firefight. "Don't let them get cover on the hillside!"

They had to stop the Klingons' advance on the hilltop if they were to have any hope of holding their position. If any of the soldiers broke through their lines, Garrovick and his companions would have to face enemies from in front and behind. Already tired from the heat and the long march through the jungle and outnumbered nearly three to one, it wouldn't take long for them to be overwhelmed.

"Stephen! Ten o'clock!" Flodin yelled from Garrovick's left. He spotted the Klingon moving through the brush and shifted the aim of his phaser. The cold blue-white beam spat forth as he pressed the weapon's firing stud, striking the Klingon in the shoulder. The soldier convulsed as the beam caught him before finally sagging to the jungle floor.

Garrovick had already spotted another Klingon near his first victim when he heard a groan of pain from his right. Able to afford only a quick glance in that direction, he watched as Sinak fell back from his firing position, clutching his leg. He'd been hit by incoming fire, and that was all Garrovick had time to process before a disruptor blast tore into a tree just a meter to his right. He felt the heat of the blast and the sting of bark and bits of wood peppering his body. Then movement down below him caught his attention. Eight dark figures raced among the trees.

"Look sharp, Cheryl! They've loaded up on this side and they're rushing us!" He attempted to sight in on a target, firing just as the Klingon leapt behind a tree less than twenty meters away. Even with the advantage their elevated position offered the fugitives, Garrovick knew they wouldn't be able to stop them all.

Movement to his right, something big crashing through the underbrush. He didn't have time to search for the source as another Klingon moved into his vision down the slope. He fired his phaser and was rewarded with the sight of the Klingon slumping to the ground.

And then something dark flashed in his peripheral vision.

He rolled to his left, away from the threat just as Khulr's foot slammed into the ground where his head had been. He tried to push himself to his feet and aim his phaser, but the Klingon was too quick. A dusty leather boot lashed out and knocked the weapon from his hand. Garrovick forgot about the phaser as he rolled away and tried once again to regain his footing.

"Stephen!" Flodin shouted from behind him, torn over her friend's peril and dealing with the advancing Klingons.

"Don't worry about me," Garrovick snapped, moving to his right and attempting to draw Khulr away from his companion. "Keep them pinned in the tree line."

Khulr for his part seemed uninterested in Flodin. Instead, his eyes were locked on Garrovick, watching as he moved away from him.

"Do not think I've forgotten about our last meeting in the mines, human," he said, his voice low and threatening.

Garrovick hadn't forgotten it either. The look on the Klingon's face told him that Khulr had no intention of "capturing" him. Accidents were bound to happen out here in the jungle during the heat of battle, after all.

He wasn't worried so much for himself but for the rest of his crew should they be taken back to the prison. With him out of the way, Khulr would have even more opportunities to pursue his perverted hatred of the other humans, especially Elliot.

There was no sense waiting for it, he decided. Time was running out for them. Inevitably, the Klingons would break through the perimeter. Outnumbered as they were and given the deteriorated condition of the *Gagarin* crew members, they stood little chance of winning any hand-to-hand combat.

So he might as well get it over with.

"I'm sure Korax gave orders that we weren't to be killed," he said. "Are you telling me you're ready to disobey him? I didn't think you had the *nagh*s for that."

And as Khulr bristled at the remark, Garrovick attacked.

The bloodcurdling cry of rage that exploded from his lips succeeded in startling the Klingon, keeping him standing in place for the extra second Garrovick needed to close the gap between them. Then he was in close, less than an arm's length away, and he struck out.

Bone crunched under the heel of his hand as he made contact with Khulr's nose, still bruised from the damage Elliot had inflicted during their previous fight in the mines. The guard grunted in pain, not expecting such a ferocious attack. He started to get his arms up in an effort to block the strike, but by then Garrovick had pivoted away. His right foot came up and struck the Klingon in the left knee.

The kick hadn't been a strong one, mostly because Garrovick had been too close to his opponent. It generated another cry from Khulr, though this one was born more from anger than pain.

His left arm swept out, slamming into Garrovick's right shoulder and the human felt bone snap. The blow spun him around as he stumbled away and fought for balance, trying to keep the Klingon in his line of vision as he fell to the ground. Jolted by the impact, his shoulder throbbed in even greater pain and Garrovick bit back an involuntary scream of agony.

Khulr was advancing quickly, giving him no quarter. Garrovick's lungs were already straining for oxygen in the stifling heat. Even without an injured arm there was no way he'd be able to keep this up for long. The Klingon simply outmatched him physically.

Then he heard the familiar click and hum of power.

Khulr had drawn his stun baton from the holster on his belt and activated it. The weapon's far end glowed hot red, telling Garrovick it had been set to deliver its most potent charge. If Khulr landed a blow with the baton, just one, he was as good as dead.

"What's the matter?" Garrovick asked as he stared down the approaching Klingon. "You can't fight a weak human without a weapon?" He doubted his bravado sounded convincing. His right arm was useless, and it took all of his concentration not to give into the pain in his shoulder.

Khulr continued to stalk him, stepping forward until he straddled Garrovick's legs. Smiling even as a fresh line of blood trailed from his reinjured nose, he looked down at the human.

"Elliot succeeded with that ploy before, in the mines." He shook his head. "Not this time. I intend to watch your eyes as I impale your heart on this." He raised the baton, waving the glowing end before Garrovick's eyes.

Garrovick spotted movement behind the Klingon and his eyes flickered toward the source. Khulr saw his reaction and started to turn just as Sydney Elliot threw her entire weight into the guard.

She struck Khulr in the back of his legs and both she and the Klingon crashed to the Earth. Elliot was the first to recover, rolling onto her side and lunging for the baton that was still in Khulr's hand.

Khulr roared something unintelligible as Elliot's hands closed around the baton and jerked it free, barely able to deflect her attack as she delivered a glancing blow with the weapon to his arm. The charged end didn't make full contact and he was able to grab part of the weapon's handle and hold it still, his superior strength preventing Elliot from pulling away and trying again. He had no leverage, though, and his other arm was trapped beneath his own body. Even with his grip on the baton, Elliot was able to use the weight of her body to keep his arm pinned to the ground.

"I wonder what your buddies back at the prison will have to say about this," she hissed even as she pulled unsuccessfully on the baton they both still gripped, her with two hands and he with one. "Beaten not once but twice by a weakling human female."

Khulr's hand remained steady on the weapon even as he struggled to free his other arm. "You had better kill me, Earther, now. If you do not, then you will beg me for death."

His body jerked again, and this time his left arm came free. Sunlight glinted off gleaming metal and Elliot saw the knife. It was large and double-edged, with a smaller blade jutting out to each side. It was a vicious weapon, designed to do more damage when pulled from its victim than when it entered.

"No!" she roared, twisting her body and putting a foot on Khulr's side as she heaved with her remaining strength, wrenching the baton free from the Klingon's hand. She rolled away as Khulr twisted onto his side and scrambled after her, his blade a blur as it swung through the air.

It was a move made in blind desperation, with Elliot swinging the baton so that it pointed directly out in front of her. Khulr's momentum carried him forward until the glowing end of the weapon jammed into his throat, and Elliot's ears were assaulted by the sounds of the baton emptying its charge into the Klingon.

Khulr's body convulsed in response to the violent assault. Spasms racked his arms and legs, and a gut-wrenching shriek ripped itself from his distended mouth. He locked eyes with Elliot, but could say nothing as his body succumbed to the savage effects of the energy discharge.

Finally he fell away from her, crumpling to the ground in a disjointed heap.

With her own body trembling in pent-up fear and exhaustion, Elliot pulled herself to her feet. She couldn't tear her eyes from the Klingon, who now lay unmoving on the ground before her. After all the torment and the nightmares and sleepless nights associated with it, she was free from her persecutor. Khulr, who had hounded her and harassed her and tortured her for years, would antagonize her no more. Elliot had only to look at the stark, wide-open eyes on his face to know that he was dead, finally.

"Sydney?" Garrovick said from behind her. "Are you all right?"

It was enough to snap her out of her reverie, and she turned back to where Garrovick still lay on the ground grimacing in pain. He was gripping his right arm, which hung oddly from his shoulder.

"I think it's separated," he hissed through clenched teeth as Elliot bent to inspect the injury. Garrovick was right, the arm had come out of its socket joint at the shoulder and would have to be reset.

"You'll need treatment with a bone-knitter for sure," she said. "I think Commander Sulu has one in his medical kit."

Out of the corner of her eye she saw telltale phaser beams firing into the jungle, but they weren't aimed downward. Instead they were being fired almost straight ahead, telling Elliot that the Klingons were beginning to break through the lines.

"Cheryl!" Garrovick shouted as he looked around frantically for his fallen phaser. "They're overrunning our positions! We've got to . . ."

"mev!"

Both of them turned at the command to halt and found themselves staring into the muzzle of a disruptor. The weapon was steady in the grip of the Klingon wielding it.

They had been overwhelmed.

The chase was over.

Despite everything, they had lost.

Chapter Thirty-six

KORAX TRIED TO FEIGN disinterest as the group of fugitives was brought before him, but he failed miserably. He attempted to appear more enthralled by the breathtaking vista offered by the plateau of the Pao'lan jungle surrounding him, but it was impossible. The sight of Koloth standing before him as his prisoner was simply too much for him to remain composed.

That he had captured a traitorous, renegade officer of such stature would be more than enough to secure his own return to a life of some merit and dignity. That the traitor was also his former commander and the one Korax viewed as the arbiter of his downfall was an unexpected bonus he fully intended to exploit.

Strolling down the line of captives, Korax came to a stop before Garrovick. The human was favoring his right arm and Korax could tell by his gaunt face that he was in extreme pain. Korax would have the doctor treat the injury upon their return to the prison. Despite all the trouble

302

Garrovick and the other Starfleet officers had caused during their captivity, he was still under Council directives to see to their safekeeping.

Of course, one of the reasons they had been so much trouble in the past would no longer plague them in the future.

Korax turned to face Elliot, who stood next to Garrovick. "One of my guards tells me you killed Khulr."

Elliot nodded, and Korax noted an edge of fear creeping into her otherwise stone-faced expression. "Yes."

After several seconds Korax simply shrugged. "So be it. He was more of an annoyance than he was worth, frankly. Thank you for disposing of him."

Ignoring the looks of shock on her face as well as those of her companions, Korax resumed his review of the captives, directing his attention to the trio who had attempted to free the prisoners.

"Hello, Koloth," he said as he stepped before his former commander, making no effort to suppress the satisfied smile on his face. "It has been a long time."

Koloth's own expression was one of smugness. "How rewarding this must be for you, Korax. I imagine this is the highlight of your otherwise mediocre career."

Bristling at the remark, Korax drew his disruptor without thinking and pointed it at Koloth, the muzzle of the weapon mere centimeters from the Klingon's face.

"I have you to thank for my career, and I've waited a long time to convey my gratitude."

Koloth acted as if the disruptor didn't even exist, his expression revealing nothing. As Korax looked down the length of his disruptor, years of hatred channeled itself down his arm and into the weapon, which began to shake visibly.

Realizing the involuntary motion made him look weak

before his adversary, Korax lowered the weapon and deliberately turned away, moving instead to study Koloth's two companions. Both of them appeared to be human.

"The life signs we detected earlier indicated three Klingons moving with the prisoners. Ingenious of you to fake those readings."

Directing his gaze back to his former commander, he said, "Have you relaxed your standards, Koloth? I didn't think someone of your status would lower himself to associate with Earthers."

Koloth didn't even bother to turn his head, but instead merely shrugged. "One does what is necessary to accomplish one's goals."

Korax looked into the face of the first human, who looked to be middle-aged. He was certain he had encountered this man before as a gnawing feeling of recognition begged for his attention. The human's face had filled out somewhat and the jawline and chin had softened, but there was no mistaking the features of the man who now stood before him.

"Kirk." Korax drew the name out in a long, slow breath. How many years had passed since he had last laid eyes on this insufferable Earther? How long had Kirk been considered a vile enemy of the Empire? And now the notorious Federation captain stood here, at his mercy.

"I never thought we'd cross paths again, Kirk," Korax said. "And I never would have thought you foolish enough to travel so deeply into Klingon territory. From what I've heard, there's quite a substantial price on your head. Not only will I return to some semblance of dignity and status, but I'll be able to do so with a modest bit of wealth." He turned his attention to the other human. "No doubt you are a member of Kirk's crew," he said before returning to Kirk himself.

"I had heard that you finally put that decrepit worm-infested dung-bucket of a starship out of its misery. Tell me, did your masters give you another ship to lord over? Is it populated with a crew of spineless lapdogs like the *Enterprise* was?"

Kirk glared at Korax, his voice low as he replied. "After all these years, I finally understand why my engineer saw fit to punch you in the mouth." Even before Korax could react to the remark, Kirk pressed on. "I have another starship, yes, and I command a crew whose loyalty and proficiency is unmatched by anyone in the fleet." Leaning closer to Korax, he added, "Yours or ours. But what would you know about leading such people? Instead you've elected to serve your Empire here, a position of some importance no doubt, given your apparently unique qualifications to command it."

It was one thing to exchange verbal barbs with Koloth, but with this insolent human? Korax had killed enemies for far less. He wanted to kill Kirk as well, right here and now.

However, restraint won out again as he remembered the rewards that would come from delivering Kirk in irons to the High Council. Korax looked forward to dragging Kirk into the Council chamber by a chain fixed around the human's neck.

Korax's communicator chirped, demanding attention. He grabbed the offending device from his belt and activated it.

"What is it?"

"This is Moqlah, Commander. The Zan'zi *has entered standard orbit and its captain is demanding to speak with you."*

Sighing in frustration, Korax shook his head in disgust. His instincts told him that the *Zan'zi*'s arrival had to be connected somehow to the Starfleet prisoners, and once again he felt the situation being pulled from his grasp. He had to get this affair under control before dealing with any outsiders if he was to maximize his own potential benefit.

Before he could answer Moqlah, Korax heard a familiar hum from behind him, and he turned to see seven columns of transporter energy appear and take on the forms of Klingons. As they materialized, Korax could see that each of them was heavily armed, with six of the Klingons carrying disruptor rifles.

The seventh one was obviously their leader, even if Korax hadn't recognized the uniform markings of a warship commander. Heavy leather gleamed in the sunlight, as did the top of the new arrival's head, which the Klingon kept completely devoid of hair. That along with a trimmed goatee helped accentuate the already prominent ridges on his wide forehead. A single scar ran down the right side of his face from his temple to his lips, turning his expression into a perpetual sneer.

"I am Jardak, captain of the Imperial cruiser *Zan'zi*. Am I to understand that you are the administrator for the prison facility on this planet?"

Korax schooled himself not to react to the unsubtle air of disdain that had permeated the word "administrator." Jardak obviously felt that such a position was unworthy of anything resembling respect.

"That is correct. I am Korax. What do you want?"

Jardak snapped his fingers and the six Klingons who had accompanied him began to fan out, taking up positions that allowed them to cover the prisoners as well as those soldiers of Korax's who were in the immediate area. Jardak himself examined the five bedraggled members of the *Gagarin*'s crew.

"Are these all who remain of the Federation ship?"

Korax nodded. "Of the group originally brought here, yes. What concern are they of yours?"

"They were taken during battle and then treated like common criminals," Jardak said. "That in itself violates centuries of tradition with respect to combat. That they were then left here to rot while those responsible for the decision lied about their actions is a heinous offense against the honor of the Empire." His eyes scanned the five remaining *Gagarin* survivors once more. "The High Council believes that continuing this deception is an impediment to the ongoing negotiations with the Federation. They wish the matter closed, once and for all."

Kirk felt a knot form in his stomach as Jardak spoke.

If the High Council was trying to rid themselves of the problem surrounding the *Gagarin* prisoners, it had to be because they were trying to deflect attention from themselves. Their best option would be to wipe away all evidence of the hostages' existence.

And that, of course, would include anyone captured during an attempt to free the prisoners.

He glanced at Koloth and thought he saw similar thoughts reflected in the Klingon's eyes. The suspicion was confirmed when Koloth spoke.

"The dishonor exists whether or not the Council chooses to acknowledge it. Doing away with the source of the problem does not free them of their responsibility."

Jardak turned his attention to Koloth and as the two Klingons faced off, Kirk watched the silent communication they exchanged. Here were two warriors who had sworn their loyalty to the Empire and, by definition, to those who occupied the seats of power. Perhaps, from time to time, their loyalty forced them to stand silently and absorb the fallout of policies and directives they felt diminished what they had pledged to defend. Kirk could see that Jardak agreed with Koloth, but how far did his loyalty go?

"You are correct," Jardak said. "There are those on the Council who would simply bury the issue and forget about it, just as there are those who disagree with that position. Fortunately for you, it is a member of that latter group that has brought me here today."

It took an extra second for the remark to register with Kirk, but then clarity returned and provided him with the answer.

"Gorkon?"

Jardak nodded. "Gorkon."

"That's impossible," Korax exclaimed. "Gorkon is a junior Council member. He cannot override Chancellor Kesh."

Calmly, Jardak turned his attention back to the camp commander. "According to the communiqué I received this morning, Kesh has stepped down after having apparently fallen victim to a sudden illness. I also gathered that certain other Council members were inclined to vacate their seats. Junior officials are filling those positions, and Gorkon himself has assumed the temporary role of Chancellor. He feels it is long past time for honor to be restored to the Empire, and such drastic changes must begin in the highest halls of power if the initiative is to succeed."

Kirk couldn't believe it. Gorkon and his allies had succeeded in engineering a coup, removing their adversaries from office, and using their vision of what the Klingon Empire should be to propel themselves into power. If what Koloth had told him was right, with views such as those held by Gorkon gaining popularity within the Empire, then Gorkon had the support of the common people behind him. In time they would far outnumber those who held dissenting opinions.

Change was in the air, but how long would it take to take real effect? How long would the Federation and other parties have to wait before they saw any tangible effects from the events occurring on this day?

"And what about the prisoners?" Koloth asked, giving voice to Kirk's next thought. "How will honor serve them?"

"They will be returned to the Federation with the apologies of Gorkon and the High Council. All information regarding the *Gagarin* will also be surrendered. No longer will the Empire deny its role in this despicable affair."

Kirk couldn't believe what he was hearing. Could it really be that simple?

"And that's it?" he asked. "After all this time, they just get sent home and the Klingons lose face with us? You can't tell me this won't have repercussions throughout the Empire, to say nothing of how the Federation Council will react."

Kirk knew the Council would demand a full accounting of all incidents between the Empire and the Federation where Starfleet personnel were listed as missing in action. He doubted the Klingons would be prepared or willing to come forward with such damaging information until their own internal problems were settled. Though the aftermath of this affair might bring the opposing sides closer together, the peace process that both parties had been crafting would suffer, at least in the short term.

Jardak regarded the *Enterprise* captain for several seconds before replying. "If Klingons see that their leaders are willing to suffer personal embarrassment for the good of our people, it will strengthen their belief in the necessity of honor above all else. Only then will the Empire attain the true greatness that Kahless envisioned for us."

As he reached for the communicator on his belt, he added, "There is much work to be done if we are to obtain that goal. It begins here, today." Activating the communicator, Jardak barked a short series of words in his native language.

Kirk could only understand part of it. "Fire on . . ."

Fire on what?

"The prison," Sulu said, grasping the rest of Jardak's order. "He just ordered his ship to destroy it."

Chapter Thirty-seven

"THERE!"

It was Garrovick who saw it first, pointing toward the horizon. Kirk turned in time to see thin slivers of crimson energy rain down from the sky toward the lone mountain in the distance, the top of which still lay shrouded by clouds. The true target of the energy beams lay at the base of that mountain. He couldn't tear his eyes from the scene as plumes of thick dark smoke rose from the distant trees, lifting into the sky and further concealing the mountain from view.

According to the surveillance data they had gathered while observing the prison, Kirk knew that over a thousand inmates had been housed at the facility, to say nothing of the garrison charged with overseeing them. Had Jardak really ordered their deaths so casually?

"Oh my god," Sulu breathed.

Garrovick and his companions were equally stunned. Sydney Elliot stepped from the line of prisoners, her expression one of total horror as the barrage of fire continued to assault its target.

"They just destroyed it?" She saw the expression on Korax's face, knowing that the camp commander was as unprepared for what had just happened as she was.

Leveling a withering glare at Jardak, she said, "What about your soldiers? They just get wiped out? Do their lives mean nothing?"

"Syd," Garrovick said, reaching out to grab his friend's arm and draw her away from Jardak and Korax. "This isn't the time."

Wrenching her arm from his grasp, Elliot whirled on Garrovick. "What about Moqlah, Stephen?" An image of the Klingon flashed in her mind, and she remembered how he had protected them and how Garrovick had saved the guard's life during the Romulan's escape attempt in the mine. A red cloud of anger just as quickly enveloped the mental picture of the Klingon who had risked so much to treat them with some measure of dignity. "Did he deserve to be eradicated like some virus?"

Jardak watched the confrontation with amusement for some moments before speaking again. "He and the other soldiers died for a greater purpose. As for the prisoners themselves, with very few exceptions they were flotsam, worthless and expendable."

"I'm sure my men appreciated being cast down with the criminals they guarded," Korax said, making a valiant effort to reign in the shock at what he had just seen.

Seemingly unimpressed with Korax's reaction, Jardak replied, "A Klingon warrior's duty to the Empire includes dying in its defense."

"Does that include dying at the convenience of its leaders?" Kirk asked. "Do those in power hold so little regard for those who pledge their lives to the Empire? And what about your orders from the Council? What about *your* duty?"

Bristling at the questions, Jardak leaned in closer to Kirk. "My loyalty to the Empire is not for you to judge, human. Chancellor Gorkon's orders are to have the Starfleet prisoners returned to the Federation, and I intend to do just that. However, the original orders given by Kesh to destroy all evidence of the prison facility were never rescinded." With a dismissive shrug he added, "Perhaps the newly appointed Council members will learn to be more precise with their directives in the future."

Sulu blanched at the casualness of Jardak's remark. "Was it really necessary to destroy it after we had rescued our people? What does it accomplish to sacrifice so many innocent lives?"

"The prison was a symbol of shame and as much a disgrace to the Empire as the actions that brought your companions here."

"That's not a reason for murder," Kirk countered, his jaw tightening in barely controlled anger. "It's a waste, no matter the reasons you've given."

Jardak flicked at a piece of dirt on the sleeve of his uniform, seemingly unimpressed with the entire conversation. "Remember, human, that we Klingons do not coddle our criminals as you do in the Federation. We punish them, treating them like the undeserving dogs they are. If a handful of them should perish, we do not mourn their loss."

He indicated to one of his men with a wave of his hand. "Prepare everyone for transport to the *Zan'zi*. Place Commander Korax and his men in detention."

Korax, who had been staring at the growing pyre of smoke in the distance, spun to face Jardak.

"This is how it ends? I have been loyal to the Empire

my entire life, though a single mistake made in my youth condemned my career to mediocrity. Even here, on this all but forgotten trash heap of a planet, I continued to serve to the best of my ability, making my mining quotas and guarding the Chancellor's terrible secret. And this is my reward?"

"You're a fool, Korax."

Koloth's simple statement drew surprised looks not only from Korax, but from everyone else as well.

"Simply serving the Empire is not enough," he continued. "Your life is what it is because you chose to do what was accepted, not what was right."

"I followed the orders of the Council," Korax replied, his jaw tightening in anger.

"The Earthers should never have been taken prisoner in the first place," Koloth countered. "But they were, because of the decisions of weak-minded cretins who abused their power. You could have taken steps to rectify the situation when the Earthers were brought here, but you hid behind those same cowards. You are no better than Kesh and Komor, and you deserve to share their fate."

Korax's body actually began to tremble as his anger continued to simmer, and Kirk thought the Klingon might lash out at his former commander. It was obvious that Korax had carried rage and frustration within himself for many years, and that Koloth was the focal point of that anger. To be powerless before the one he viewed as responsible for the downward turn his life had taken had to be maddening indeed.

Then, to Kirk's surprise, Korax simply fell to his knees, slumping to the ground. His gaze remained fixed on the horizon where smoke continued to rise from the treetops. The prison, like his once-proud and promising career, had been reduced to smoldering ruins.

"Am I an outcast in the eyes of the Empire I have served for so long, with no chance for redemption?"

"It would appear so," Jardak said simply, obviously disinterested in the defeated, plaintive look Korax directed at him. Instead, he turned to two of the Klingons who had accompanied him.

"Take him. It disgusts me to look at him."

Kirk was stunned at the harshness of Korax's removal as the prison commander was led away.

As if forgetting what had just happened, Jardak turned to Kirk. "Captain, I invite you to board the *Zan'zi* as my guests. We will return you to Captain Koloth's ship."

Flabbergasted, Kirk replied, "And that's it? Korax is to be punished because he didn't measure up to your notion of honor? That deserves a prison sentence or execution?"

Jardak shrugged as if dismissing the question. "He deserves the fate created by his own actions." With that, he turned on his heel and walked away.

"I don't understand any of this," Kirk said as he watched Jardak's retreating back.

"Klingon honor is a matter best left to Klingons, Kirk," Koloth replied. "Do not judge us by your human standards."

It was Sydney Elliot who stepped forward, her voice tight with anger. "And your standards are better? Animals like Khulr are allowed to roam free, beating and torturing those who are weak or helpless, and those like Moqlah get tossed aside? He told us about Kahless and Klingon honor, and he did everything he could to treat us according to those philosophies. He was nobler than any Klingon I've ever met, including you."

Kirk saw the smoldering look in Koloth's eyes and raised a hand toward Elliot, indicating for the ensign to ease off. Looking to Garrovick, he said, "Commander, prepare your people for transport to Captain Jardak's ship."

As Garrovick led his friend and their crewmates aside, Kirk felt a momentary sense of relief and happiness for the *Gagarin* officers. After surviving years of tremendous hardship, they were finally going home.

Any satisfaction he felt, though, was offset once again by the price that had been paid to gain the prisoners' freedom.

"Koloth, you told me once before that I shouldn't view Klingons through my human eyes. You said that not all Klingons were alike, that they were as diverse as humans or any of the races in the Federation. So tell me, do you agree with Jardak? Should the prison have been destroyed?"

"It does not matter what I think." Koloth's reply was quick and sharp, but Kirk thought he saw uncertainty in the Klingon's eyes.

He pressed on. "Are you prepared to stifle or even kill those who don't subscribe to the views you've now decided to hold dear? Is this how you intend to spread your message across the Empire?"

"Take caution, Kirk," Koloth said, pointing a thick gloved finger at the *Enterprise* captain. "You have earned a measure of respect from me, but do not abuse what I offer. The prison is gone, and my duty is to the Empire, especially now. Chancellor Gorkon needs warriors to serve him who value honor above all."

"Honor?" Kirk didn't even bother to hide the disgust on his face. "Where's the honor in killing or silencing those who don't share your beliefs?" He pointed to the smoke-shrouded mountain in the distance. "What about obliterating a group of people merely for convenience so that they won't remind you of the mistakes you've made?

You can't learn and grow as a people by wiping out innocents."

Innocents. *Innocence.*

Emotions Kirk thought he had buried came rushing to the surface, boiling with an intensity he hadn't felt since . . .

. . . since the last time he had been forced to watch as innocence was crushed beneath the foot of power. It had been innocence born out of the desire to help, not harm. It had wanted to create, not destroy, and those who would pervert what it represented had snuffed it out.

David.

The image of David Marcus filled his vision, lying on the ground as the Genesis planet tore itself apart around him. He saw the ghastly knife wound in David's chest, mocking him and symbolizing the opportunities Kirk had missed. Though he had not known David as a child, he had been given a second chance to build a relationship with his son. No sooner had the opportunity arisen, however, than it was robbed from him by a Klingon's blade, the same one that had taken David's own life.

"Is this the way it will be throughout the Empire, Koloth? Simply eliminate those who represent an inconvenient reminder of actions you're ashamed of? And what about outside the Empire? There are hundreds of races in this galaxy who know all about the Klingons. Do you think they'll believe you've simply turned over a new leaf? What about those Klingons who decide not to play along? What about those who strike out on their own, attacking and intimidating those who get in the way of their goals, even when those same people pose no threat to them? Where's the honor in that?"

And then it exploded from Kirk's lips, delivered with

such unrestrained fury that it actually caused Koloth to step backward.

"Where was the honor in murdering my son?"

His eyes clouded by the rage that had come over him, Kirk nevertheless saw Sulu standing to his side, the helmsman's mouth open in mute shock. It made him realize for the first time since his son's death just how far he had buried the pain of that loss. He had stifled it, pushed it aside almost from the moment it had happened, when he had been forced to deal with his crippled ship orbiting Genesis while facing down a renegade enemy vessel. There had been no choice except to ignore his personal tragedy for the sake of his crew.

"Captain . . . ?" Sulu began, but said nothing else. Kirk hadn't heard him, anyway.

Even after the initial shock of David's death had subsided, he had continued to suppress his anguish. Instead he channeled the emotions into his career, choosing instead to focus on the two constants that had seen him through other personal tragedies during his life: the *Enterprise* and her crew.

But they weren't with him here, now, in the oppressive heat of the jungle on this all but forgotten world. His ship and his crew had been, temporarily at least, replaced by Stephen Garrovick and his companions. But they were rescued now. He had done what he'd come here to do, hadn't he? It was over, and he could return home and he could focus once again on the *Enterprise,* rather than letting his emotions run amok.

No, he commanded himself. The situation was *not* over. Garrovick and his people were still a long way from home, the jungle having not quite released its stranglehold on them just yet. Koloth's word aside, they really had no guarantee that they would make it back to Federation space.

There's still a job to do, he reminded himself harshly. His priority still had to be on securing the safe return of the *Gagarin* survivors. Slowly, but then with the same determination that had always guided him, he started the process of battling back the pain and the grief yet again.

Koloth's expression softened somewhat as Kirk fought to reign in his surging emotions. "The Empire is in a state of change, Kirk. There will be growing pains and uncertainties as a new course is charted for all of our people. There will also be many actions taken that we will regret.

"Your son was an unfortunate casualty who fell victim to the actions of cowards. Take comfort in knowing that the Klingons responsible for his death have been cast into *Gre'thor* where they will spend eternity at the mercy of Fek'lhr."

Kirk heard the words, but the battle he was still waging within himself refused to let them register, to dilute the bitterness and pain he felt. Those words, along with the noble actions of more than one Klingon who had seen a grave injustice and who had risked their careers and possibly even their lives to set things right, rang hollow in the face of what he had seen here today.

"As far as I'm concerned, every last one of you can go to *Gre'thor,* or hell, or wherever it is that Klingons burn best."

With that, he turned abruptly and marched toward the far side of the plateau.

As he watched Kirk walk away, Sulu was tempted to follow after him and offer support. He stopped himself, however, certain that the captain would prefer solitude for the moment.

In all the years that he had served with him, Sulu had never seen his captain so distraught. Possessing what could only be described as a supreme force of will, Captain Kirk had never allowed any personal feelings to interfere with his command decisions. He had always provided an emotional anchor for his crew in even the most trying of times. It was one of the traits that had made him a great leader in Sulu's eyes, and one of the many reasons he had followed the man time and again to hell and back.

However, the explosive outburst that Kirk had unleashed on Koloth had sent a shiver down the helmsman's spine despite the stifling heat of the jungle and the perspiration streaming freely from his face and body. He saw that it wasn't a stalwart commander who stalked away from him now. Instead it was a man who had repeatedly triumphed on behalf of countless people he would never meet, yet had been forced to stand by and endure the loss of his only son in a single instant of cruelty.

Moving to stand beside Sulu, Koloth said, "If I could undo his son's death, I would. Unfortunately, all that is left to Kirk is his son's memory. He must keep that close to his heart during future battles. It will remind him of why he fights."

"Captain Kirk only fights when there are no other options," Sulu countered. "It's not something he takes lightly, but he doesn't shy away from it, either."

As he regarded Kirk's retreating back, Koloth nodded in admiration. "That is what defines the honor of a true warrior."

Chapter Thirty-eight

ON THE VIEWSCREEN in the *Enterprise* officers' lounge, Kirk was pleased to see that Stephen Garrovick and Sydney Elliot bore little resemblance to the man and woman they had rescued from Pao'la. Two weeks of medical and dental care at Starbase 49 as well as improved nutrition had succeeded in easing their gaunt, exhausted features. Kirk knew that within a few months, the former prisoners' bodies would be healed.

As for their minds, only time would tell.

Kirk wanted to believe that the rescued survivors could leave their ordeal behind them and resume normal lives, but what were the real chances of that happening? He had been held prisoner before, had even been tortured by the enemy, but he knew that nothing he had experienced could compare to what Garrovick and his companions had endured. He had to hope that their strength of will, along with Starfleet medicine and the support of their families, would see them through the difficulties that lay ahead.

"Mr. Spock tells me you're resigning your commission, Commander," Kirk said to Garrovick. He noted that Garrovick's brown hair had already started to grow back, and he was also showing the beginnings of what promised to be a full beard.

Garrovick nodded. *"At least temporarily, sir. I thought I might spend some time at home. My mother can't wait to see me and I figure that after all that's happened, she deserves to have me around the house for a little while. I doubt I'll be bored, though. She'll probably have a list of chores for me that's about a kilometer long."*

Despite the way he felt, Kirk was unable to keep from smiling. "Well, we'll just have to do our best to get along without you."

"That's okay, sir." Garrovick indicated Elliot with a nod of his head. *"With Sydney back in action, the Federation will be well protected from tyranny."*

Kirk turned his attention to the former *Gagarin* security officer. Like Garrovick, hair had begun to cover her scalp, and her once pasty skin had reclaimed its rich ebony luster. The top she wore left her arms bare, and Kirk could see that she had already begun to regain some muscle tone.

"Congratulations on your promotion, Lieutenant," he offered.

"Thank you, Captain," she replied. *"For everything. Starfleet promoted me to full lieutenant, but I like the shore leave I racked up a whole lot more. But don't worry, sir. I've been told that I'll get a ship assignment as soon as the doctors clear me."*

Behind him, Kirk heard the quiet hiss of the doors parting and turned to see Spock and McCoy enter the lounge.

He nodded to his friends before returning his attention to the screen.

"Well, if nothing turns up, give me a call. I think Mr. Chekov would benefit from an officer with your talents."

Elliot smiled at that, but it was a smile that quickly faded. *"Captain, has the Klingon government provided any information about any more of our shipmates? Are there more of them being held somewhere?"* Kirk's own features soured at the question, as they had at every mention of Klingons over the past two weeks.

Ignoring McCoy's questioning look, Kirk instead focused on Spock, who merely had to shake his head slightly to provide the answer Kirk needed but didn't want.

"No, Lieutenant. So far, Chancellor Gorkon and the High Council haven't been able to provide any further information, either on the *Gagarin* or any other ship that might have disappeared over the years. The replacement of Chancellor Kesh and members of the Council has caused major disruption in the Klingon government. It could be a while before things stabilize there, and longer still before we get any kind of helpful information."

The words were an understatement, Kirk knew. Civil unrest had erupted in pockets throughout the Empire. Gorkon had legions of supporters, but there was still the reality that many Klingons would not easily accept the changes Gorkon and his followers represented. They would undoubtedly cause strife and difficulties in the near term, and the new government's priorities would not include answering questions from a party that was still, in theory at least, an enemy.

"At any rate," he said, "that's a concern that has been handed off to Ambassador Joquel and her diplomatic team. It's their job to worry about the Klingons for now, and it's your job to continue your recovery and return to your lives, something I imagine you're all anxious to do."

"Amen to that, Captain," Garrovick replied. *"I plan to contact the families of every crew member. If you could find us, then there's a good chance that others are still out there somewhere."* His gaze fell for a few seconds before he added, *"Besides, I think I also owe something to the ones who won't be coming back."*

Kirk nodded in understanding. How many such calls had he made during his career?

Spock and McCoy continued to wait for the next few moments as goodbyes were exchanged. Only when the communication was severed did McCoy saunter forward in his usual nonchalant manner and drop into a chair next to Kirk. As he opened the front panel of his maroon uniform jacket and adopted the more casual air he preferred, the doctor studied his friend, who continued to stare at the now blank viewscreen.

"What's on your mind, Jim?" he asked after nearly a minute spent in silence.

At first Kirk resisted the doctor's question. "I'm just tired, Bones."

"Bull. You've been acting like this since you got back. Every time someone mentions Klingons, you get all stone-faced."

Spock stepped closer to his companions and added, "Dr. McCoy has given a succinct if not entirely accurate assessment, Captain. You have exhibited a most reserved demeanor since your return to the *Enterprise*. Based on conversations the doctor and I have had with Mr. Sulu, we know what happened on Pao'la. Perhaps you could elaborate."

His expression grim, Kirk still didn't look away from the dormant viewer. "So you've been checking up on me."

"We wouldn't have to if you'd talk to us," McCoy snapped. "We're your friends, in case you've forgotten. Sulu told me how you nearly bit Koloth's head off on that planet. So, how's about you tell us what's eating you?"

The words penetrated the barrier Kirk realized he had thrown up around him since his return to the ship. He saw the look of concern tinged with irritation on McCoy's face. Coupled with the implacable expression Spock exhibited, Kirk knew he wasn't getting out of the room until he satisfied his friends' concerns.

"Koloth told me that Klingons have always valued honor and character. Their entire culture was built upon those beliefs. They apparently went through a period where those values seemed to lose their importance, but he says that's changing now. I try to reconcile that with what I saw on Pao'la, and I can't. It was barbaric." Pausing momentarily, he shook his head in frustration and rose from his chair to begin pacing the lounge.

"With such casual disregard for life, I can't believe they won't destroy themselves before we ever get to achieve peace with them, honor or not. I mean, is such a radical shift in fundamental beliefs and values possible? Are the Klingons willing to risk everything they've built and plunge the Empire into civil war in order to reaffirm such an arcane notion?"

Spock replied, "Humans have asked themselves those questions many times in their history, Captain, as have my own people. Both our civilizations managed to affect drastic philosophical change in a relatively short period of time. It therefore seems logical to assume that such a feat is possible for the Klingons as well."

"If it weren't for Klingons with honor," McCoy said, "Garrovick and the others wouldn't have been rescued, and the peace conference would probably have failed."

But Kirk wasn't so sure. "We rescued the hostages, with the help of Klingons, but at what cost? They wiped out hundreds of lives on that planet as a matter of convenience. They tried to sabotage the conference, and they were willing to destroy one of their own ships and kill hundreds more of their own men just to keep their secret. Was all of that really in the name of honor? If you have to kill indiscriminately in order to possess something, is it worth having? Does the end truly justify the means?"

"Obviously, that is not an accepted value system in our society," Spock said. "However, we cannot judge the Klingons by our societal standards, Captain."

"How can you say that?" Kirk countered. The accusatory tone of the question was not lost on him, but he pressed on anyway. "How little value will Klingons place on life when it's in conflict with their goals? We've already seen how they treat their own people, and we certainly know how they feel about humans."

He saw the stunned expression on McCoy's face, and immediately realized how forceful his response had been. Spock's expression was almost unreadable, but Kirk thought he saw pain and perhaps disappointment in the Vulcan's eyes.

"Jim," McCoy finally said in a gentle voice, "all Klingons didn't sabotage the conference, and all Klingons aren't against the idea of peace." He paused a moment before drawing a deep breath and adding, "And all Klingons didn't kill David."

The words knifed into Kirk just as he imagined the honed Klingon blade had impaled his son's chest. Anger rushed forth as he was once again reminded of how helpless he had been to prevent David Marcus's death.

"Maybe they didn't," he said. "But it was their way of life that allowed it to happen. Conquering the weak and destroying the defenseless; that's their nature. How many more innocent people have to die before you see the Klingons for what they really are?"

Turning away from his friends, Kirk stalked across the floor of the lounge to stand before the large forward-facing viewing ports and the centuries-old sailing ship's wheel positioned before them. In this forwardmost area of the ship, the plexisteel windows looked outward into the twisting vortex of stars as the *Enterprise* traveled among them at high warp.

Instead of the solace he usually found here, he felt alarm at the anger he had displayed so openly. McCoy's stalwart support should have brought forth reason to battle his rage, just as Spock's logic should have allowed him to see the detrimental effects of his rampant emotions. His friends' compassion and understanding were supposed to help him drive back his pain.

What it could not drive away was the image of David Marcus's lifeless body that was forever seared into his mind. Just as his son had been taken from him, so too had the optimism that blinded him and made him believe that peace would be soon in coming between the Federation and the Klingon Empire. A few gestures of good faith weren't enough to undo the treachery and deceit he had seen perpetrated by Klingons with his own eyes.

So until peace finally arrived, he would be watchful. No one else's innocent son would be lost because he failed to see the true face of the enemy.

Staring out the viewports into the void surrounding his vessel, he knew his anger would soon fade. Eventually he would refocus his energies on whatever challenge or obstacle presented itself. But even as the *Enterprise* surged forward through the vast expanse of space, James Kirk felt the seeds of pain, shame, and hate planted within the center of his own heart, dragging him backward into the chaos of rage and despair.

He could only hope that, one day, the dream of peace between his people and the Klingons could be accomplished before the dark emotions he harbored finally engulfed him.

About the Author

Dayton Ward has been a fan of *Star Trek* since conception (his, not the show's). After serving for eleven years in the U.S. Marine Corps, he discovered the private sector and the piles of cash to be made there as a software engineer. His start in professional writing came as a result of placing stories in each of the first three *Star Trek: Strange New Worlds* anthologies. With Kevin Dilmore, Dayton also co-wrote the *Interphase* duology for the *Star Trek: S.C.E.* series of "eBooks" as well as that series' upcoming *Foundations* trilogy. Though he currently lives in Kansas City with his wife, Michi, he is a Florida native and still maintains a torrid long-distance romance with his beloved Tampa Bay Buccaneers. Feel free to contact Dayton anytime via E-mail at **DWardKC@aol.com**.

Look for STAR TREK fiction from Pocket Books

Star Trek®: The Original Series

Star Trek: The Next Generation®

Star Trek: Deep Space Nine®

#19 • *The Tempest* • Susan Wright
#20 • *Wrath of the Prophets* • David, Friedman & Greenberger
#21 • *Trial by Error* • Mark Garland
#22 • *Vengeance* • Dafydd ab Hugh
#23 • *The 34th Rule* • Armin Shimerman & David R. George III
#24-26 • *Rebels* • Dafydd ab Hugh
    #24 • *The Conquered*
    #25 • *The Courageous*
    #26 • *The Liberated*

Books set after the Series
    The Lives of Dax • Marco Palmieri, ed.
    Millennium • Judith and Garfield Reeves-Stevens
        #1 • *The Fall of Terok Nor*
        #2 • *The War of the Prophets*
        #3 • *Inferno*
    A Stitch in Time • Andrew J. Robinson
    Avatar, Book One • S.D. Perry
    Avatar, Book Two • S.D. Perry
    Section 31: Abyss • David Weddle & Jeffrey Lang
    Gateways #4: Demons of Air and Darkness • Keith R.A. DeCandido

Star Trek: Voyager®

    Mosaic • Jeri Taylor
    Pathways • Jeri Taylor
    Captain Proton: Defender of the Earth • D.W. "Prof" Smith
Novelizations
    Caretaker • L.A. Graf
    Flashback • Diane Carey
    Day of Honor • Michael Jan Friedman
    Equinox • Diane Carey
    Endgame • Diane Carey & Christie Golden
#1 • *Caretaker* • L.A. Graf
#2 • *The Escape* • Dean Wesley Smith & Kristine Kathryn Rusch
#3 • *Ragnarok* • Nathan Archer
#4 • *Violations* • Susan Wright
#5 • *Incident at Arbuk* • John Gregory Betancourt
#6 • *The Murdered Sun* • Christie Golden
#7 • *Ghost of a Chance* • Mark A. Garland & Charles G. McGraw
#8 • *Cybersong* • S.N. Lewitt
#9 • *Invasion! #4: Final Fury* • Dafydd ab Hugh
#10 • *Bless the Beasts* • Karen Haber
#11 • *The Garden* • Melissa Scott

Enterprise™

Star Trek®: New Frontier

Star Trek®: Starfleet Corps of Engineers (eBooks)

Star Trek®: Gateways

Star Trek®: The Badlands

Star Trek®: Dark Passions

Star Trek® Omnibus Editions

Other Star Trek® Fiction